DISCARD

Bennington Girls Are Easy

ALSO BY CHARLOTTE SILVER

Charlotte au Chocolat: Memories of a Restaurant Girlhood

The Summer Invitation

Bennington Girls
Are Easy

CHARLOTTE SILVER

DOUBLEDAY

NEW YORK LONDON TORONTO

SYDNEY AUCKLAND

Copyright © 2015 Charlotte Silver

This book is a work of fiction. Names, characters, businesses, organizations, places, events, and incidents either are the product of the author's imagination or are used fictitiously. Any resemblance to actual persons, living or dead, events, or locales is entirely coincidental.

All rights reserved. Published in the United States by Doubleday, a division of Random House LLC, New York, and distributed in Canada by Random House of Canada Limited, Toronto, Penguin Random House companies.

www.doubleday.com

DOUBLEDAY and the portrayal of an anchor with a dolphin are registered trademarks of Random House LLC.

Jacket design by Emily Mahon
Jacket photograph by Andrew B. Myers

LIBRARY OF CONGRESS CATALOGING-IN-PUBLICATION DATA
Silver, Charlotte.
Bennington girls are easy / Charlotte Silver. — First edition.
pages cm
1. Female friendship—Fiction. 2. Women college graduates—Fiction. I. Title.
PS3619.I5467B46 2014
813'.6—dc23
2014009865

ISBN 978-0-385-53896-1 (hardcover)
ISBN 978-0-385-53897-8 (eBook)

MANUFACTURED IN THE UNITED STATES OF AMERICA

1 3 5 7 9 10 8 6 4 2

First Edition

CHARACTER LIST

BENNINGTON GIRLS

Cassandra Puffin: Sylvie Furst's best friend

Sylvie Furst: Cassandra Puffin's best friend

AND THEIR PEERS . . .

Pansy Chapin: that bitch!

Bitsy Citron: diamond-mine heiress

Penelope Entenmann: coffee-cake heiress

Dorian Frazier: hired by Sotheby's because of her cheekbones

Gala Gubelman: famous campus beauty and kleptomaniac

Chelsea Hayden-Smith: modern dancer

Vicky Lalage: worth staying in touch with for family real estate

Fenna Luxe: from Malibu

Fern Morgenthal: from Portland

Angelica Rocky-Divine: red-headed, bisexual, cross-dressing ringleader of the modern dancers

Jude St. James: off in Africa

The notorious Lanie Tobacco: she of the wine-stained bathrobe and halo of fruit flies

Beverly Tinker-Jones: another one of the modern dancers

Bennington Girls Are Easy

PART I

Dances of the Young Girls

CHAPTER 1

How can somebody actually dance themselves to death?"
Professor Sobel, taking a drag on his cigarette, thought to himself: I left that gig at Columbia for this? The setting was Bennington, Vermont. The subject: Stravinsky's *The Rite of Spring*. An afternoon in early March, the doldrums of mud season: the bitterness of the cold mattered little to Professor Sobel, who insisted on teaching all of his classical music courses outside in a meadow, no matter what the season, so he could smoke unlimited cigarettes in a pleasing, rhythmic continuity. Questions and comments were not encouraged in Professor Sobel's courses, though in the free-wheeling spirit of progressive education were nevertheless volunteered. The students, among them Cassandra, sat crouched in the mud awaiting his response to Chelsea Hayden-Smith, the Bambi-eyed sophomore who had interrupted him in the midst of a majestic monologue about the finer thematic points of Stravinsky's masterpiece.

"Are you from Kansas?" he asked, his large shaggy frame towering over her. "Have you absolutely no imagination to speak of?"

He put out his cigarette, disgruntled. God, was he looking forward to class being over so he could go meet that leggy cello student he was banging for a quickie in the Secret Garden. And so:

"Class dismissed," Professor Sobel announced without further ado.

But one year later Cassandra wondered whether or not Chelsea, during her final moments on earth, may have thought back to *The Rite of Spring*, as she and her best friend Beverly Tinker-Jones plummeted to their deaths through the wide glass windows of the fifth-floor dance studio of the college's performing arts building. Cassandra wondered, too, if when Professor Sobel first heard the news he guffawed, cried, or simply, as was most likely the case, lit another cigarette and never thought of Chelsea Hayden-Smith ever again.

Chelsea and the poor, fawnlike Beverly, both of them ethereally beautiful young girls, ages twenty and nineteen respectively, were said to have died immediately on impact. The coroner in Bennington, Vermont, was long used to handling the college's many overdoses and suicides, but this latest tragedy was something new. He had never known, previously, of anybody dancing themselves to death. But he, unlike Chelsea, was not so young or so impertinent as to question the unexpected twists of this cruel universe.

The cause of Chelsea's and Beverly's deaths was said to be an accident, and yet the rumor mill began swiftly, and with inexorable force, from the minute the news hit the dining hall, where the students who were not still in bed sat spreading Tofutti cream cheese on their bagels and nursing their hangovers with grape Pedialyte. People said that the girls had been pushed through the window. People said that the Wiccans on campus might have had something to do with it, though this theory did not hold up when you stopped to consider that none of the Wiccans, almost all of whom were overweight, had anything to do with the modern dancers; what the Wiccans mostly did was hang out in the house living rooms and braid one another's hair and eat chocolate cake. (Cassandra knew this for a fact, having once crashed a meet-up of theirs just because she was hungry.) Other people said that ghosts were involved, and if you had ever been on the Bennington campus late at night, why not? It was a ghostly, godless place. There was actually a name for it and its peculiar geography: the Bennington Triangle. This had been given to it on account of a number of individuals who had gone missing from this supposedly serene corner of southwestern Vermont in the last century, including but by no means limited to a Bennington sophomore who had disappeared from one of the hiking trails near campus. And now, just look at what had become of the dancers—not a disappearance per se but an otherworldly turn of events that was queer and creepy nonetheless.

Cassandra learned one thing from all of this, anyway: that modern dance at Bennington was a dangerous discipline and that she had been right to steer clear of the performing arts building all these years. Not to mention the hiking trails.

She was an English major.

And, as such, throughout the years she often thought back to Chelsea and Beverly. The spring she graduated was the spring the dancers died. There seemed, in retrospect, to have been some kind of warning, for her and all of the other young women of Bennington who graduated with the class of 2003, in the unforgettable image of those tender white feminine bodies slain on the black pavement.

CHAPTER 2

J ust like those two ill-fated young women, Chelsea Hayden-Smith and Beverly Tinker-Jones, Cassandra Puffin and Sylvie Furst were best friends. Before ending up at Bennington together, both girls had grown up in Cambridge, Massachusetts. Right from the beginning, in high school, theirs was a fast, fiery friendship, a brief, beautiful phenomenon particular to the golden-green wilds of adolescence. Cassandra fell in love with Sylvie—for romantic love is the forte of teenage girls. It happened one afternoon after school, as they were sipping raspberry lime rickeys in the Sunken Garden at Radcliffe in the first, bewitching hours of getting to know each other when they were just fourteen years old. They learned in that single afternoon what it would have taken two grown women to learn in a year: the elaborate subtleties of tortured family dynamics, traumatic holidays, and, this being Cambridge, shrinks, medications, and so on. They didn't tell each other any sexual secrets that afternoon because there were none, yet; those came later.

One night that spring, the spring the dancers died, Cassandra was lying in bed in her dorm room when she got a phone call from the security booth. It was Alphie, the avuncular head of campus security, whose primary job responsibility appeared to be passing out candy canes in the dining hall during the holidays and who knew every student by name, saying: "Cassandra, Sylvie is here."

Sylvie? thought Cassandra, waking up from a nice, long nap. Sylvie? As far as she knew, Sylvie was supposed to be still abroad in Florence. Or was she in Madrid or Barcelona by now? Maybe. She'd had plans to travel all over Europe by train after her program ran out. Also, she craved a change of scenery in order to get over the tumultuous affair she'd been having with the photography TA, the spellbinding saga of which Cassandra had been privy to over a series of outrageously expensive international phone calls.

"But if you're in Italy, then for God's sake why aren't you sleeping with an Italian?" Cassandra had wanted to know, and Sylvie had laughed and said, "Good question! I guess I'm just being perverse that way."

Well, in any event, Florence or Barcelona or whatever, Sylvie was supposed to be off in Europe. And now here she was, appearing quite without warning in Bennington, Vermont?

Still lying on her twin bed—the exact spot where she had spent the better part of her ruinously expensive education—Cassandra sighed and looked out her window. It was one of those enchanted mid-May evenings, that time of year when the fragrance of the roses is beginning to drown out that of the lilacs. On the lawn, students were doing all of the usual unchallenging outdoor activities: tai chi, Ultimate Frisbee, topless sunbathing—though the sun, at this point, was beginning to set. No matter; certain Bennington girls could be counted on to take their tops off in any weather short of a blizzard. And there was no need, by the way, for even a blizzard to stop them: it was a "clothing-optional" campus. Beyond the lawn was the view of the Green Mountains spoken of with dark, all-knowing irony as "the End of the World."

Oh! I'm going to miss this place, thought Cassandra with one of the sweet pangs of nostalgia that were so becoming to her melodramatic sense of herself. She got up and brushed out her hair, which she was still wearing, in those days, quite long. Then she walked across the lawn to meet Sylvie at the security booth. On her way over, she passed a beautiful redhead pedaling a blue Schwinn bicycle. On closer inspection, it was none other than the bisexual, cross-dressing ringleader of the modern dancers, Angelica Rocky-Divine, whose long, indolent white body could frequently be glimpsed entirely unclothed in all its plush splendor while doing cartwheels at the End of the World.

Angelica's bright, unshackled beauty, redolent of the meadows themselves, seemed to Cassandra to evoke the original spirit of the college when it was founded in the year 1932 as a suitable refuge for the wayward daughters of good families. Bennington girls even today were proud of their saucy reputation, and not one of them on the entire campus could have failed to be familiar with Salinger's description in *Franny and Zooey* of a Bennington-type chick on her way to New Haven for a Yale football game who "looked like she'd spent the whole train ride in the john, sculpting or painting or something, or as though she had a leotard on under her dress." Angelica had gone so far as to trump that fictional girl, having once had boisterous sex in the john of an Amtrak train on a jaunt to New York City to see some show at the Guggenheim with her architecture class, the object of her flamboyantly predatory designs being a short, yet somehow still Lawrencian, wood-making student, whose consistently upright cock she thought was very, very good-looking, a real piece of aesthetic human construction.

Oh! thought Cassandra again. This place is just so charming, like something out of a Salinger story. Was she ready for the Real World?

The answer came to her in a snap. The answer was *not at all*.

Even then, and this was several years before the world economy collapsed, Bennington alumni were a remarkably nonresilient lot. The boys lucky enough to be dating students a couple years younger than them could be found squatting in their girlfriend's dorm rooms; these saintly young women could be seen, at mealtimes, packing up bananas and oatmeal cookies to bring back to them.

In the distance, Cassandra could finally make out Sylvie, a small brunette figure in a white dress waving from the foot of the security booth. They squealed and hugged, as girls will do. It had been almost a year now since they had seen each other, the longest they had ever been apart.

"You could have *called*! I had no idea. I thought you were still in Europe."

"You know me, Cassandra. I don't call," said Sylvie. It was true, and that was part of her charm—the way she thrived on the drama of the last minute. But the most delightful thing about Sylvie was that she was always up for anything.

It was then that Cassandra did a double take and stepped back to look at her best friend. Until recently, Sylvie had been pretty but underdeveloped. Her voluptuous, Victorian-era dark hair had overwhelmed her tiny body; she was like a little brown velveteen mouse. A late bloomer—coming back from Italy, that tiny body had ripened and was filling out a white peasant dress with red rick-rack trim. Cassandra complimented her on the dress immediately.

"Oh this," said Sylvie, glancing down at her firm brown breasts set like two precious jewels in the sloping white neckline, "yeah, I picked it up at this market in Barcelona."

"Oh, so you did make it to Spain then?"

"Oh yeah. I went all over." Then she touched the top of her head and said, "Oh my God, Cassandra, you haven't said anything! My haircut! I was hoping you'd like it."

Sylvie's haircut—so that explained it: shorn and gone, that black, horselike plait of hers. Now she had a pixie cut, a style that Cassandra upon closer inspection decided became Sylvie's petite style of beauty better than any other. And, on the right girl, a good pixie cut can be incredibly sexy. Sylvie was the right girl. Her skin took the sun well and her arms were strong and brown.

Cassandra, in contrast, was the peaches-and-cream type, soft around the edges. She was pretty but klutzy and there was a certain failure of carriage that prevented her from being, like so many other girls at Bennington, what is ruthlessly known as "hot." She had this foggy, underwater look in her big blue eyes: a look that marked her as someone who had spent entirely too much of her childhood alone. Perhaps it was because, as she and Sylvie had discussed at length, her father had died when she was a little girl. They both agreed that girls who had grown up without fathers often bore this rather crippled air.

Tonight, Sylvie was carrying a vintage set of watercolors in a blue waxed-cotton tote bag with a pattern of California oranges. She might have been in a catalog, Cassandra thought: the beautiful American art-school girl, back from time abroad, the beneficiary of a magnificent sentimental education—sex and sunshine and red wine and pasta and a good European haircut. That photography TA must have been pretty good in the sack, she decided, even if he wasn't Italian.

"I love your haircut!" she insisted to Sylvie, hugging her again. "Oh my God, it's just so chic! You look," she said, with what Sylvie noticed was actually rather a mournful expression on her face, "absolutely beautiful."

And the two young women walked arm in arm out onto the lawn, breathing in the roses and what remained of the lilacs.

ater on that same evening, Sylvie and Cassandra sat in
Adirondack chairs all the way out at the End of the World.

"So," Sylvie said to Cassandra, "what's the latest around
here?"

"Hmm. Well, sexually speaking, black boys are all the rage on
campus."

"Oh, great. All two of them."

"Well. Pansy Chapin's sleeping with that guy Kojo, you know,
the one who played Mercutio in that production of *Romeo in the
Hood*."

"But wait, what about that tall, handsome boyfriend of hers,
the one she's always visiting with the duplex on Central Park
South? She'd better not let him go! He must be *loaded*."

"Oh, he is loaded, really, really loaded, and he's still in the picture. They're engaged now. He popped the question on Torcello,
this island off the coast of—"

"Venice! Oh my God, I went there. It's gorgeous."

"I bet it is! Actually, she's in the Hamptons with him this weekend. Kojo's just something on the side."

"That poor guy. She's always cheating on him."

"Pansy says it's true."

"What?"

"What they say about black guys."

"What they say about their cocks?"

"Uh-huh. The morning after she first slept with him, we were
all sitting around at brunch and Pansy held up *a banana* to demonstrate."

"Jesus. I didn't think that any intelligent heterosexual woman actually thought that size mattered. Do you think it matters?"

"Oh no. Not at all! Sex is a really mental thing with me." Cassandra liked her men upper-class and intellectual, with a fine, sadistic verbal edge. She had a long-term Harvard boyfriend who sometimes came and visited her on campus. In spite of his existence and the status of their supposedly monogamous relationship, she was forever urging her friends to go crash frat parties to meet men at nearby Williams College, though out of the lot of them, only the aforementioned Pansy Chapin and Gala Gubelman, famous campus beauty and kleptomaniac, had been up for tagging along, and that was just because Pansy, from a young age, was always on the lookout for a rich husband and Gala was generally held to be a nymphomaniac.

"Me, too," Sylvie agreed.

"Oh! I can't believe I forgot. You heard the one about the modern dancers?"

"Yes!"

"Those poor girls. And now their parents are suing."

"What for?"

"Damages. They say the school should have put up a sign in the dance studio saying not to get too close to the windows."

"Oh, come on. What idiot would need a sign telling them something like that?"

"But modern dancers *are* idiots."

"Oh, right. Of course they are. Isn't that why we've always hated them?"

"Yeah, well that, and they always get all the guys. Not that I want the guys you have to pick from at Bennington! But still."

It is often remarked that friends and lovers need to like the same things. What is less frequently remarked upon—but is a far more enduring bond, in the long run—is that they need to hate the same things, too. Sylvie and Cassandra did, with a high, sparkling vehemence that never got old. Having attended, long before Bennington, a progressive arts high school in the Boston suburbs, notorious for the high number of students who did stints in the chic mental institution McLean, they had been given a wealth of material. If you are lucky enough to attend a progressive school at an impressionable age, you will have things to loathe for a lifetime.

Sylvie yawned and asked: "By the way. Those girls. Were the two of them lesbians, do you think?"

"So what if they were? Does it matter? They're *dead*."

"I just wondered. It would be kind of a nice romantic twist if they were. Dying that way. Together."

"Well, I guess it would be kind of romantic if you put it that way. It would be like something out of a ballet! And they were both so incredibly beautiful, I have to say. Chelsea had these amazing curly long lashes." She sighed, remembering.

"I don't know. All the modern dancers at Bennington are so incredibly beautiful. After a while they all just blend together."

"Yeah." Cassandra paused. "You know something? I've always just hated the name Chelsea."

"That matters?"

"Well, it just occurred to me as I was thinking about them. Chelsea! You know what it reminds me of? When some stupid person dares to call me Cassie! Cassie!" She shuddered.

Sylvie thought of admonishing Cassandra for being such a vain little bitch when two of their classmates were dead. Then, because Cassandra was her best friend and because they could say anything to each other, decided against it.

"I don't like the name Beverly either, to tell you the truth," Sylvie said.

CHAPTER 4

Jobs, even back when Sylvie and Cassandra graduated, were getting hard to come by. But it was not yet impossible to find one, as it would be for the Bennington girls who followed after them in just a couple years' time. Cassandra managed to find employment before Sylvie did, in some vague administrative capacity, untaxing to her fragile mental health, at a cultural nonprofit in Harvard Square: the less said of the specifics of this job, like most jobs, the better. Because most jobs are boring. After graduation, Sylvie also landed back in Cambridge, but only temporarily, she sincerely hoped. Because for as long as she could remember, she had hated the city of Boston. Many years ago now, her grandmother had taken her to the Isabella Stewart Gardner Museum, long lauded as one of the crown jewels of Boston but, to the discriminating Sylvie, nothing all that special; she sniffed in its grand and gloomy rooms a certain fustiness, a residual, mothy scent, perhaps, of the city's Puritan legacy in spite of the gallant efforts of the more flamboyant Mrs. Gardner herself. "Make a wish," Sylvie's grandmother had commanded, handing her a penny and pointing to the fountain in the middle of the Venetian-style courtyard. Sylvie braced herself and closed her eyes and tossed the penny into the fountain. Then announced:

"I wish I wasn't here."

She was six years old at the time.

Still, sometime over the course of that first summer after college, she announced to Cassandra, "So, I found a job."

There was a note of gloomy caution, nothing resembling elation certainly, in her voice.

"Oh, Sylvie, that's wonderful!" Cassandra said, refusing to listen to it and trying her best to be encouraging.

"No, it isn't. It isn't wonderful *at all.* It's at Black Currant."

"Oh."

And now Cassandra was the one who sounded gloomy.

Black Currant was a bakery in Harvard Square, generally held to be the crème de la crème of such establishments among the dreary postdoc and professorial set of which Cambridge society consisted. Cassandra often went there for coffee and the very excellent raisin-pecan rolls they had—not that she would have been caught dead working there. But best to keep that to oneself right now; Sylvie needed her support, obviously. So she tried to change her tone, hoping that it wasn't too obvious. It was, of course. Sylvie picked up on it immediately and felt faintly condescended to. Sylvie hated feeling condescended to! And she was forced to listen to the inanity of Cassandra prattling on:

"Oh my God! I'm so happy about this. That means that you'll be working in Harvard Square, too, Sylvie. So we can have lunch, like, every day together!"

But already Sylvie was thinking: Like hell I'm happy about this. I'm getting out of town.

From her very first day on the job at Black Currant, she began to plot her escape. The wheels, the wheels in her head were turning. Which was worse, she wondered, the staff or the customers? The two groups coexisted in a state of low-level hostility in which there was seldom any actual yelling but plenty of complex anger clotting the atmosphere. Maybe the customers resented the staff for the indignity of a place where you had to pay a full seven bucks for a slice of vanilla-bean pound cake. There was no bathroom, and if you asked where the bathroom was, you were sure to get a really dirty look. Maybe the staff, making $7.50 an hour, resented the customers for spending a full seven bucks for a slice of vanilla-bean pound cake. (A whole pound cake cost twenty-three dollars.)

All Sylvie could take away from the situation was: these people are fucking miserable. An ex-convict, having taken a job as the night baker, confessed to Sylvie that being in the clink was nothing compared to the likes of *this*.

But *I* could do this, thought Sylvie. She meant that maybe one day she could run a bakery, though not here in Cambridge—no way. But maybe someday in New York . . . For, of the many things that Sylvie was naturally good at, one of them was being an excellent cook; Cassandra had often marveled at how she could turn something as mundane as a tuna fish sandwich into something absolutely delicious. The girl was born knowing how to dress a salad in the correct amount of French olive oil and how to toss off a perfectly silky chocolate soufflé.

And so, *I* could make these jams, Sylvie was thinking, looking at the stout glass bottles of chunky apricot preserves selling for seventeen dollars a pop. *I* could write out those labels. She imagined her pretty, sloping handwriting; she imagined tying a white grosgrain ribbon around the lid . . .

This place must be making a killing, thought Sylvie, trying to crunch the numbers in her head. She and Cassandra had first become friends back in high school while skipping out on geometry class together. She wasn't good at math, but she was shrewd with numbers on a practical level, and she could grasp how they broke down in a business. This one broke down entirely to the owner's advantage and not to the staff's—why, they didn't even get free coffee!

But in those days, Sylvie was young and idealistic and given to making people feel good; she hadn't yet learned to *want* to take things away from people. But she soon did learn that hospitality in any form was to be distrusted at Black Currant, as when she gave an elderly sculptress an extra scoop of cranberries on top of her eight-dollar oatmeal and afterward was reprimanded by Tish, her manager.

"Sylvie," said Tish in the weak, trailing voice that never varied, no matter what the emotional pitch of the situation, for perhaps in Tish's diminished universe there was only one. "Sylvie, we don't give away freebies here. Of any kind."

"Oh, I know," began Sylvie, tossing her shiny black head with its glamorous, Italian pixie cut and figuring that she personally could get away with anything because she was young and because she was beautiful, "but I just thought, it was this nice old lady, and she's a regular, and it was only a couple of cranberries, so—"

"A cranberry is a cranberry," said Tish, and from then on this became a phrase of hilarity between Sylvie and Cassandra: *A cranberry is a cranberry*. How appropriate, remarked Cassandra, that Tish should hold dear this most bitter of fruits, for the two of them, with the glittering callousness of twenty-two, thought she was the last word in grimness: something of a withered fruit herself.

"Now most of the time she never smiles," said Sylvie. "A frown is, like, her default expression. She already has these frown lines and you know what I found out—she's only twenty-eight! You'd think she was forty-two already." Sylvie pressed her hand to her own satiny brown cheek and continued, "But what I wanted to say is, when she does smile, and it isn't often, it's actually really creepy. It makes you more uncomfortable when she smiles than when she scowls, you know?"

Later on, the girls howled when they discovered a Yelp review in which Tish was described by a disgruntled customer as "the I See Dead People manager." There really was something rather haunted about her pinched white face and the dusty black pigtails, which by now she was far too old to be wearing.

Before Sylvie met Tish—not to mention all of the regulars at Black Currant—she had always assumed that you grew up and had a sex life. Of course there were unfortunate cases who didn't, but they were the exceptions. Now, however, it occurred to her that there might be a whole seedy underclass of people to whom nothing sexual ever happened; life went on without even the possibility of magnetic eye contact or melting touch. She felt, in general, that living in Cambridge past a certain age threatened to enclose her and her still-beautiful flesh in a gray crust of sexlessness. She felt that to stay there too long might prove fatal.

The sad, mauve-colored streets of Cambridge were thronged with women who had, to Sylvie's mind, just plain given up. She wanted to go and shake them. She wanted to ask them point-blank: What happened to you? Did you wake up one morning and just decide that there was no damn point in pretending anymore?

And then there was her family. That didn't help. All of Sylvie's relatives had been born in and elected to stay in Cambridge for reasons that were to her frankly bewildering. One afternoon that summer, when the girls were taking their lunch breaks, she announced to Cassandra:

"Oh my God. Get *this*. My mother told me last night that Aunt Lydia and Uncle Billy and my grandparents have pooled their money together and bought a plot at Mount Auburn! Turns out they don't come cheap either. Nothing does in this town. That's another strike against it! Cambridge: incredibly boring and incredibly expensive, to boot. But seriously, Cassandra, can you imagine? Aunt Lydia and Uncle Billy and my grandparents laid away in a tomb for all eternity! *A plot in Mount Auburn!* Talk about never getting out of Cambridge! I ask you. Is that all those idiots have to look forward to?"

Cassandra's reaction to this bombshell was not quite as Sylvie had hoped.

"Do we want to get out of Cambridge?" she asked.

"Absolutely," said Sylvie flatly. There could be no question of that.

CHAPTER 5

One weekend, Sylvie got an invitation to go and stay on Martha's Vineyard at the fabulous beach-front property of a Bennington classmate named Vicky Lalage. Aside from the beachfront property, which had been in her family for generations, Vicky herself was nothing much to write home about, a dim, honey-blond creature with spectacles, the good-egg type often found at Bennington sitting under an apple tree with a group of similarly undistinguished girls and a pile of knitting. Nevertheless, Cassandra was jealous not to have been invited to go with, and was most put out to discover that their good friend Gala Gubelman just happened to be on the Vineyard, too.

"She's not staying with Vicky, though," Sylvie reported over the phone once she got there. "She's been dating this anorexic slut from Bryn Mawr and *that's* who she's staying with, not Vicky. Turns out her parents have this big place out in Edgartown."

"Wait, Gala is dating a girl *after* graduation?"

"I know, right? That's what I said! I said: Gala, you are being *ridiculous.*"

"What's the girl like?"

"Absolutely impossible—" Sylvie began, before launching into an exquisitely detailed tirade about the finer points of the anorexia from which she was "supposedly" in recovery, and what a drag it was to have to go out to eat with her; the girl's name was Tess Fox.

Exhibitionists all, this quartet of lithe young girls—Sylvie, Vicky, Gala, and Tess—spent the better part of that weekend on the nude beach. On Sunday afternoon, just before she had to go and catch the ferry, Sylvie was lying there and feeling stricken at the thought of having to go back to Black Currant. It was August by now; September, that month of new beginnings, fresh starts, was coming. Worse, it appeared that almost everybody she knew was going to be in New York City that fall except for her. Tess said that Gala could move into the studio apartment her parents had bought for her in the East Village, no problem, the two of them would be so cozy there; and Vicky revealed that she had just signed the lease on a loft in TriBeCa.

"Wait," said Sylvie to Vicky, remembering something, "you're a native New Yorker, aren't you?"

Vicky nodded.

"You grew up in Greenwich Village, right?"

"Well, when I was born we actually were living upt—"

Sylvie got right to the point.

"Your parents, though. Do your parents still live there? In Greenwich Village?"

"My *mother* does. My *father's* dead, remember."

Sylvie was so carried away with her ulterior motives, she didn't even bother to say *I'm sorry*. Instead, she rolled over on her stomach and sulked. So obviously this meant that nobody would be living in Vicky's childhood bedroom come September. The thought filled Sylvie with emptiness on this splendid summer's day. Then—rage! Why should Vicky's bedroom go unused, in the most fashionable neighborhood in New York City, with so many people desperate for housing? It wasn't fair!

She sat up straight, looked down at her sleek brown breasts and belly, then scooped up a palmful of sand and let it cascade through her fingertips, enjoying the soft heat of it against her skin. She felt full to bursting with life.

"Oh my God, did you hear the one about Penelope Entenmann?" Gala was now saying.

Penelope Entenmann was the name of the leggy cello student who was famous for letting Professor Sobel nail her in the Secret Garden.

"Oh no, what is it?" Vicky asked, being the good-egg type, genuinely concerned.

"*Pregnant.*"

It was presumed to be the professor's child, and in fact was. Sylvie made a note to tell Cassandra, who had had a crush on him back at Bennington and would surely be interested in the latest about him and Penelope.

"Oh, no! What is she going to do?"

"Keep it," said Gala authoritatively. "Rumor is she's going to have it in Hawaii."

"And what, like, give it up afterward?" Sylvie wanted to know. "Why doesn't she just have an abortion already?"

"That's, like, really judgmental of you," Tess Fox cut in. Over the course of that weekend she and Sylvie had not exactly hit it off, so to speak, and this was too bad, since they were in for a long ferry ride together, during which, as things turned out, they would bicker almost incessantly.

"No, no, she wants to *keep* it, she says. She wants to *raise* it in Hawaii, she says."

Idiot, thought Sylvie to herself. All of her classmates were idiots. But then she turned to Vicky and in her sweetest, most charismatic tone of voice said: "Hey, that's so cool about the loft in TriBeCa. I forgot if I mentioned it already, but *I'm* going to New York, too. Any day now." (*Bullshit!* Gala Gubelman was tempted to hiss, as she narrowed her eyes at Sylvie behind the lenses of her Italian sexpot sunglasses.) "But!" Sylvie carried on in all innocence. "I haven't figured out where I'm going to be living yet. Do you think there's any way that maybe I could crash at your mom's till I found a place?"

Sometimes there can be much wisdom in asking for things directly because so few people do it, and in this case it worked. Vicky was pleasantly surprised by Sylvie's candor, especially coming from this pretty, upbeat girl who made the most delicious tuna fish sandwiches anybody had ever tasted. Just the kind of girl who could stay with one's mother, she thought. The room was available, and it would be no trouble at all. Also, she still felt a good deal of guilt over the trust fund left to her by her dead father, an aristocratic French art collector. Letting Sylvie stay in her bedroom at her mother's would ease her conscience about getting the place in TriBeCa.

Sylvie has guts, Cassandra thought to herself on hearing the news that come September she was going to be living rent-free in a brownstone in the West Village. I would never have dared ask Vicky that. But she hugged her and said:

"Oh my God! New York! Sylvie, that's so wonderful! And who knows? Maybe I'll move there someday, too. After all—everyone from Bennington's already there anyway."

Sylvie thought this was just like Cassandra, making someone else's news all about herself; and the thought came to her that maybe she didn't want her best friend ever since high school to come to New York. Maybe she wanted New York City all to herself.

er first month in New York, Sylvie got a job at Petunia Bakery, in the West Village. Later on, of course, she would feel a mixture of emotions around that first job and what it said about her. On the one hand, she felt that its being a famous bakery—the one responsible for igniting the cupcake craze all over the city—conferred on her a certain cachet. But on the other hand, that was just the problem. Because some people—some of the die-hard New Yorkers whom Sylvie tried to emulate—blamed the cupcake craze, and places like Petunia, for gutting the soul of the city. Years after she had left Petunia, whenever the subject came up, she would always make sure to say that she had worked at the "original" location in the Village, and not one of the ones that sprang up later on in Rockefeller Center or around Columbus Circle.

But in the beginning anyway, Petunia was a confectionary paradise, its red velvet cupcakes and saucy, ruffled vintage aprons the perfect antidote to the Colonial austerity of Black Currant. Also, there were plenty of guys there, and all of them had crushes on the cute new girl, having long since tired of the other ones behind the counter. And Sylvie, herself, hadn't yet learned to find the kinds of guys who worked at Petunia annoying. By those kinds of guys, she meant adult men who were not ashamed to be caught dead working in the vicinity of cupcakes. But then, let it be said that in their generation, masculinity was not what it once was; just recently Gala Gubelman had had all of her friends in hysterics at an account of a date she had gone on during which the boy had tried to impress her by offering to share his homemade peanut brittle recipe. *Peanut brittle recipe?* the girls had repeated to one another, incredulous.

Sylvie made $8.25 an hour working at Petunia. But that was okay—everything was okay. Having gotten out from Tish and company alive was enough of a triumph to keep her in an excellent mood for a long time.

And she was living rent-free in a beautiful four-story brownstone in the Village! With a grand piano, and fluffy white couches, and all of the fabulous French paintings Vicky's father had spent a lifetime collecting. The windows of Sylvie's bedroom faced an iconically leafy Greenwich Village street, which was just as it should have been.

When Cassandra came to visit her at that apartment, the two of them passed hours in that bedroom with the view of the nice, leafy street, talking and talking, stopping only to eat the occasional cupcake from Petunia. That was another good thing: unlike Black Currant, Petunia let their employees get away with some freebies. Sylvie brought home boxfuls of cupcakes, and she and Cassandra could be found, toward the end of their evenings together, moaning at the deliciousness of it all and licking fat curlicues of chocolate buttercream frosting from their fingertips.

"Do you think you'll ever move to New York one of these days?" Sylvie asked Cassandra one night, because she wondered how she could bear to go on living in Cambridge.

"Maybe," replied Cassandra, who did sometimes envy Sylvie the comparative coolness of her lifestyle. And yet at the same time, because she was still in her early twenties, she believed that her options as to where she might live or what she might do with her life were limitless. Besides, her life in Boston was nothing if not comfortable, and Cassandra was big on having her creature comforts. She also liked having a steady boyfriend, and Sylvie had reported back to her that in New York these were not quite so easy to find because everybody knew that single women outnumbered the men. Then, too, Sylvie said, so many of the men you met there were short: "Manhattan," she had once fumed to Cassandra over the phone, "is an island of short men!" Cassandra's Harvard boyfriend was very tall and she liked that. It had been a point of pride when he came to visit her at Bennington. He's a big one, Alphie the security guard had murmured, with evident approval, on checking him in. It had been a long time since Alphie had seen a male specimen so strapping.

"If you moved here," went on Sylvie, "you'd have so many *connections.* You could get a job *like that.*" Doing what, Sylvie didn't know and Cassandra didn't ask: another perk of being twenty-two is that you still believe that things will just work out. For you anyway, they'll work out. "Like, for instance. The other night, there I was doing Zumba at Crunch—"

"Doing *what* at *where?*"

"*Zumba. Zumba dancing.* At Crunch. Crunch is the gym I go to. Gala and I go to the one on Lafayette," she added, with that peculiar desperation of people who are new to New York to show that they can get street names and addresses right. Cassandra failed to deduce, as quickly as Sylvie would have wanted her to, that Lafayette meant SoHo.

"Oh," Cassandra said, suddenly feeling left out. It wasn't that she wanted to go to the gym. Cassandra didn't exercise, and had avoided gyms ever since the day at Bennington when Pansy Chapin had convinced her to work out with her and she had fallen and bruised her knees when trying to get off the treadmill; Pansy never invited her to go again. No, it was just the thought of Sylvie and Gala going somewhere together without her that rankled.

"Yeah, and guess who I ran into? Gala wasn't there that night, she was off cheating on Tess with some guy."

"Oh, God. Oh, no. Please tell me it wasn't the guy with the peanut brittle recipe."

"No, no, he's ancient history. Peanut Brittle! That's what Gala and I decided to call him: Peanut Brittle. Sometimes when we meet a new guy, we say: He seems kind of Peanut Brittle. Peanut Brittle! It's the new crunchy granola."

"Hmm."

"But what I wanted to tell you is, I ran into Bitsy Citron! At Crunch."

"Bitsy Citron? What was *she* doing there?"

"Teaching, actually. Apparently she teaches this class called Beach Body."

"She would," said Cassandra, thinking of how Bitsy had been known, at Bennington, for her tight muscle tone, sexy hair, and her family's reportedly owning diamond mines somewhere in South America.

"Anyhow—afterward in the sauna together we started talking and I had forgotten, but! Bitsy's older brother is this really successful artist named *Ludo* Citron. Like, finance guys are starting to collect his work and he just did this really cool limited edition collaboration with Puma."

"Is that what being a successful artist means?"

"Hello, it's the twenty-first century, Cassandra! What the hell else could it mean? Triumph of capitalism and all that."

My, Sylvie sounds like a real New Yorker already, thought Cassandra, alternately impressed and horrified.

"But the point is, Cassandra, the point is that Bitsy said that maybe I could work for him! Like, maybe I could be an artist's assistant. Wouldn't that be cool if I were an artist's assistant?"

"I guess so."

Cassandra continued to feel left out. Peanut Brittle, she was thinking to herself. So Gala and Sylvie were making up their own adjectives and catchphrases now! Not so long ago, she and Sylvie had been the ones doing that.

"You guess so! Cassandra, Bitsy said it's a really great gig if you can get it, like, all his assistants ever do is hang out at his studio on the Bowery and listen to the Rolling Stones and eat roast chicken from FreshDirect."

"That does sound kind of great actually, Sylvie," Cassandra admitted, visions of free roast chickens dancing like sugar plums in her head.

"And! If you moved here," said Sylvie again, bolstered by the prevailing mood of optimism, "we could live together. Maybe."

Cassandra was touched by this. The thought of living with Sylvie was as sweet to her in that moment as any love nest, and she forgave her for making up catchphrases and doing Zumba with Gala.

"But you're living at Vicky's," she said, remembering reality, which, as always, was utterly inconvenient.

Sylvie shrugged and reached for the last of the cupcakes, carefully splitting it in half with Cassandra.

"Yes, but not forever," she said.

Meanwhile, Vicky's mother and Sylvie's landlord, Rosa Lalage, was a former opera singer. She had tawny-blond hair and the brittle beauty of a well-manicured woman past a certain age. On several occasions, Sylvie had observed her through the French doors of the living room doing her vocal exercises while wearing nothing but a pink thong. She still had her figure, at least. One of Sylvie's chores for living in the brownstone rent-free—and there were many of them, she was to discover—was to keep her refrigerator stocked with low-fat Greek yogurts, just about the only food she ever ate. And as the summer wore on, living with Rosa Lalage and her white silky terrier, Fabergé, was her first experience of just how bitter it was to be on the bottom end of the totem pole in New York City—at the receiving end of the whims and patronage of those more fortunate than you.

Death turned out to be the theme—the recurring note—of Sylvie's first few months in New York. One night, Cassandra got a phone call. It was Sylvie, and she was crying.

"Oh my God. What happened?"

"Fabergé!"

"Fabergé?"

"The dog! Rosa's dog!"

"Oh, *Fabergé*. The obnoxious little terrier. Right."

"She's dead."

"Dead! Oh my God. What hap—"

"I was supposed to be watching her while Rosa was on the Vineyard, is the thing."

Then Sylvie sobbed girlishly, beautifully; her sobs formed lovely moaning silver bells. She was twenty-two years old and in New York City and life was an adventure. Even this—especially this—was an adventure! When you got right down to it, what Sylvie and Cassandra had in common above all else was a lust for misfortune, the more ridiculous the better. A favorite phrase of theirs: *This would happen to us!*

"And I *was* watching her. Well, not all the time, but you know—"

Cassandra did know. *She* wouldn't have left a dog with Sylvie, who was always up to something or other at the last minute.

"Well, what happened?"

"Well, I'd been out a lot, there's this guy, Jasper, at the bakery, oh my God, well—wait, I'll tell you about Jasper later. Anyway, I'd been out one night. One. And when I got in this morning, I saw her. *Fabergé.* On the living room floor. I saw her through the French doors."

Sylvie shuddered, then continued: "Not that I was sorry exactly. I always hated that dog."

"God, me, too. Rosa just *would* have to have a dog like that."

The next motif of death happened when Rosa—fresh off the Vineyard and nonplussed that her dog had upped and kicked the bucket under Sylvie's care—banished her to sleep not in the guest room but in a tiny room on the fourth floor that once upon a time had been Vicky's nursery. Getting in the bed that first night, Sylvie was puzzled to find something hard underneath the pillow. It turned out to be a small wooden box, wrapped in a French flag. She unwrapped the flag and read the label on the box.

"*Cassandra!*" she screamed into the phone, having picked it up to call her immediately. "Cassandra! You are not going to believe what I am holding in my hand. What I found, under my goddamn pillow—"

"Your pillow?"

"Yeah, the bitch stood there in her pink thong and waved her golden wand and exiled me to, get this, Vicky's nursery! I haven't figured out what the significance of that is, but it's definitely kind of sick, right? So okay, there's this, like, lump, not a normal lump, under my pillow. Like, you could hurt your head on it. It turns out it's a box. A box in a French flag, okay? So I take the flag off and the label on the box says"—Sylvie paused appropriately—"'Contents: Marc Lalage.'"

"'*Contents: Marc Lalage*'! You mean—"

"I mean, this woman made me sleep in a bed with her husband's ashes! Yes! That's what I mean. Jesus Christ! I've got to get out of this place."

It was after the episode of "Contents: Marc Lalage" that Sylvie first learned one of the important lessons of life in New York City, or anywhere else as a grown-up for that matter: the lesson of hoping not to run into people you have had fallings-out with. For years, long, long after leaving there, she dreaded the threat of running into Rosa Lalage and her daughter Vicky, too.

CHAPTER 7

One weekend not long after this, Sylvie came home for a visit. On Saturday night she and Cassandra had stayed up so late talking at Sylvie's mother's house that Cassandra had ended up spending the night there, which had necessitated her using Sylvie's toothbrush—pink, with Tom's of Maine cinnamon toothpaste (Sylvie's parents were hippies and had been using this stuff for years)—and having to borrow a pair of her underpants the following morning. They were slightly too small for her but mercifully clean and they even smelled of lavender sachets from the dryer: how sweet to share things with Sylvie, Cassandra thought, to wake up on the sheets of her childhood bedroom, strewn with faded buttercups. It was a purplish gray winter morning, faintly drizzling.

"Come on, let's go to Black Currant," Cassandra begged her.

"Cassandra."

Sylvie did not relish the thought of returning to the site of her old workplace, ill-fated as her brief tenure there had been.

"Oh come on, you know that you haven't worked there in ages."

Cassandra was right, because when you are young, even a period of six months can feel like a lifetime. Sylvie was convinced. And also, she consoled herself, she would be sure to get an iced Americano as well as some of that wonderful creamy oatmeal with the cranberries, so long as Cassandra was paying. Cassandra was often in the habit of paying for things, Sylvie had noticed, and thought that this was a most useful quality to have in one's best friend.

On arriving at Black Currant, they were struck by a most

gratifying sight: Sylvie's long-ago nemesis, the dreaded Tish, once upon a time described on Yelp as "the I See Dead People manager," standing behind the counter, her tiny, ruined body aslant on a pair of crutches.

Tish! On crutches! The girls choked back a furious desire to laugh.

Sylvie regained her composure and strode up to the counter with a confident roll of her Zumba-toned hips and said, "Hey, Tish," with a big smile on her face. And then Tish did something truly distressing and smiled herself. Cassandra saw right away what Sylvie meant about Tish's scowl being preferable to her smile.

"Hey," said Tish, her low-affect voice no match for Sylvie's exuberant force of personality. For Tish was thinking: So she did go to New York, that hot, flaky girl with the pretentious French name. What was it: Sheri, or Sido, or something? Giving your American-born daughter a French name was just asking for trouble, Tish felt. She was sure to go through life with the most romantic and outlandish expectations. It never paid to hire girls like that. They had too many opportunities, those ones. They never stayed.

And furthermore, Tish could tell that Sylvie had gone to New York because she just had *that look*. You couldn't miss it, in Harvard Square, where so few people had it. It had to do with a certain fearless way of carrying yourself that was hardly necessary in Cambridge, where nothing, except for boredom and a kind of quiet death of the soul, was to be feared. Tish noted with scorn Sylvie's black leggings and motorcycle boots, and the deft way she'd tied her scarf. Also: her beautiful, clear skin and beautiful, compact body.

"So, how are things with you, Tish? And how's business?"

Sylvie considered asking her about the crutches, but then decided against it. She thought it was more enraging actually not to, as though to meet Tish again in this wretched state was only to be expected.

"Fine. *Fine.*"

"You know what I'm in the mood for," Sylvie went on shamelessly, "a large iced Americano, please, and also—a large oatmeal! You guys just have the best oatmeal, Tish. I've always said this bakery was so good, it could almost make it in New York City. So! A large oatmeal, with extra cranberries, if you don't mind. Thanks, Tish."

Now, ordinarily, Tish gave out extras and freebies under no circumstances. But there was no telling just what this Sido-Sheri girl might do; Tish recalled her unbecoming sense of self-respect back when she was an employee. So she gave her the damn extra cranberries, a wholly extravagant deluge of them on top. She did it because she just wanted to get her out of there as fast as she could.

"Oh my God, Sylvie, that was fabulous!" Cassandra applauded her afterward. "I'd never have thought of that little extra touch of asking for the cranberries. Do you remember—"

"*A cranberry is a cranberry!* Cassandra? How could I forget?"

"And another thing, you look really hot today, Sylvie. Your hair, the boots, everything. You just look *so New York*. I'm sure she noticed."

Sylvie thought how nice it was to return to Cambridge once in a while, just for a boost to the ego. In New York, everyone was hot. In Cambridge, no one was.

She took this exact moment to ask Cassandra about something that had been on her mind recently. As a matter of fact, her coming home this particular weekend had not been random; she had come home in part because she wanted to ask Cassandra the following question in person.

"Hey, so there's this really great apartment I found," she said.

And then before Cassandra could say anything she proceeded to describe it in great detail, making sure she understood how darling it was before she got to her eventual point, which was to ask her for the security deposit; Cassandra could never resist anything that appealed to her sense of aesthetics.

"And it's so cute," Sylvie heard herself saying, "it has this really pretty molded white ceiling and oh! You'll love this, when you come visit. The bathroom even has a claw-foot tub. The water pressure is really weak, though, but no big deal. Every apartment has to have *something* wrong with it."

"Yeah, and especially in New York City. Oh Sylvie, Sylvie, I think it sounds practically perfect for you!"

"It used to be a studio, but the landlord just added a partition to make it a two-bedroom, so he could get more money." Cassandra nodded, thinking how helpful it was of Sylvie to give her a crash course in the mercenary ways of New York City real estate. "So, after I sign the lease I'll have to get a roommate."

"Who are you thinking of?" Cassandra asked her, imagining that it would be one of their Bennington classmates.

"Oh, I'll be sure to find someone," said Sylvie with her typical aplomb, and in fact, over the years that she went on to live in that apartment, none of her many roommates would be former classmates but instead almost always strangers. Furthermore, as Sylvie would go on to discover, almost none of them were satisfactory. There was the cheap, slightly-older-than-Sylvie single woman—a veritable spinster—who worked for a human rights organization and after work would come home and make "bad, white-people Indian food" (thus did Sylvie describe said cuisine over the phone to Cassandra, who understood where she was coming from immediately). There was the overzealous, quite possibly manic-depressive theater girl who covered the refrigerator with magnets ("Magnets, Cassandra! *Magnets*"). There was the midwestern publishing girl who demanded that the apartment be absolutely quiet so that she could concentrate on reading manuscripts. Not to mention an NYU graduate student, from Tel Aviv, who served Sylvie with papers threatening to sue her over some vague misunderstanding about a mattress.

Sylvie decided here to drop the matter of the security deposit casually, without any alarming or predatory emphasis, in the blameless tones of a plucky young thing all alone in the big city. Cassandra thought: It's for Sylvie. I love her. And that was that. She made up her mind that she would be happy to give her the money, and said so. Also, she thought to herself, if one of these days she ever did move to New York, as Sylvie was always begging her to do, it was just possible that she would move in with Sylvie in that very apartment. So why not help her to get it? It would be a shame to let it go over a little thing like the security deposit when she, Cassandra, had the money and her beloved Sylvie didn't.

"Tomorrow," she said firmly, and Sylvie's heart leapt. Success! was what she was thinking. "I'll write you a check tomorrow, before you go back to New York. I wish I had known! I don't have my checkbook on me today."

"Actually"—Sylvie hesitated—"I was thinking cash."

"Cash?" echoed Cassandra uncomprehendingly. She was not in the habit of turning down people who were so kind as to offer one checks herself.

Sylvie reiterated that yes, if there was one thing she had learned so far in New York City, it was that it was always better to have cash; cash, Sylvie reported to Cassandra, was king.

"All right," Cassandra said, prepared to take her word for it. "But"—she found herself suddenly curious about something—"I thought you said you started working for Bitsy's brother at his studio. Has he not paid you yet, or what?"

"He's not going to pay me, Cassandra. It's just an unpaid internship, to start. You have to understand how it works. He's such a big deal! Everybody wants to work for him."

"Do you like his work?" Cassandra asked her, genuinely curious because she respected Sylvie's opinions and because they were close enough to being out of college that they actually believed that art still mattered. That it was sacred, even.

"Not at all, actually," said Sylvie promptly, but this had not prevented her from agreeing to work for him for free or from falling into bed with him, either. A regime of regular, highly aerobic sex, much of it taking place amid collapsed cardboard boxes and unfinished canvases, had contributed to her looking so radiant these days. She hadn't told Cassandra about Ludo, thinking that she might be jealous and because Gala, so much more experienced than either of them, was her chosen sexual confidante; one of those was enough, Sylvie felt.

The following afternoon, Sylvie met up with Cassandra on her lunch break and the two of them went and drank raspberry lime rickeys in the Sunken Garden at Radcliffe. After that they walked across the square to Cassandra's bank, Cambridge Trust. It was a wonderful, homey, trustworthy, shabby-prep old bank of the kind that doesn't exist anymore. Cassandra had opened a modest savings account there a number of years ago now, when she was still in high school. This was the reason she had the money to give Sylvie now. The picture on her Cambridge Trust bank card showed her in a peppermint-striped sundress, her fine blond hair worn long and parted, rather virginally, in the middle. At the time that photograph was taken, she was fourteen years old.

Cassandra got Sylvie cash out of the bank. The security deposit was one thousand dollars. Sylvie, taking that amount of money with what would have been to anyone but Cassandra a disturbing sense of casualness, entitlement even, remarked, "You know, I just closed my account here."

"Oh, so you opened up a bank account in New York?"

"Yeah, Bank of America. It's a chain, but—" They were sweet, diligent, well-trained Cambridge girls, given to saying things like *It's a chain, but.* Sylvie went on, "It's a chain, but I mean, that's the way the world works now. And I just figured, you know, it's not like I'm ever coming back here again, so . . ."

"No," said Cassandra, accepting this.

Years later, when they were both nearly thirty, Sylvie and Cassandra had a conversation in which they both remembered Cambridge Trust fondly. And Sylvie, sitting on the kitchen counter of her apartment in Fort Greene, took a puff of her joint and remarked, "Actually, I think that the day I closed my account at Cambridge Trust was the day my childhood ended. And you know something?" She laughed. "It's been all downhill ever since."

Then Cassandra laughed, too. They laughed, that night, until they cried.

CHAPTER 8

Even though she was nearly always broke and had no health insurance, Sylvie had three indulgences that even under dire straits could not be ignored. They were iced Americanos, marijuana, and fine lingerie.

Cassandra loved lingerie, too, and when Sylvie had any money to spare, which was not often, she would hit all of the sample sales and buy matching pieces for Cassandra and herself. French lingerie. Italian lingerie. Lingerie that, to Cassandra, had been bought in New York, not Boston, not Cambridge, and so had the pixie dust of Manhattan on it. Every year on Cassandra's birthday, Sylvie showered her with satin tap shorts, crepe de chine camisoles, rosebud or bluebell garters. Her packages to Cassandra were always beautifully wrapped, in lilac or celery tissues, in brown paper with a pink cotton bow.

They knew each other's cup sizes and measurements—having been acquainted with the nooks and crannies and delicate variations of each other's blossoming bodies ever since they were just fourteen years old: Sylvie, 34B, extra-small to small in bottoms, Cassandra, 36C, medium to large. They knew how their bodies and mood swings reacted to different brands of the birth control pill and how frequently (or not) they had orgasms and doing what and with whom.

Sometimes they'd trot around Sylvie's apartment trying on the lingerie they'd just bought, pulling their stomachs in and thrusting out their boobs in bustiers and thigh highs in front of the dusty mirror. Then they'd plop down at the kitchen table and polish off another jar of Nutella, spreading it on pieces of burned toast they heated up in Sylvie's oven because she was too poor in those days to own a toaster.

"Goddamn it, are we really that low on Nutella? Desperate living!" *Desperate living* was a catchphrase of theirs, to be employed in many a situation that the average individual might not feel warranted it. "Hey, Cassandra, go down to the bodega and get some. No, it's okay, just go in your slip and throw a coat over it, you think that little Chinese guy who owns the bodega hasn't seen worse at two in the morning? I can't go, I'm totally high."

"You are?"

"Cassandra."

Sylvie was so animated, Cassandra always forgot that her best friend was actually a huge pothead.

"Anything," said Cassandra, stopping to put her camel-hair coat on over her pink silk slip, "for Nutella."

"It's better than sex," said Sylvie slyly, and although by now she had racked up a modest number of lovers, some of whom, like Ludo, were even good, it was still, in some private, girlish way, true.

Every February, the girls sent each other vintage valentines. Inside the valentines they wrote: "Guess who?" or "Your (not so secret) admirer" or, because they were both children of divorce and did not necessarily believe in the bonds between people being everlasting, "Don't worry! At least *somebody* will always love you."

Sylvie went just about everywhere in leggings, French sailor shirts, and motorcycle boots. Cassandra marveled at how great she looked even after traveling, the sight of her back home in Cambridge for the holidays after the grueling Fung Wah bus ride, in a black minidress and white lace tights, shaking snowflakes from her cap of dark hair.

During these years, Sylvie was still wearing her black hair in a dashing, insouciant pixie cut and was so abundantly, effortlessly sexy that she could pick random clothing off the floor of her apartment and get dressed and still look great; a true New Yorker by now, she applied silver eyeliner with expert fingers standing on the subway.

And Sylvie, during these years, her early, delirious years in New York City, the years in which she still deemed it worthwhile to apply silver eyeliner, fell in love with ease: there was a series of boys with supple young bodies and curly hair and names like Jasper and Angus and Max and she had loved them, in her fashion, loved them, loved them all.

And yet when, later on in her life, she thought back to this time, it wasn't the boys she had been in love with that she remembered. It wasn't those boys that came back. No, it was her apartment. The boys were blurry, where her memories of the apartment persisted in being almost unbearably specific. Yes, years, years later she was disconcerted to find that she could still remember nearly everything, from its wedding-cake ceiling to the rosy Chinese lantern she had splurged on at Pearl River Mart and hung up in the middle of the room, to its extraordinary natural light. That light could trick you into believing that you were in Florence—or the French countryside—or Athens—anyway, not America. Waking up there was like waking up in a jar of lavender honey. It was an apartment that was high on charm, light on convenience—not a single closet; the weakest water pressure in the world. Sylvie's landlord, Pete, was a piano teacher of the fading hippie variety, who had bought the building long ago and was thoroughly uninterested in making improvements.

And Sylvie, who not infrequently fell behind on her rent, didn't demand them.

Most bathrooms in the kinds of apartments people live in during their twenties are charmless, neon-lit squares; the faster you get the hell out of them the better. But Sylvie's bathroom, ah Sylvie's bathroom, it was a most romantic spot, with that lavender-honey light streaming in through long windows overlooking one of the ramshackle gardens of Brooklyn. The sink was an old-world shade of terra-cotta, and luxuriously deep. But for all that Sylvie's bathroom was beautiful it was also, in a way, lonely; tinged with decay, or the foreboding of decay.

A decay that could only be feminine.

A bathroom where, washing one's face late at night or in the cool thin light of morning, Sylvie sometimes would look at her reflection staring back at her in the mirror and suddenly have the presence of mind to remember that she was getting older after all.

CHAPTER 9

During these years, the years right after Bennington, Cassandra spent many weekends in New York. How she looked forward to the adventure of hailing a Fung Wah bus on a side street in Chinatown on a Friday night, armed with the navy blue L.L.Bean Boat and Tote she'd had ever since freshman year. She didn't, however, look forward to the experience of taking the Fung Wah itself; nobody in his or her right mind could have looked forward to that.

The inconveniences of the Fung Wah were many, and bemoaned not only by Sylvie and Cassandra but by the young and the poor the whole East Coast over. Every couple of months, it seemed, a brand-new article appeared in *The Boston Globe* about the latest scandal: one of their buses bursting into flames, a number of others failing inspections. It was true, as Sylvie once remarked to Cassandra, that the people who worked for the Fung Wah spoke English only when it suited them, and that was rarely. Otherwise, it was all Chinese, all the time. The girls, coming off a hammering onslaught of this least melodic of languages, had a terrifying thought, which they dared voice only to each other: *What if Chinese becomes the universal language?*

"Why Chinese, when it could be, you know, Italian?"

"Because that's not where the money is."

"What isn't where the money is?"

"Italy, you idiot. Hadn't you heard? The future belongs to the Chinese."

On Sunday afternoons in New York, when she was supposed to be going back to Boston, Cassandra used to get this knot in her stomach. Sylvie and she, both familiar with this feeling, called it the Fung Wah Blues, as in, "Oh, no, I feel sick to my stomach, I must be coming down with the Fung Wah Blues . . ."

Then they would laugh and order another twelve-dollar cocktail neither one of them could afford, though often Cassandra, having more money, paid quite happily for Sylvie. Back then, twelve-dollar drinks with numerous, not necessarily complementary ingredients were still a lot of fun to splurge on, and they hadn't yet woken up enough mornings with splitting hangovers to learn to distrust sugary cocktails. Even the overpriced, sometimes white trash–inspired comfort food on the menus of Brooklyn restaurants was still cunning, back then.

One Saturday afternoon right around Christmastime when Cassandra was visiting, they met up with Gala Gubelman, famous campus beauty and kleptomaniac. Alphie the security guard had once caught her red-handed stealing the tip jar from the Upstairs Cafe, but one look at Gala's lascivious baby face and he let it drop. This resulted in a nearly mythic bout of campus drama when, sometime afterward, Gala pinned the abduction of the tip jar on the notorious Lanie Tobacco, she of the wine-stained bathrobe and halo of fruit flies over her head, suspecting, correctly, that people would believe Lanie capable of just about anything. (One of Lanie's feats of mastery had been selling coke to this hot young Italian professor, Marcella Davini, the night before the midterm exam; she passed out in Lanie's room and forgot to give the exam entirely.) Lanie had then confronted and blackmailed poor Gala in the game room, luring her into the role of accomplice in a series of darker and darker intrigues for the remainder of the school year.

That Saturday, the three young women spent a harmonious afternoon strolling around downtown, stopping to buy five-dollar pashminas from a street vendor in SoHo. Cassandra bought one in lavender and Sylvie bought one in cream right away. But Gala couldn't make up her mind. Did she want gold? Or red? Or how about this turquoise one? The only word for Gala Gubelman's style of beauty was *ripe*; even her head of chestnut hair seemed to suggest the promise of fertility. On top of this, she heightened, rather than downplayed, her lavish physical good fortune by always dressing in bright colors; Gala was the sort of woman who would not buy a pair of black tights if a pair of kelly green ones could be had instead.

"The turquoise looks cheap," weighed in Sylvie.

"No," said Cassandra, "it could be almost Indian . . ."

"Indian? Since when do you like things that are Indian?"

"Indian culture can provide some really elegant visual inspiration sometimes. If you don't overdo it."

"Yeah, but I hate all of that cheesy beading they do."

"I'd get red if I were you," said Cassandra, who, being a blonde, had always believed that the color red belonged to brunettes.

"But I just don't know," cooed Gala, who could make the most mundane of sentences come out sexy. She even had a dainty, provoking little lisp. Then, as if the sound of her own voice had reminded her of her own goddesslike power in the world where men were concerned, she turned to the nearest one she could find. It was the pashmina vendor, who had been getting impatient with the windy deliberations of these young women mussing up his merchandise.

"You," said Gala, her plump lips curving into a honeyed, deadly smile. "Which color would *you* get if you were me?" She cocked her head, cradling the soft fabrics to her throat.

He pointed to the gold one and that settled it. Gala bought the gold pashmina.

Afterward the girls burst out laughing and Sylvie chided her: "Gala! You needed to ask the pashmina vendor for color advice?"

"When we were standing right there," said Cassandra.

"And you had to ask, like, this random Haitian dude for his opinion. I was an art history major!"

"We have great taste!" added Cassandra.

Gala shrugged.

"You *are* boy crazy, Gala. This just goes to prove it."

"Boy crazy? Boy crazy? Actually, in case you've blocked out our Bennington days, I'm a complete and total slut!"

They all laughed, remembering.

Sylvie said: "Hey, we were trying to remember something the other day. Did you ever have a threesome with Pansy Chapin?"

"Oh, no. You must be thinking of me and Bitsy Citron."

"Oh, yeah, people always used to get Pansy and Bitsy mixed up," said Sylvie. "Same physical type. But Bitsy had that little white dog named Brioche, remember? She used to bring him with her to Coffee Hour."

"Is Bitsy a native New Yorker?" Cassandra wanted to know.

"Oh, yeah. She and Ludo grew up on Park Avenue, remember?" Sylvie had since stopped sleeping with Ludo and was no longer working for him, but considered herself to still be an authority on the Citron family nevertheless. "This one time the whole family got tied up *for ransom*. The guy who did it was wearing a ski mask and everything. He must have had some interest in their diamond mines. They never did catch him, I don't think. But, moving on. Is Pansy an heiress to anything? She certainly *looks* like one."

"No," answered Cassandra promptly. "Old money. Bar Harbor. You get the picture. It ran out."

"Oh. Well, anyway. Bitsy Citron and I had a threesome with that Bulgarian sculptor guy, what was his name, the guy who used to wear those really skinny purple velvet pants."

"Oh yeah, that character. What *was* his name?"

"Does it matter? To tell you the truth, the only damn thing I can remember about him now are those purple velvet pants. Honestly, if I saw a lineup of twelve naked male bodies, I wouldn't have a clue which one of them was his."

Later on that same afternoon, Gala and Cassandra found a coat on sale that they both liked at a boutique in SoHo. Luckily, there were two of them left in just the right sizes.

Cassandra turned to Gala and asked her: "Would it be okay do you think if we had the same coat? I mean—with you being in New York, and me being in Boston?"

For Gala, a confident, pleasure-seeking creature, there had never been a question that both of them would buy the damn coat. She said: "It's fine. I don't care. In fact, we could wear them out of the store today, I wouldn't mind."

After buying the matching coats, the three of them sprang into the campy spirit of the coincidence. The thought of Cassandra and Gala posing in their coats immediately brought to Sylvie's mind Diane Arbus's portraits of twins. It didn't hurt that the coats in question verged on the outlandish, being royal blue felt with Peter Pan collars and black velveteen bows on the pockets.

"You know what these remind me of?" exclaimed Cassandra. "*Madeline!* I'm going to call this my *Madeline* coat."

"Oh my God, *Madeline!*" Sylvie trilled.

And then Gala was trilling, too: "Oh, *Madeline*, my sister and I used to love those books! She was our hero!"

Everyone's mood brightened at the nostalgic thought of *Madeline*, the Parisian comfort food of their upper-middle-class childhoods, and Gala and Cassandra swirled out of the boutique in their matching coats, striking poses for Sylvie's camera. People stopped to look at them on the street, these charming, round-faced young women looking years younger than they really were in these rather ridiculous coats of theirs, one with long chestnut hair, the other's bobbed and golden. (Cassandra had cut hers after graduation.) Then, as if they truly were in a photo shoot for a catalog, snowflakes began to fall—the first snowfall of the year. And then several months later, a photograph of Gala roaming down Mercer Street in her *Madeline* coat and a leopard miniskirt appeared on the website of *Italian Vogue*. That figured, the girls complained. Gala got all the breaks.

Soon, they passed the window of a woman's clothing store called Endless Flax.

Sylvie pointed at the sign and said: "Oh God, that place just looks so depressing. More like it should be in Cambridge than New York, right? And anyway—who would want to shop at a store named Endless Flax? I mean, come on. *Endless Flax.* Pretty fucking bleak already."

"Oh no," said Gala, wrinkling her nose. "Is everything in there, like, hemp?"

Oh, how she hated earth tones.

With a sense of creeping horror, the three of them peeked in the window.

"Imagine it coming to that," said Cassandra, with a sad shake of the head.

"What?"

"Elastic-waist pants."

"Endless flax," Sylvie repeated in sheer wonderment. "Endless flax!"

For the three attractive young women standing in front of the window, those two words said only endless boredom, aging, disappointment, failure. They laughed for a good long while that afternoon, unable to conceive of their own lives ever being anything other than fantastical, beautiful, richly and expensively textured.

CHAPTER 10

Next, while warming themselves up over cups of Valrhona hot chocolate indoors, Gala asked her friends: "So. Feel like going over to Orpheus's place with me? He invited me for this, like, little karaoke evening he's having later on."

"Orpheus! Are you still hooking up with that hipster doofus?"

"Hey! That's not fair, Sylvie."

"Ah! So you are hooking up with him or you'd be perfectly fine admitting that he's a hipster doofus."

"*Sylvie.* But you're going to come with me, aren't you?"

"Where is his apartment again?" asked Sylvie, who considered all invitations from the vantage point of geographical convenience, or lack thereof.

But to Cassandra the question of greater importance was: "Why karaoke? Why must people in our generation persist in liking karaoke so much? It's one of the trends I just can't get behind."

"One of the trends? One of the trends? Cassandra, you can't get behind *any* of the trends of our generation."

"Oh, and you like karaoke, I suppose?"

"Karaoke? I fucking hate karaoke. But that's not the point. The point is—"

"*Sylvie. Cassandra.* Please. You have to come. I beg of you. I need your protection. Strength in numbers! Orpheus is sleeping with this new girl and I'm going to have to meet her for the first time tonight."

"Is it another Bennington girl?" Cassandra wanted to know. Orpheus McCloud was one of their few male classmates, and it only followed that even after graduation, there would be untold numbers of willing and ready Bennington girls whose sweet, wild privates were left for him to plunder. He was a not entirely failed folk musician and not even bad-looking, either. Not even bad-looking was the best a girl could hope for in summing up the opposite sex at Bennington.

"No, she's somebody he met in the real world, can you believe it? I don't know what her story is. But I'm dying to find out."

"But Gala," Sylvie said, "I just don't get why you are always so incredibly possessive about your exes. It's not like you don't move on quickly enough yourself—you're always sleeping with somebody new."

Gala considered the magnitude of Sylvie's question with the respect it deserved. While winding a chestnut curl around one of her fingers, painted with sluttishly chipped purple polish, she said finally: "Yeah, well. There are plenty of people you can find to *go to sleep with* in this city. Finding someone you want to *wake up with* is another story. I like Orpheus, I'm still kind of hung up on him. You know what he used to do? He used to actually *make my bed* sometimes. In the morning, before he left for class. Don't you think that was really sweet of him?"

"No," said Sylvie.

"No," agreed Cassandra. "I'd think it was only gentlemanly courtesy."

"Please! You two must not know what's out there. You haven't *lived.*"

After much deliberation and more begging from Gala, it was agreed that the girls would accompany her to Orpheus's place in Astoria.

"Astoria? Where the hell's that?" demanded Cassandra. It sounded so foreign. Another country, almost.

"Queens, you idiot. Gala's right. You haven't lived! Try getting off Brattle Street much?"

"Only when I come see you," Cassandra confessed.

"Yeah, I keep wondering why the hell you haven't just moved to New York yet," Gala pointed out, reasonably enough. "It feels like you're always visiting."

Cassandra shrugged and reminded Gala that she had a boyfriend in Boston and wanted to be with him, an explanation that she thought Gala, being by her own admission a complete and total slut, would accept.

And Gala did accept it, saying: "He's, like, incredibly tall, right?"

"Six foot five," said Cassandra, happy to enumerate.

"That's hot, Cassandra. That must be really hot."

"It is."

"Manhattan," groaned Sylvie, not for the first time. "I've told you and told you! It's an island of short men."

"What do you think brings them here?" Gala asked.

"I've been thinking about that very question and I have a theory. Money! They're at an evolutionary disadvantage being short, see, so they have to do *something* to help them get the ladies. So, they all decide to come to Manhattan to try to make money."

"Hmm," murmured Gala and Cassandra, convinced.

They left the café and picked up the train at Union Square. It took too long to get to Astoria, and it was in the wrong goddamn direction, Sylvie realized: you had to get on an uptown train and cross the Fifty-Ninth Street Bridge. It was going to be a schlep getting back to Fort Greene at the end of the night. It occurred to her that she was already getting a little jaded, compared to when she'd first moved to the city. Back then, she was up for going absolutely everywhere. Now she liked keeping her entire life below Fourteenth Street, if she could help it. Even invitations to openings in Chelsea were getting all too easy to say no to. Plus, nobody ever actually has any fun at openings, and anybody who persisted in saying that they did must be, in Sylvie's estimation, either a liar or a pretentious moron.

Cassandra, on the other hand, had never seen anything like

Astoria before: another country indeed and not one she would have traveled to by choice. No, it was more like the kind of country where you'd have to get your shots taken care of before they'd let you in. The streets were thronged with sticky brown children running untamed. No trees, no history, no apparent charm; even the fresh fallen snowflakes, which were always so enchanting in Cambridge, did precious little to coat the sordid ambience of a place like this. There were skinned lambs slung in the windows of the butcher shops and, at the foot of the subway, something that went by the ominous words of *taco truck*. Who could possibly eat food from a truck? thought Cassandra, daintily stepping over the wet strands of garbage. Who dares to risk it?

"A lot of Greeks out here," said Gala. "Some of the guys are pretty hot to begin with, but I've noticed that they have a way of aging fast and getting all jowly. You have to stick with the really young ones. See"—she gestured to a sculpted young man unpacking a crate of clementines at an overflowing fruit stand; it was nearly Christmas and citrus in all its quenching splendor was appearing everywhere—"that place is open twenty-four hours, which is cool. I love combining fruit and sex. Have you ever had a guy feed you chunks of mango right after doing it?"

The girls shook their heads.

"*Sexy!* You really ought to keep it in mind, for future reference. Okay, I think it's this way to Orpheus's place, if I remember correctly . . ."

They stopped en route and bought him a bottle of prosecco, which Sylvie, for one, resented, because she remembered afterward that his family was loaded. Also: since when did Bennington boys ever remember to bring anybody a hostess gift? They just brought themselves and that was supposed to be the ultimate prize. Well, but who could blame them? It *was*.

"Gala, do you have any insight into why Orpheus lives out here? I thought that his family, like, once owned the state of Kentucky or something like that. Like, really old Southern money. Right?"

"Orpheus McCloud," said Cassandra dreamily. "With a name like that . . ."

"He just likes living out here, I guess. You know how guys are. They don't care if things are clean."

"But still. You'd think it would be inconvenient, living all the way out here. Like, even getting somebody to come home with you. They'd have to go all the way to Queens."

"But even if Orpheus's family does have a ton of money, so what? I've always thought it was cool that he lives pretty modestly, all things considered."

"Oh, right, why, because living in Queens when you could actually afford to live somewhere else is so 'authentic'?"

"Well, okay. I did always wonder what the hell he was doing in Queens."

When they got to Orpheus's apartment, they walked in on him and the new girl he was sleeping with, as if the two of them were in the middle of a date. The girl, whoever she was, turned out to be some blonde in a black leotard popping a lamb roast into the oven. The apartment was fragrant with spices—tarragon, thyme. Meanwhile, Orpheus lounged at the table, a lock of long strawberry-blond hair in his eyes, drinking whiskey. He radiated the sleepy comfort of a man for whom a woman was presently cooking a good meal. The girl, Cassandra noted, wasn't sleepy—anything but. There had been a certain striking pertness to the pose her body struck when she'd popped the roast into the oven. Confidence, Cassandra was thinking. This girl struck her as being overconfident. She moved around Orpheus's kitchen with an air altogether lacking in the mincing apology and accommodation Cassandra was long used to observing in women around men, and nearly always favored herself.

"Are you two wearing the same exact coat?" asked Orpheus,

squinting at Gala and Cassandra. He thought so, but couldn't be sure and didn't want to risk getting it wrong. If there was one thing he'd learned at Bennington, it was that girls' egos were fragile. They could take offense at the tiniest things *like that* and then before you knew it there would be hell to pay all over campus. The Bennington female, Orpheus thought: Desire and drama incarnate.

"They're our *Madeline* coats!" Not to be outdone by this strange woman and her lamb roast, Gala did a twirl, nudging Cassandra to join her. Cassandra, with rather less natural flair than Gala for this sort of thing, complied. Jesus, thought Sylvie, relieved to be staying out of this one in her plain black peacoat.

"Madeline?" Orpheus still couldn't get with the program.

At this point the mystery chick spoke up. "*Madeline*," she said to Orpheus, assuming a suave, patient tone. "The children's books. You know. The little French schoolgirl. The redhead."

"Oh, the redhead! Right. The redhead with the yellow hat. Huh." He would have continued this line of thought but was getting distracted by the sight of Gala, peeling off the *Madeline* coat and propping her boobs up at a bursting angle. Goddamn it, thought Orpheus, pouring himself another glass of whiskey. As luck would have it, Gala just happened to have on a leotard, too. Red, though, not black. With it she was wearing a thrifted tartan kilt, sloppily missing its pin. There was always something a little slapdash about Gala's appearance, but being so beautiful, and still young, she could get away with it. In her case men would take in the sight of missing pins and torn stockings not as lapses in personal grooming but as come-hither cries for their help, a prelude to disrobing, even.

"Orpheus . . ." she started to coo. Where was she going with this? she asked herself. What did she have left to say to him? She didn't know, she realized; she just fancied the sound of herself lisping his name.

"You two are so cute in your coats," said the other girl, finally putting out her hand to introduce herself because somebody had to do it. Lee, she said her name was.

Lee, thought Cassandra, sizing her up. A breezy, cool girl's name and a breezy, cool kind of girl: her platinum hair was worn in a boyish crop. Black eyeliner, pale lips. Petite—about Sylvie's size: no match for Gala's goods.

"You know what else your coats remind me of," Lee went on. "You know that old movie—that old movie with Peter Sellers and the young girls who follow him all around?"

"*Lolita*?" asked Cassandra, failing to see what Lee was getting at. Gala didn't care because Gala at this moment was too busy making saucer eyes at Orpheus.

"No, no, not *Lolita*, no way! It's from the sixties, it's about these two young girls in New York City who get obsessed with Peter Sellers and follow him around. He's, like, a famous concert pianist or something—"

"Oh! I know. *The World of Henry Orient.*"

"Yeah, yeah, that's it."

Cassandra recalled seeing that movie once as part of a Peter Sellers weekend at the Brattle Theatre, in Harvard Square. The girls in that movie were incredibly young and, if memory served, really fucking annoying: just what was Lee getting at, anyway?

What a crummy evening this was shaping up to be, Sylvie was thinking, going ahead and opening the bottle of prosecco and helping herself to a glass that was rather notably generous in its proportions. Coming all the way out to Queens, and it didn't look like that lamb roast was going to be ready in *forever*, or that once it was there would be enough of it to feed all five of them.

Cassandra sized up Lee again. Gala meanwhile was pulling Orpheus down onto the sofa, right on top of the sumptuous contours of her lap. Giggles. What was it about this chick, this Lee creature, standing there with a mysterious, not clearly earned sense of authority in Orpheus's kitchen? And this sense of authority didn't dovetail with her face, which, Cassandra decided, was actually rather faded for someone who still dared to flaunt a black leotard without a bra on underneath. There was something about her that was a wee bit tragic and it wasn't just that she was going to all of that silly effort with the lamb roast.

CHAPTER 11

B y the time karaoke was over, the girls were thoroughly drunk and decided to go to one of the many Greek restaurants in the neighborhood for taramosalata and warm pita bread, and deep blue bowls of avgolemono soup.

"So, I got the scoop," said Gala. "Also, is Orpheus totally going to get back together with me, or what? Mission accomplished! Anyway, get *this*. She's thirty-three."

"Who is?"

"Lee."

"Lee?" repeated Sylvie. "The chick Orpheus is sleeping with?"

"Wait, hold on a second." This from Cassandra. "Orpheus is sleeping with a thirty-three-year-old?"

"Uh-huh. See. There's no way he's not going to get back together with me. And I made myself perfectly—available."

"Did you ever," muttered Sylvie, helping herself to more taramosalata. "You know, I'm just crazy about Mediterranean food. You could almost consider living out here, just for that. This stuff is *cheap*."

"Yeah, but," said Cassandra. "I mean, I know Orpheus's apartment is, like, enormous by New York standards, but this neighborhood—it's ugly and it *smells*. You might want to eat ethnic food sometimes, but you wouldn't want to have to smell it, day in, day out."

"Nobody lives in Queens," said Sylvie definitively, for nobody they knew, aside from the perverse Orpheus, did. Also, Sylvie couldn't help but be proud of herself for getting in on the Fort Greene wave before everybody else did. This way, she had that uniquely New York satisfaction of being proud to say she had lived in a neighborhood before it got gentrified and reaping the benefits of still living there after it did.

"Sylvie! Cassandra! Let's dish. What the hell do you think that Orpheus is doing with a thirty-three-year-old?"

"I think the better question is, what is a thirty-three-year-old doing with Orpheus?" Sylvie offered.

"Oh, come on. Orpheus is *hot*. He's a musician."

"Bennington boy hot. Not real world hot. That's different."

"What makes me sad," mused Cassandra, "is the idea of a grown woman being reduced to sleeping with a Bennington boy. In the real world. Aren't there any other men she could meet in all of New York City?"

"Maybe older women are good in the sack," said Sylvie. "You hear about that sometimes. Sexual peak and all that."

The girls had heard about it, but that does not mean that they believed it. They shook their heads and agreed to order some pistachio baklava for dessert, the conundrum of Lee and her thirty-three-year-old charms, or lack thereof, forgotten altogether. And as soon as possible they returned to the subject of their own sex lives, so much more fascinating and fulfilling than any older woman's could possibly be.

"What ever happened with that guy you mentioned the last time I saw you, Sylvie? It sounded like maybe there was a new guy."

"What guy?"

"Oh, I think you said he was, like, this really up-and-coming fashion photographer or something . . ."

Sylvie now had a lackluster day job touching up photos of celebrities at a fashion agency in the meatpacking district and was felt by her friends to be "in" with fashion people as a result. (This was how she had come to let drop to Cassandra once, over the phone, "The other day, Scarlett Johansson stopped by the office to see this guy Federico, he's her personal makeup artist. And guess what? On a good day, your figure is really pretty much exactly like Scarlett Johansson's!" "Oh my God, really?" Cassandra had squealed, not stopping to ask just whose figure Sylvie thought her's resembled on a *bad* day.)

"Oh, that guy," Sylvie said now. "Him. The one I met at one of those pretentious loft parties in SoHo, right. He keeps texting me and begging me to come over, but."

"But what? Wasn't he any good?"

"I *guess.* But wait! Didn't I tell you? I know I told Cassandra."

"What?" Gala pounced, praying for something dirty.

"Ugh, well, this is embarrassing, but. I drank a ton of sangria, back at the loft, back when we were dancing. That stuff was delicious! And *free.* Anyway the point is—we didn't use protection. We ended up having sex in the backseat of a cab. The funny thing was, that was way better than the sex we had once we got back to his place. I think it was exciting just because, you know, I never take cabs since it's not like I can afford them. So it seemed all *glamorous* at the time. But when I got to his place, to tell you the truth I just wasn't that excited anymore. And then, the next morning, I had to hightail it to Duane Reade with a hangover and get the morning-after pill, ASAP. He paid for it, though. Thank God! Or I would have been screwed."

"Ah! That was really thoughtful of him, Sylvie! Guys don't always do that, you know."

"They don't?" asked Cassandra, thinking, as she did so, how very grateful she was to have a steady boyfriend back in Boston and to not have to have casual sex, as Sylvie and Gala evidently did. So degrading, she thought. Which, for the record, is what people who have not yet had casual sex always think until they try it out for themselves.

"So," she heard Gala asking Sylvie now, "was he as good as Ludo was? Or can nobody else compare?"

"Ludo! That bastard. The last time I ever saw that guy, it was when I quit, remember? We were all having lunch at his studio and I had just figured out he was sleeping with that new girl I couldn't stand, Katarina, the one who always used to wear those stupid python pants, and I decided right then and there to give my notice and throw a roast chicken in his lap!"

"Oh, that's right, he always used to give you guys roast chicken from FreshDirect!"

"Uh-huh, that was his idea of payment. Bastard," said Sylvie again, really stewing this time. "When you stop to think that his family owns diamond mines!"

"Wait, did you sleep with Ludo?" Cassandra said, furrowing her brow. "Because if you did, you never told me."

"Oh, what, do I have to tell you everything?"

"Well—yes."

"She told me!" piped up Gala, not very helpfully, Sylvie thought. Gala loved getting in the middle—of best friends or of couples: it didn't matter which.

Sylvie sighed, annoyed with the both of them right now.

"It was just a fling, Cassandra."

"Oh, Sylvie! Come on! It was just the best sex of your life."

Both girls glared at her.

"What?" demanded Gala Gubelman. Selfish, she polished off the last piece of baklava. Pistachio was her favorite. "After all! Flings always are."

Later on that night, while the girls were on the long train ride all the way back to Brooklyn and chattering among themselves, Lee bedded Orpheus briskly and left his apartment, not in the least in love but fully delighted with the experience nonetheless, only to stop at the taco truck for a salted tongue empanada. Such bliss, treating oneself to a greasy, solitary meal after a good bout of meaningless sex. As she bit into the empanada, savoring the little touches of the radish and lime sprinkled on top, she recalled the spectacle of those poor, desperate younger women prancing around Orpheus's apartment earlier that evening. Bennington girls! thought Lee to herself, digging into her empanada. She herself had graduated many years ago now from Sarah Lawrence, so she knew what she was talking about. They were so incredibly young and really fucking annoying.

PART II

Clementine's Picnic

Professor Sobel asked to see the wine list. It was April in New York and he and Cassandra were having lunch together at a French restaurant.

"Champagne, it seems to me," said Professor Sobel, scanning the menu. Cassandra had no opportunity to scan it herself. This was not so casual or collaborative a lunch as that. Professor Sobel was paying, and as such, in charge, which was the way both of them liked it.

The French restaurant was one of those that have a storied past but are seldom spoken of in these days of competitive dining and celebrity chefs. It was even in midtown, on a rather dowdy stretch in the East Fifties, a neighborhood in which Sylvie, for one, would not be caught dead. But Cassandra would be, and Professor Sobel knew this, just as he knew that she would think that an invitation to an illicit lunch was much more chic than dinner.

He ordered two glasses of champagne. After the waiter left, he dropped his voice to a whisper and said to Cassandra: "Ordering wine always reminds me of a favorite joke of mine. Oh, you might remember from my classes what a weakness I have for telling the occasional bad joke. So. A man walks into a bar. One woman says to another: 'Hey! Check out the size of the wallet on that guy.'"

Cassandra laughed, and then looked down at her menu.

"Cheese soufflé," she said immediately. It cost twenty-five dollars *at lunch*. Just wait till she told Sylvie. Sylvie wouldn't approve, because when a man was paying, you ought to make the most of it and order meat—the ideal outcome of any date in Sylvie's view being not getting laid but getting to tuck into a big rare steak.

For otherwise she lived on bloodless, spinsterish things like Wasa crisps, lentil soup, carrots, and raisins.

But to the more romantic Cassandra, the pleasure of being in the moment was the goal; and cheese soufflé, a delightfully old-fashioned dish, straight out of the pages of Julia Child and not much seen on menus anymore, seemed to her exactly *the* thing to order at a French restaurant on a spring afternoon. The elegance of her selection was not lost on Professor Sobel, who, being an old fogey himself, went with frogs' legs Provençale.

Cassandra made a note of this, thinking that there *was* something slippery and sinister, rather like frogs' legs, about Professor Sobel. Professor Sobel's energy was very masculine but, at the same time, subtle: an unusual combination. Surely a more obvious man would have ordered the filet mignon. But there was nothing transparent about Professor Sobel, nothing stable. A deep ocean, Cassandra thought with approval, not a shallow pond.

Cassandra had just turned twenty-eight years old and was now officially living in New York City. That February, she had seen Professor Sobel for the first time since graduating from Bennington. The two of them had locked eyes with each other during intermission at this concert she was attending with her new boyfriend, Edward Escot. Cassandra had been introduced to Edward at a dinner party the year she was twenty-seven, about six months after the fallout of a broken engagement to her first boyfriend. She and Edward had been together for nearly a year when she decided to move to New York, to get closer to him. Edward was a Harvard man and he and Cassandra did grown-up things together like go to chamber music concerts at Bargemusic. The program that night was called "The Complete Bach Cello Suites Part I."

Professor Sobel thought that Cassandra, who, back at Bennington, had been a pet of his because she was one of the handful of students there who actually could write a cogent analytical paper, was looking very fetching and that being on the arm of a man, as is so often the way with a woman, much enhanced her appearance. He found her far more lovely and poised than she had been at college. She had on big turquoise beads and a décolleté black dress. Great tits, he thought, and went up to her to reintroduce himself.

The boyfriend obviously wasn't a Bennington boy. For one thing, he was wearing a blue blazer, and for another, he had a firm handshake. He might, almost, be a figure to be reckoned with as competition. But, no, Professor Sobel reminded himself. It won't matter if she has a boyfriend. Bennington girls are easy.

During intermission, they drank gin and exchanged e-mail addresses. And come April, that stirring season of young love that can make a smoky, disheveled man with a tall, once lean frame so nostalgic, he sent her an e-mail headed "Henry James in Manhattan," because he happened to recall a conversation at Bennington in which Cassandra had said he was her favorite author.

Dear Cassandra,

May I take you to lunch sometime? I believe the Classical cuisine is French, and I know what a Classicist you are, as am I.

Yours,
Solomon Sobel

Solomon, thought Cassandra to herself. It would be sexy to get the opportunity to call a man Solomon in bed.

Sylvie had been at home while Cassandra was getting dressed to meet Professor Sobel earlier that afternoon.

"Liquid eyeliner? Really, Cassandra? Remember, he's an asshole!"

Sylvie had never forgiven Professor Sobel for the nasty comments he'd scrawled across a paper on Wagner she'd knocked off while thoroughly stoned.

But Cassandra continued applying the liquid eyeliner in a smooth, feline swoop, then added an extra coat of mascara. She also put on perfume before leaving the apartment, something she didn't usually do during the daytime; and when Professor Sobel kissed the palm of her hand at the restaurant, she couldn't help but notice him drinking the scent of it in.

When the champagne arrived, he raised his glass and, searching for something or other to celebrate, came up with: "Fancy us both loving Bach so much . . . and meeting again."

The champagne went to Cassandra's head and suddenly she felt very happy. The waiter had told her to allow extra time for the cheese soufflé, and this news, which might have been an inconvenience to some people, was to her just another sign of a most pleasant decadence: she thought how nice to be living in New York and not Cambridge, and to have time to enjoy a long lunch on a weekday afternoon.

Evidently, the champagne was going to Professor Sobel's head, too—he was now on his second glass—because he was murmuring across the table, "Cassandra, Cassandra . . ." He loved her name, too, as it happened; he found it lushly dramatic, and the chord of doom it struck, going all the way back to the ancient Greeks, very much to his taste for tragedy. "We ought to go to Germany."

"Germany?"

"Yeah, ever been?"

"No."

"Well. See. We ought to go one of these days. We ought to go together."

Cassandra blushed; Professor Sobel noticed the deepening, thrilling pink roses in her cheeks. Still blushing, she admitted, "Well. I do have German heritage, you know."

"You would. Is that where you get your exquisite sense of *tristesse*, Cassandra?"

"That's a French word."

"So it is. But you're a Francophile, aren't you? So. I'm onto something. *Tristesse, tristesse* . . . The point is, both of these cultures have a fine sense of the tragic. They're not—Caribbean! Would you ever want to go on a Caribbean vacation, Cassandra? No? I didn't think so. Neither would I."

Their food arrived with a soothing, old-world flourish, Cassandra's cheese soufflé, Professor Sobel's frogs' legs Provençale. Deftly Professor Sobel's lips slid the skin off one of those legs, savoring it with what was to Cassandra an exciting, nearly narcotic degree of focus.

He said: "Me, I only like the great civilizations of Western culture. Berlin, Rome, Vienna . . ."

Then he talked for a while of his fantasy of sweeping her off to the Glyndebourne opera festival in England, describing all of the details he thought a girl whose favorite author was Henry James would lap right up, from the perfectly cold salmon they served to the white gloves the waiters wore. That she expected to be swept into bed with him as well was not in question. She was attracted to older men, always had been.

"Oh, it sounds absolutely like paradise!"

Paradise, thought Professor Sobel, stopping to ravish the last of his frogs' legs. It was to him a striking word. Suddenly, even though here he was drinking champagne with a very attractive and delightful former student in the middle of a spring afternoon, he felt this wash of Wagnerian sorrow come over him. The last several years had been unkind to Professor Sobel. It all started with Penelope Entenmann getting pregnant. She had gone off the birth control pill without telling him because she wanted her body to feel more "natural." This was right around the time when her friends started to notice that she was going round the bend in general, sitting for long spells at the edge of the brook while claiming to be giving Reiki to butterflies. The president had found out about the affair and sacked him. Changing times, thought the professor, and not for the better . . .

Worse, just as Gala Gubelman had reported to her cohorts on

the nude beach of Martha's Vineyard way back when, Penelope had insisted on *having the baby*. Going so far as to give birth to it on a beach in Hawaii, with another Bennington girl, trained as a midwife, helping. Then she'd had the audacity to name his child—his firstborn son!—Prajeetha, which means "precious gift" in Sanskrit. If he'd had no interest in the baby before that, after that he really didn't.

Nevertheless, Penelope, though she tried not to let on, was the heiress to the Entenmann's coffee-cake fortune. If you were going to knock up a Bennington girl, it was only common sense to knock up one who had a trust fund.

He then realized that Cassandra wasn't one of the Bennington girls with a trust fund. Culture and taste, he thought, recalling the pretty, touching sight of her in that décolleté black dress at the Bach concert, but no trust fund. Suddenly it came back to him that her father was dead, a misfortune that was entirely to his advantage. Professor Sobel murmured: "Paradise, paradise . . . I suppose that paradise for me was the Secret Garden at Bennington. I used to call it 'the little college on the hill where nothing bad ever happens.' So you see, childhood is ending all the time."

"Remember how the head of psych services at Bennington had this poster on the door of her office that said 'It's never too late to have a happy childhood'? Do you think that's true?"

"Bullshit! I think one often finds that it's too late for a hell of a lot of things."

Afterward he was smoking a cigarette outside when, feeling emboldened by his old friend nicotine, he kissed Cassandra's hand again. She wondered if he could still make out her perfume—if after their lengthy lunch any of its flirtatious essence remained.

Suddenly, she thought of something she hadn't thought about in years. Maybe it was just because it was the month of April; maybe it was just the gentle lull of the weather and being in the company of one of her old professors that carried her back to her college days. It was almost as if, standing there on the streets of New York City, she could sniff the lilacs of Vermont.

"Do you ever think of the dancers?"

"Dancers?"

"The modern dancers. The girls who died, falling through the window. It happened the spring of my senior year. Chelsea Hayden-Smith and Beverly Tinker-Jones."

"Terrible, a thing like that," he muttered, shaking his shaggy old head. "Terrible, terrible, terrible."

"She was in your class. Your class on Stravinsky."

"Who was?"

"Chelsea. Don't you remember her? She had these amazing curly long lashes. She was just so incredibly beautiful."

But Professor Sobel thought the same thing Sylvie did. All of the modern dancers at Bennington were so incredibly beautiful that after a while they all just blended together.

"No," he told Cassandra, "I don't remember her. I don't remember her at all."

CHAPTER 13

S ylvie babysat every afternoon. That was what she was doing to make a living now: babysitting. Over the course of the last year, she had built up her own business among the wealthy families gobbling up the beautiful, tarnished old brownstones of Fort Greene, positioning herself perfectly to swoop in and make a winning impression on their children. And she did— make a winning impression. None of these parents ever suspected that beneath the sparkling brown eyes, smooth white skin, and upright, can-do carriage of this delightful young woman, the wheels, the wheels were turning. For instance, this one time while the girls were standing in line at the dry cleaner's, Sylvie struck up a conversation with a Russian woman and her toddler. The toddler took an immediate shining to Sylvie. The mother then asked her if she would be available to babysit, adding that she was hoping to find somebody who was bilingual in English and Russian. Was there any chance that Sylvie spoke Russian? she wanted to know.

Sylvie faltered and said: "Oh, that's so too bad! Because I am fluent in Italian and French, actually, but my Russian is kind of middling." In fact, Sylvie's Italian and French were kind of middling and her Russian nonexistent, but no matter; she managed to imply, thanks to the gentle, apologetic dip in her voice, that the loss was all the woman's own.

Afterward, Cassandra chided her: "Oh my God, Sylvie, I can't believe that you admitted that."

"What?"

"Well, that you weren't fluent in Russian. I mean, I thought for sure you would just pretend and then somehow get away with it."

"Goddamn it! You're right, Cassandra. I *so* could have just pretended I spoke Russian and gotten away with it!"

"You're normally so much quicker on your feet than that, Sylvie," said Cassandra admiringly.

"Totally, totally!"

Sylvie now relished the sway she held over these unsuspecting families of Fort Greene; a good nanny, much like a good man, is hard to find, and Sylvie was a good nanny. Children thought so, and children would know. Also, how egotistically gratifying was this turn of events, when for the better part of the last two years—commencing with the great economic collapse of the year 2008—Sylvie had been unemployed after being let go from her day job at the fashion agency in the meatpacking district and had fallen so behind on her rent that even so spineless a character as Pete the landlord, who was supposed to be a hippie for God's sake, had been compelled to threaten her with eviction. (Sylvie, on coming home one day and discovering that she had been served with eviction papers, merely crumpled them up and hoped that this, too, would pass. It did.) The couple of jobs she did find during this desperate time lasted only briefly and were either corporate and in midtown and the only place to eat lunch was Chipotle, a fate that the girls agreed obviously was not to be endured, or else they were sketchy and out of people's home offices in Brooklyn and the exact nature of one's payment was not to be discussed.

"What is being unemployed like?" Cassandra had wanted to know in that tone of radiant curiosity that people always use when inquiring about the misfortunes of others.

"It's like this. When you are unemployed, every twenty-four hours will feel like seventy-two."

"Wow," said Cassandra, who would not have any reason to recall this particular insight of Sylvie's until some time later when she was in similar circumstances herself.

CHAPTER 14

After having lunch with Professor Sobel, Cassandra got off the train to go meet Sylvie and some of her charges at a playground. Today she was watching a brother and sister named Quinn and Imogen. Part of the fun of having Sylvie babysit was that there was plenty of juicy human material in it: she and Cassandra loved discussing the kids and what problems they were doomed to have when they grew up. In the case of these two children—Quinn was four and Imogen seven—the verdict was in: Quinn was homosexual and Imogen a bitch.

Quinn, it went without saying, the girls liked much better. He was a beautiful child with long, pale yellow ringlets and a face that, no matter what the situation, never dared convey any emotion beyond a wan, sulky boredom; Cassandra could well picture those sour lips smoking a Gauloises. His parents dressed him well, as was only the norm with four-year-olds in Brooklyn. How poignant his shoulders looked underneath his thin, hipsterish T-shirts; at this rate, he'd be wearing oversize glasses in no time. Quinn adored Sylvie, as children usually did, drawn to her physical energy and her noncondescending candor. The two of them did art projects, Quinn exquisitely sensitive to the colors he used in his watercolors. Like Sylvie, he gravitated toward a soft, sophisticated palette—pale blues and mushroom grays. No primaries! Ever. Primary colors were for other children with lesser taste.

Today, Sylvie and Quinn were sitting together, doing pastel chalk drawings on the pavement. Cassandra, seeing them, thought: Oh God, am I going to have to sit *on the ground*? This babysitting business sometimes got a little too rugged for her, even as a spectator. She looked down at her shapely navy blue dress—much more chic than black on a spring afternoon—worn to show off her figure to Professor Sobel. It was going to be difficult to kneel in that dress without the fabric tugging.

Quinn, seeing Sylvie's friend coming, the blonde with the big boobs and the name he couldn't be bothered to remember, thought: Oh no. She was going to spoil everything; she was going to take Sylvie away from him. And Sylvie was *his* babysitter. Sylvie was getting *paid*. Sylvie had to watch him and Imogen for *money*, which his parents had plenty of and Sylvie did not. Already, he and Imogen had these things all figured out; they were New York children and they knew the score.

"Hello, Quinn," said Cassandra, with the phony voice she always used when speaking to children. The girls didn't know this, but Imogen, who was an excellent mimic, did a fantastic imitation of Cassandra behind her back, saying: *Hello, Quinn. Hello, Imogen. How are you?* The syrupy emphasis Imogen placed on that last word, *you*, was lethal. Whenever she imitated Cassandra, she could count on putting Quinn in stitches. She never did it in front of her parents, though. Her parents were such fools, they liked Cassandra; they actually fell for that voice the way no child ever would. Parents just thought she had good manners.

"Hello, Quinn," said Cassandra again, having failed to get even a perfunctory response the first time around. "How are *you*? Oh, and what are you doing? Drawing? Oh, I just love pastels, I remember those."

Now this was another annoying habit of Cassandra's around children: she was always waxing nostalgic around them. Every banal detail—a stick of pink chalk, a child's green galoshes—could send her, madeleine-like, into a frenzy of reminiscences. Whenever Cassandra began a sentence with the words "I remember," it meant the death of the conversation in the eyes of any child. What did *they* care about some chick's old party dress, or forgotten birthday cake? They did not care, for they had not yet learned what Cassandra had at far too young an age—that all could be lost; that these banal details would be remembered with an aching heart forever afterward.

There are beautiful children and then there are beautiful children. Imogen belonged to the latter category. She had the kind of silky blond femininity, combined with a straight-backed confident carriage, that marked her already as the prettiest girl in the class. Even Sylvie was intimidated by the directness of her arctic blue gaze and had decided against telling her parents about the girl's breathtaking tantrums. Like so many parents today, they considered their child flawless and would have considered the tantrums to be Sylvie's fault.

Right now, Imogen was in the midst of practicing cartwheels, or perhaps *practicing* is not the word, for Imogen's cartwheeling technique had long since been perfected. Her long legs spun in gorgeous circles. She was demonstrating for some other hapless little girl, who was rather on the chubby side and did not seem to get it. "Like this," Imogen kept on insisting, bouncing up and down on the balls of her little blue Keds—Keds were an "in" sneaker this season, in Brooklyn, edging out even Converse. "Like *this*." And then she'd do another cartwheel.

"Clap for me, Sylvie! Clap for me!" she called once she was finished. "Why aren't you clapping?"

"I'm clapping, Imogen," said Sylvie with great weariness, and then she did just that. Cassandra joined her, a little too late, which Imogen noticed, thinking: *I hate Cassandra.* Like her brother, she thought it was obnoxious that Sylvie let a friend of hers tag along when she should have been paying attention to them.

Cassandra was looking at Imogen doing cartwheels and, as usual, making it all about her. She had been quite hopeless not only at cartwheels but also at hand-clapping games and four square and . . . well, you name it. She sighed, remembering. It was true that childhood was a kingdom of many lost pleasures. But it was also a kingdom populated by other children, and other children could be so cruel. Maybe there was something to be said for surviving into adulthood after all.

Then Imogen, finally sick of doing cartwheels and hoping that Sylvie would cook up something exciting for her to do, threw her arms up in the air and ran toward the two young women. She braced herself for the inevitable, Cassandra saying: "Hello, Imogen. And how are you?"

"Why is your face so red?" demanded Imogen. She had cool, soap-flake coloring herself and already wondered what was the matter with the skin of so many grown-ups, when hers was so perfect.

Cassandra, whose naturally rosy skin *was* red from all of the champagne, put a demure hand to her burning cheek. God, she hated this kid. *Imogen.* No wonder Sylvie was so bone-tired these days, having to put up with her.

"Actually . . ." said Sylvie, addressing Cassandra, "I was wondering that myself. Are you . . . ?"

"Drunk? Well. Tipsy anyway."

Imogen's ears pricked up at the word *drunk.* Now *this* was getting interesting. One thing she did kind of like about Cassandra: once she got the phony *hellos* out of the way, she often forgot that children were there in the first place and started letting all kinds of adult tidbits drop. At times like that Cassandra was worth paying attention to, or you might miss out on something good. Imogen's parents were careful never to say things like "drunk" in front of the children and that kind of attitude got pretty damn boring after a while.

Quinn couldn't be bothered to pay attention to any of this. He was deep in his drawing, massaging various tender shades of blue into the pavement, quite pleased with the results.

"Oh, Cassandra!" exclaimed Sylvie. "Don't tell me that you and Professor Sobel . . ."

Aha! thought Imogen, picking up on the words *Professor Sobel,* almost as compelling and forbidden as *drunk*. So there was a man involved. This was going to be great.

"No, no! Professor Sobel is very subtle. He thinks it's sexy to prolong things, I have this feeling."

Imogen, having no idea just what it was this Professor Sobel fellow might want to prolong, listened to the two women hungrily.

"Subtle! Subtle! Is that what you call it? This, about the man who once did a baboon impression in front of you? Sitting on top of his desk in the music building? Do you remember that, Cassandra, or have you blocked it out?"

Cassandra now took a moment to recall the time when Professor Sobel, wearing a black cashmere sweater pitted with moth holes, hoisted himself up on top of his desk and crossed his legs. She had watched as Professor Sobel, still sitting cross-legged on top of the desk, started beating his chest and waving his arms and making these queer, animalistic, broken, moaning sounds. That episode lasted a good long time and had an almost operatic quality about it. Once he had finally stopped, he had looked long and hard at her with the *I've got you* gaze of the animal kingdom, and explained, "Every so often, a man just has to get in touch with his inner primate."

Afterward, he'd sighed and put on a Beethoven string quartet and the two of them had never discussed the incident ever again.

"Oh that," said Cassandra now. "Well, there is something kind of animalistic about the attraction between Professor Sobel and me—I've always felt that Professor Sobel has just a touch of this very male dominance and cruelty, combined with this veneer of verbal sophistication . . ."

All this was lost on Imogen, but she did think a grown man doing a baboon imitation sounded pretty cool. She loved imitations, being so good at them herself.

"If that's a fantasy you have, you'd best be rid of it."

"Oh, but I agree! By acting it out, right?"

"No, Cassandra, that is not what I—" Jesus. Sylvie stopped, realizing that she often found herself speaking to Cassandra in the same tone of voice she used on Quinn and Imogen. Quinn and Imogen! They were right there. They had heard everything, probably. She turned to the little girl and said: "Hey, Imogen, why don't you show us your cartwheels again?"

There it was, staring her down, the fearless arctic blue gaze. No way Imogen was going anywhere. Oh, the hell with it, Sylvie thought, remembering her own wretched childhood. Kids always figured out what was up with the adults anyway.

So Sylvie turned to Cassandra and got to the point: "But Cassandra. You have a boyfriend, remember."

"Oh, Sylvie, you're being awfully—unimaginative about this. You know I've never necessarily believed in monogamy. I think there can be far worse betrayals between people than *that*."

Monogamy. Imogen didn't know what that meant, but even so, she was with Cassandra on this one: that didn't sound too hot. Monogamy. It sounded like being forced to do something boring, like going to bed on time. Like something her stupid parents would believe in.

"Infidelity can hurt people, Cassandra."

"Everything can hurt people," Cassandra shot back, and Imogen, thinking, Well then, grown-ups must be wimps, because nothing ever hurt *me*, sighed and went back to doing her cartwheels.

CHAPTER 15

Cassandra's boyfriend, Edward, lived in Philadelphia. When she first met him, she was still living in Boston, and for many months now, they had been having a glamorous long-distance love affair, featuring classical music concerts, regattas, why, even corsages and bouquets of long-stemmed white roses, which Edward was bold enough to send, from time to time, to Cassandra's office. They also attended, the previous November, the storied Harvard-Yale game. Cassandra met Edward on the train platform in New Haven, just, as she related to Sylvie over the phone, "like something out of *Franny and Zooey!*"

"Hey, wait a minute. Didn't Franny go *insane* after the weekend of the Harvard-Yale game?"

"Oh, Sylvie, Sylvie, must you be so *unromantic?*"

"Yes, actually," said Sylvie, and laughed. "If experience has taught me anything, yes."

There is no good time, really, for one's friend to get a new boyfriend, unless you happen to have one yourself. And Sylvie didn't, at the moment. She hadn't been in love or had a torturous crush, even, in quite some time. Torturous crushes were fun; she missed them. Just recently Gala Gubelman, who, while she was on her computer at work, loved to stalk other people's exes online, had discovered that Ludo Citron was now dating a washed-up nineties movie star who had her own clothing line of ungainly separates sold at Opening Ceremony and had expected Sylvie to be jealous. But she wasn't—she only felt a remoteness from that part of her past. The days when she had been involved with guys like Ludo seemed a long, long time ago. The idea that she could have been attracted to an artist was preposterous to her now. Sylvie had come a long way since college, and she no longer believed in art. It wasn't sacred anymore. Nothing was. Money, maybe. Yes, money to Sylvie was starting to feel sacred.

As for Edward, he was an academic and handsome in a rather stiff, professorial style. He was several years older than Cassandra—in his thirties already—but Sylvie, upon hearing Cassandra's description of him, said, "Wait, wait, wait, I think I get the picture. He's a guy of our generation, but he has more in common with someone who's sixty?"

"Yes!" exclaimed Cassandra, not in the least insulted. She just had that sweet, cozy feeling she got—that rush of serotonin—whenever Sylvie immediately understood what she was saying.

Meanwhile, now that she was finally living in New York, Cassandra figured that living with Sylvie would be only temporary. The plan was that she would stay there for the summer, then move to Philadelphia, once Edward proposed. Being the old-fashioned type, he didn't want them to live together before marriage. Sylvie disagreed with Cassandra's plan. Sylvie thought that Cassandra should move to New York City for good.

"And live with you?"

At the back of Cassandra's mind was the thought of the security deposit that she had given Sylvie so many years ago now: she didn't expect to get it back but she did think that there would be a kind of justice—good karma accrued—in getting to move into the apartment for a while.

Sylvie murmured her assent on the other end of the line, preoccupied with the evening ritual of rolling a joint.

"That would be nice," Cassandra said. "That would be great!"

"Well, why not? We've always wanted to live together, and we haven't, have we? Ever since college, I mean."

"Is there anything you need?" Cassandra asked her, eager to appear to not be a mooch. Sylvie was sensitive about people being mooches, she knew. She was swift to complain if roommates used her shaving cream or if they preferred to get takeout at the soul food joint down the street rather than split the groceries: Sylvie was always trying to save money by eating at home and, being the child of hippies, favored a healthy diet. That anybody should treat themselves to takeout, ever, was a personal affront to her values, particularly fatty, low-rent takeout. "And now the whole apartment smells like barbecued chicken wings!" she had thundered to Cassandra once, over the phone. I will be different, Cassandra vowed. I will be the ideal roommate. (There is no such person, in fact. They do not exist.) "I mean, is there anything you need for the apartment?"

Everything, Sylvie thought to herself. I need everything. She had a bare, ragtag collection of silverware and dishes, none of which matched. She *still* didn't own a toaster. Or facecloths; she took her mascara off with paper towels at the end of the night. That is, assuming she had a roll of paper towels on hand in the apartment. Sometimes she didn't. Paper towels are expensive, too. Everything is expensive, Sylvie had found. Even things, like paper towels, that in her considered opinion had no right to be.

"Well . . . I could use more cooking stuff," she said carefully, thinking that cooking stuff was only the beginning. Cassandra was known by her friends to be generous and a soft touch with money, and Sylvie felt that she might be convinced to spring for just about anything.

"How about a Le Creuset pan? My mother gave me this really beautiful old Le Creuset pan. It's kind of a mustard color, on the bottom. Would you use it?"

"Oh, definitely!"

"All right then, I'll bring it."

"Can I ask you a question, Cassandra? It isn't about the Le Creuset pan."

Smoking pot had made Sylvie contemplative.

"Sure."

"It's about Edward."

"Edward . . . ?"

"Do you like him?" asked Sylvie, because she wasn't convinced, from the way Cassandra talked about him, that she did.

"Like? Like . . . Well, that depends. Do you think it's possible to like a man *and* be in love with him?"

"Of course it is!" shrieked Sylvie, to whom even the suggestion of such a contradiction was outrageous.

"Hmm. I'm starting to wonder. The sex is much better, I think, without all of that just hanging out and trying to be best friends with each other stuff. Because I don't think I like Edward all that much, actually, but I *am* in love with him. And he's in love with me."

"Oh, so does that mean he doesn't like *you*, either?"

"Maybe!"

The girls laughed.

Cassandra had this orange suitcase. Hermès orange, she called it. It was a very fancy suitcase and exactly the kind of thing that Sylvie, leading her threadbare twenty-something life, didn't own. Cassandra first got that suitcase when she started dating Edward and it was the most potent symbol of her happiness. It was her vehicle out of the past and into the future—everything that the poor, discarded *Madeline* coat had failed to symbolize to Cassandra, the orange suitcase did.

Another symbol of her happiness was that ever since meeting Edward she no longer stooped to taking the Fung Wah bus; those greasy, perilous days of her youth were over. The first time she visited him in Philadelphia, she had mentioned the possibility of taking it. With his detached academic's eye, he had compared traveling by the Fung Wah to traveling by steerage class, not that he had ever taken the bus himself.

"But, Cassandra! The Fung Wah was good enough for you to take when you came to see *me*."

"But Sylvie, just imagine it . . ."

"What?"

"Just imagine traveling by the Fung Wah to go see a *lover*. Remember that weekend when my hair smelled like chicken vindaloo?"

"Oh God! Well, now that you mention it. Or you could end up smelling like McDonald's . . ."

"Pork fried rice . . ."

"One time I was on this bus they were *totally* using to transport dried fish."

"Not really!"

"Yes, really! Did I ever tell you about this one time, we pulled off at that hideous bus stop in Connecticut, you know the one, the one with the McDonald's. I was sitting up front that time. So the driver turns to me and says—*in English*—apparently he actually could speak English when it suited him: "'Hey, I'm going to take a smoke. Do you mind pumping gas?'"

"Oh my God! What did you *say*?"

"I pumped the gas."

"You did?"

"Cassandra! Think about it. What if I didn't do it, and the guy took his smoke break and forgot or something? Would you have wanted to run out of gas on the highway?"

Cassandra thought that was like Sylvie all over—petite but indomitable, pumping gas on a lonesome stretch of Connecticut highway.

"See, Sylvie. I have to go see Edward by Amtrak. *I have to*. And taking the train is so nice! I always go to the club car and order myself a Scotch and soda and potato chips. It's the perfect combination."

Scotch, thought Sylvie. Drinking Scotch on the train. Cassandra really was living it up, these days.

She had left Boston on April 1. That day, it had been raining, but then, as she might well have remarked to Sylvie, it always seemed to be raining in Cambridge, Massachusetts. Cambridge was a melancholy town. She wheeled her orange suitcase across the streets of Harvard Square, a young blond woman in a trench coat making, she fancied, an *Umbrellas of Cherbourg* type exit. Oh, the songs she might have sung! The child, the young girl she used to be!

That night, Cassandra and her orange suitcase—as well as her monogrammed navy L.L.Bean Boat and Tote, at the bottom of which, weighing it down, was the wonderful old mustard-colored Le Creuset pan of her mother's—traveled by Amtrak to Philadelphia. It rained, and rained. Good-bye Massachusetts, good-bye Rhode Island, good-bye Connecticut . . . Outside Cassandra's window, the Connecticut shoreline was shrouded in gray. When the conductor announced that soon they would be at Penn Station, Cassandra rubbed sleep from her eyes and thought, Good-bye, New England.

She got in so late that Edward did not come meet her at the station, something that a woman who was not in love—the pragmatic Sylvie, for instance—might have recognized as a very bad sign. What it might have told her was that Edward did not understand what an immense night this was in her life. When she got out of the cab at his apartment, though, he apparently didn't think it was too late to go upstairs and have vigorous sex right away.

But Cassandra just wasn't into it, that night. She remembered how, in the days of more simple, drowsy lovemaking with her very first boyfriend, she used to doze in the crook of his long arm; something not necessarily sexual but soothing. Something more in that mode was what she wanted right now. She was going to have to remember all of this to tell Sylvie; they were both fascinated by how different sex was with different people, or even with the same person, depending on the way you were feeling. Sex is so *textured*, Cassandra would say. I know, it's *amazing*, Sylvie would say, smoking a joint.

The next morning, it was clear and beautiful. To someone who had grown up in Boston, spring came early to Philadelphia. The magnolia blossoms were out on the well-groomed streets of Rittenhouse Square. Cassandra put on a pale blue shirtwaist and moccasins and she and Edward went for a long, leisurely breakfast, reading sections of *The New York Times* like a real adult couple, at their favorite French café. Afterward, they went back to his apartment and had sex on the original Colonial floors of the living room. It was fantastic. Cassandra adored him. This was her new life and it was going to be splendid.

When she got back to Brooklyn, Sylvie asked her: "Do you think you'll get married? He seems like the marrying kind."

"Oh, yes." Cassandra sighed sumptuously. "Absolutely."

"But then, you might end up getting divorced."

"Sylvie!"

"Well? Don't pretend like it doesn't eventually happen. Just look at my parents."

"Yeah."

At this point in their lives, Sylvie and Cassandra were both big on judging the messes their parents had made of their lives because they still believed that they, themselves, would do no such thing.

"I wonder what it's really like," Sylvie went on. "Divorce. Loving someone and then *not* loving them, and how with divorce you have to make it so official. You know. I've never been able to forget this. My mother once told me that the day she had to sign the divorce papers was the saddest day of her whole life."

Cassandra never forgot that, either.

CHAPTER 16

n the mornings, Sylvie babysat a delectable little toddler named Clementine, Clementine of the black ringlets and fat cheeks the color of French radishes. Sylvie said she was in love with Clementine; she said Clementine was her soul mate. She said that Clementine was her good luck charm and that ever since meeting the little girl, her life had started to turn around for the better.

Cassandra tagged along with Sylvie when she babysat, for something to do. Anyone could see that as children go Clementine was delightful, but still—Cassandra had no natural tenderness with, or for, children. She feared that Edward, being so traditional, would want to have them. She didn't. She wanted to have French breakfasts and make love on the living room floor forever and ever, no children waking up and waddling in.

The way Sylvie acted with Clementine was beginning to disturb Cassandra. She felt that the attention she paid her was excessive. Was this her way of detecting that the unconditional love that was once her due had shifted, as in a love triangle, to Clementine? For here was Sylvie, no longer paying attention to her but to Clementine—feeding her snap peas ("Clementine already eats all of her vegetables") out of a plastic bag, picking her up out of her stroller and hugging her at what were to Cassandra quite random intervals, singing her songs in French. *"Alouette,"* she sang, *"gentille alouette,"* which once upon a time Sylvie and Cassandra had sung together in high school French class.

Sylvie needs to get laid, Cassandra was thinking; it had been quite a while, hadn't it? Sometimes, giving in to ennui, Sylvie had one-night stands, not that she ever seemed to enjoy them all that much. It had been a long time now since the giddy, reckless era of the silver eyeliner, of Jasper and Angus and Bertram and Max ... Sex wasn't sacred, either. In fact, Sylvie had found, it was often more trouble than it was worth, and then! And then there was the fact that all of the guys she met in New York were so lame.

Cassandra and Sylvie wheeled Clementine in her stroller all over the neighborhood: to get *pain au chocolats* for her and lattes for them (which, hoping to turn her into an avid coffee drinker later on in life, they encouraged her to take tiny sips of); to florist shops (*See, Clementine, tulips, yellow tulips, can you say* tulip?); and, inevitably, to the Brooklyn Flea, where they whittled away whole Saturdays sorting through old wooden boxes of vintage buttons. Would Clementine like this one, or would Clementine like that one? Buttons were a passion of hers, little red ones especially. Button! she would exclaim. Button!

Clementine's voice was absolutely delicious. Bouncy and bell-like, the cartoon voice of a beautiful child. "Clementine is so lyrical," Sylvie said. And so, when Clementine said the word *Button!*, that sound, like the plaintive chords of a string quartet, sent silvery shivers of recognition down Cassandra's spine.

"It's sad," said Cassandra.

"What's sad?"

"Clementine's voice. It's sad."

"No, it isn't," insisted Sylvie.

"It is. It's so ... mournful."

"Jesus, Cassandra, Clementine's voice is *not* sad. Clementine is *not* sad. Clementine is a beautiful little girl and it's a beautiful spring day and anyway *I* make her happy." She got down on her knees and wiggled her nose against Clementine's: "Don't I? Don't I? Doesn't Sylvie make you happy?"

"Sylvie," repeated Clementine, giggling.

"But *happiness* is the saddest thing in the world. And as an adult to try to recapture happiness—"

Then all of a sudden Clementine was crying—Clementine, who, according to Sylvie, never cried. Sylvie thought: Cassandra really is lousy with kids. She's going to have to come up with a hell of a good excuse when Edward wants to start having them. And he will, she thought, the stuck-up preppie bastard. Sometimes Sylvie thought that Cassandra's relationship would stand a chance only if Cassandra could continue to conceal her real self—that being the self she had no shame in revealing to Sylvie.

"Oh, look what you've done, Cassandra!" Sylvie stooped down again and flooded the child with the daintiest of kisses, on her forehead, her lashes, her nose. *"Alouette,"* she sang to her darling Clementine, *"gentille alouette . . ."*

"Oh my God. Sylvie? Sylvie Furst!"

The girls looked up only to see a dim, honey-blond creature squinting at them from behind her spectacles. A pang of recognition startled Sylvie—then, fear: some old, unrealized fear that, although long past the point of logic, still carried a powerful emotional charge.

It was Vicky Lalage.

Sylvie hadn't laid eyes on Vicky Lalage since the disastrous series of events beginning with letting her mother's dog die on her watch and being exiled to the nursery with her father's ashes ("Contents: Marc Lalage"). Since then, Sylvie had hightailed it to Brooklyn and never looked back. She was twenty-two years old then and twenty-eight now. It came to Sylvie, looking at this young woman who she had once been friends with and who was now a stranger, that it felt like not six years but whole decades had passed.

I was so young then, she thought, remembering her first year in New York.

"Vicky!" she exclaimed. The two women hugged. Vicky, after recognizing Cassandra, too, gestured to Clementine and then to Sylvie, saying: "Oh my God, is she—"

"Mine? Oh no."

"You wish," said Cassandra, and the three of them laughed, on innocent ground because the presence of Clementine erased the thorny past and put everybody in a good mood.

"Everybody does say we look alike," said Sylvie, to whom nothing could have been a greater compliment. "But no, I'm just her babysitter."

They do kind of look alike, Vicky was thinking, but Sylvie seemed so different. She seemed like a whole other person. She couldn't put her finger on it at first, then she realized what it was. Her haircut. Vicky stopped for a second to recall the carelessly gorgeous, brown-skinned girl on the nude beach at Martha's Vineyard: the one with the black Italian pixie cut. But Sylvie was wearing her hair long now and Vicky thought that it weighed her down. Vicky thought that she looked tired.

"What are you up to these days?" Cassandra asked Vicky, feeling that it was only good manners to do so.

"Oh, I've been running this studio for this artist . . ." Cassandra here recalled that Vicky had been a fine arts major—ceramics or something frumpy like that. She saw flakes of plaster dotting the honey-blond hair. Vicky rambled on a bit, and then the girls heard her say: "And! I just moved into an apartment in Boerum Hill with my girlfriend. Actually . . ." She singled out Sylvie. "My girlfriend. Tess Fox. You know her."

Afterward:

"Oh my God. Tess Fox. That's that anorexic slut from Bryn Mawr!"

"*No.*"

"*Yes.*"

"The one who used to date Gala, right? The one you got into that screaming match with on the ferry coming back from the Vineyard?"

"Uh-huh. Oh my God. I'm going to text Gala and tell her *right now.*" Sylvie reached for her BlackBerry and began tapping away.

"Also, I know that was totally harmless, but I've been dreading running into Vicky Lalage for *years*."

"Well? You two are out and about in New York City. It had to happen sometime."

That song, Cassandra thought, later that night when she was lying in bed unable to fall asleep. She couldn't get it out of her head. She tried to resurrect her rusty French to translate the lyrics. It wasn't a very nice song, was it? But then children's songs so often weren't nice. Childhood was a brutal kingdom, where only the fit and the selfish survived. "*Skylark, nice skylark / Skylark, I shall pluck you / I shall pluck your head . . .*"

CHAPTER 17

Cassandra picked up her cell phone to call Sylvie, as in the old days when they were living in different cities and loved more than anything to talk on the phone to each other. Sylvie was off babysitting, and Cassandra had just woken up and was drinking coffee alone, savoring the angelic light of Sylvie's apartment, thinking: How good life is.

"Oh my God, guess what?"

In the background, children were shrieking. Sylvie said: "Can I call you—"

"No, no, I wanted to tell you. I've been thinking about it. I can handle it now."

"Handle what?"

"Having an affair with Professor Sobel. I've decided that I can handle it."

"Well, I don't know what to—I'm coming, Quinn, I'm coming. It's a friend of mine, she needs my help, too. Okay! Hold on a sec. Cassandra. Are we talking about the same man who *knocked up* Penelope Entenmann?"

"Oh, whatever, Sylvie! I'm on the pill."

"That's not the point. The point is—"

"And anyway, she's the heiress to the coffee cake fortune! She could afford to keep the baby."

"You couldn't, Cassandra! You couldn't afford to keep a baby if you got knocked up and neither could I."

"Enough about Penelope Entenmann, I beg of you! Are you actually comparing me to a girl who used to give Reiki to butterflies? I've been sitting here drinking coffee and figuring it all out. What with me having Edward in Philadelphia—"

"That isn't a plus, Cassandra. That's a complication. And anyway—that's terrible! You love Edward. Why would you want to cheat on him?"

"You're being so uptight about this, Sylvie!"

"You know what, Cassandra? I don't think you *do* love Edward. And another thing! I don't think he really loves *you*. You two don't know each other; you're not even close! All you ever do is have a ton of sex and dress up and go to black-tie events! *That's* one hell of a basis for a relationship."

Cassandra, to whom it seemed a most excellent basis for a relationship, hung up the phone feeling pissed and thought for the first time in her life that Sylvie was jealous of her. It was so sad, Sylvie not having a boyfriend right now. But why? Sylvie was so pretty. Sylvie was beautiful! Cassandra recalled the sight of her arriving back home in Cambridge in a little black dress and white lace tights, shaking snowflakes from her cap of dark hair . . .

Later that afternoon, Sylvie got home from work to find Cassandra sitting at the kitchen table in a pale blue baby-doll nightie, her plumpish white legs bare and blond hair rather naughtily tousled. Had she spent the whole day like this? Sylvie wondered.

"Oh my God, I'm so hungry," she said. "Quinn made me come into the bathroom and wipe him today. He's *four*."

Cassandra shuddered. It wasn't the talk of bodily functions that upset her. It was the talk of children. Children! How she hoped that Edward wouldn't want them.

Sylvie went into the bathroom, where she was overwhelmed by the baroque splendor of Cassandra's lingerie going *drip, drop, drip* into the famous claw-foot bathtub. And at the foot of the bathtub was a white French champagne bucket, which the girls had been so delighted to find for a steal at Marshalls, and which they took turns using to handwash their underthings. But the bucket, tonight, was full to the brim with an indeterminate garment of pink-and-apricot lace and rich with the scent of hyacinth soapsuds. So no way Sylvie would be using it anytime soon, even though she was running low on clean underwear.

Then she discovered that they were out of toilet paper. That figured, the way the day was going. She'd have to remember to steal some. In Sylvie's opinion, only suckers ever bought something you could steal so easily in a restaurant or a train station or even from other people's houses. She was forever cramming rolls into her tote bags and nobody ever noticed. Keeping the apartment in paper towels, which had given her so much grief, was harder because you couldn't steal them quite so easily as you could toilet paper. You usually had no choice but to pay for them, damn it.

"Cassandra," she called from the bathroom, "the next time you go out, remember to steal us some toilet paper, if you happen to think of it."

"Oh yeah, I keep meaning to. But I just don't feel comfortable stealing from local businesses and you know how I pretty much never go to chains." Cassandra was still, at heart, a sweet, diligent, well-trained Cambridge girl who said things like that.

But Sylvie laughed and said: "Oh, I got over *that* years ago. It's a jungle out there! It's every man for himself."

She came out of the bathroom and opened the door to the refrigerator.

"Have you bought any groceries yet?"

Groceries, thought Cassandra. *Groceries*, rather like *children*, a word she dreaded. They smacked to her of the same granola-colored domesticity, the same death of the soul.

"Didn't we talk about you buying groceries? I thought we made a list the other day, didn't we?"

Cassandra recalled the crumpled list, which, earlier today, she had thrown into the trash hoping that Sylvie wouldn't remember. It had listed the usual single girl suspects: dried cranberries, Wasa crisps, ginger tea (good for menstrual cramps), and hummus. Sylvie was actually expecting her to pay for the likes of this? If one was going to spend money, much better to go out to dinner and enjoy it, Cassandra thought.

Sylvie was thinking: *I could really go for some hummus right now.* Sylvie was thinking, of her best friend, Cassandra: *Fuck you.*

"Oh, let's go out," said Cassandra, stretching her arms. They were looking especially creamy and touchable right now, she couldn't help but notice, pleasantly filled with the thought of her own ripe, late-twenties beauty. I am just entering my sexual peak right now, she often reminded herself, for, like all lovely things, it would not last for long in this world. The supreme softness of her arms could be attributed to her having rubbed her entire body earlier that afternoon with a concoction of brown sugar and baby oil: a beauty tip of Pansy Chapin's, first passed on to her at Bennington and filed away in her memory with deathly seriousness ever since. Pansy used to do that before departing campus for assignations with her fiancé on Central Park South. *I'm primping*, she would announce, and then vanish from the dining hall for days before the visit, cocooning herself in the luscious temple of Santa Maria Novella floral waters and monogrammed Swiss linens that was her dorm room. "I'll go and put something on. What do you feel like?"

"Something Mediterranean sounds good."

"Oh, I'd like some of those yummy Greek dips! You know. Taramosalata, tzatziki . . ."

She was thinking as she said this of that day—but it was years ago now, it was the day they found the *Madeline* coats, it was the day of the first snowfall, the day they drank mugs of Valrhona hot chocolate and, thus fortified, trudged out to Orpheus McCloud's place in Astoria—when she, Sylvie, and Gala Gubelman had ended up at a Greek restaurant for that midnight snack of taramosalata and warm pita bread, and those heavenly deep blue bowls of avgolemono soup. She had felt so close to Sylvie that day and somehow did not feel so close to her right now. Was it possible to feel more close to someone when you did not, in fact, live with them? Cassandra wondered. When the two of you were not in the same city, even?

"Tzatziki!" she heard Sylvie saying. "And that's so easy to make. Let's go to the store and pick up cucumbers and stuff."

Groceries again! But Sylvie insisted, and off they went. Cassandra paid. She thought that maybe since she was always paying for things, Sylvie would do the cooking, at least. But when they got back to the apartment, Sylvie put a knife in Cassandra's hand and instructed her to start chopping the cucumbers.

"Do you think it's *really* cheaper buying groceries?" she asked. Groceries in Fort Greene never did come cheap, was one thing she had discovered. "I feel like, just picking up a carton of tzatziki would have been—"

"Cassandra! I've been living in New York City for *years.* I know how to manage a food budget. You can't go out to eat all the time. You just can't."

"But I feel like New York actually has a lot of good cheap food, too, if you just—"

"That's not really true. Not if you like to eat healthfully anyway. You eat a lot more meat and fatty stuff than I do, I guess. What I mostly eat are fresh vegetables. Oh! That reminds me. How would you feel about buying us a juicer?"

A juicer? She could think of nothing she would like less.

"What do you want a juicer for?"

"I was thinking we might do a cleanse one of these days. And now that summer's coming, we can get such great stuff to juice at the farmers' market. We can make, like, beet juice, carrot, kale . . ."

Kale? Kale juice? Now this, this was to Cassandra the death of the soul.

"Would kale juice actually taste good, do you think?"

"Why wouldn't it?"

"Because it's fucking *kale juice*."

"I love kale. I make really good kale."

"Kale is not delicious. It's just one of those things that simply isn't. Kale is anti-delicious. If you ask me."

"Well, I didn't ask you."

"But you did ask me to pay for the juicer that's supposed to juice the said kale."

"Well, Jesus, Cassandra! We can use it to make fruit juices, too. I'll drink the kale juice and you can drink, like, peach juice or something when peaches are in season. Don't you think that fresh peach juice sounds delicious?"

"Not if I have to go through a bunch of effort to juice a bunch of damn peaches to get, like, a thimble full of liquid . . . And anyway! I just drink coffee. I'm a coffee drinker and proud of it. So are you! Whatever happened to your iced Americanos?"

"I was thinking I'd replace them with juice."

"Going from coffee to juice! That's like replacing fucking with cuddling. Isn't that, like, what lesbians are supposed to do? Lesbian bed-death and whatnot. There's no comparison."

Sylvie tried again, seeking this time to appeal to Cassandra's vanity, which she knew to be a soft spot.

"But we're pushing thirty now! Don't you want to stay in breeding condition?"

"Breeding condition?"

"Don't you want to stay healthy and—well, fertile?"

"Fertile? Fertile, Sylvie? I don't like to think of myself as fertile. It's such a gassy old word, somehow. *Fertile.* I hate it! Anyway. I don't want to have children."

"No, but you want to get laid."

"I *am* getting laid."

There followed a long silence between the two women. Afraid

to look into the eyes of her best friend, Cassandra found herself staring intently at the Chinese paper lantern hanging from the ceiling, which seemed to her as good a way to avoid confrontation as any. The delicate, whimsical girl who had splurged on that lantern at Pearl River Mart during her first year in New York and proudly shown it to Cassandra when she came to visit—Cassandra exclaiming: *Oh my God, Sylvie, it's magical!*—seemed but a memory right now.

"I've been thinking . . ." said Sylvie at last.

"Thinking what?"

"I've been thinking I drink way too much coffee. We both do. I've been thinking . . ."

"What?"

"I've been thinking that there are going to be some changes around here. Changes in my life."

When she said this, Sylvie's eyes sharpened like big brown jewels in her pale face, so much more hungry and haggard now than it had been when she was younger. She was still a good-looking young woman by anybody's standards—her body still yogic and firm and capable of turning heads on the streets of the city—but Cassandra noticed that her face was beginning to show the toll of hours spent running after other people's children and lifting their strollers; of years without steady income and health insurance and balanced meals; it was beginning to show, in short, the toll of spending one's youth in, or perhaps one should say *on*, New York City.

Sylvie was wearing a pair of black leggings underneath a Norwegian fisherman's sweater of her grandfather's; this look on her was appealingly gamine, or ought to have been. But the pair of leggings she had on today was streaked through with desperate-looking runs at the seams, runs so big even a casual observer could see them. Cassandra sighed. She looked at a lemon chiffon cocktail dress of hers hanging on her bedroom door, crystallized in the

April light. She owned so many beautiful pieces of clothing, and Sylvie so few.

"Oh, I'll buy us the damn juicer," said Cassandra airily, too convinced of the richness of her life, compared to Sylvie's, to begrudge her anything.

CHAPTER 18

Sylvie was always thinking ahead and, in fact, there was an
ulterior motive behind her asking Cassandra to buy them
a juicer. The following week, they were having lunch at a
fashionable restaurant claiming to be on the local foods bandwagon, which she thought was a most excellent setting in which
to announce her latest money-making scheme, in which the juicer,
she hoped, was going to play no small part.

Sylvie liked this place but Cassandra didn't, even though she
was the one who was paying. She sometimes thought she didn't
like *any* of the restaurants in Fort Greene all that much and yet
they were all so expensive. There was just this meagerness to them.
Here was her rule of thumb, and it had never yet failed her: if a
restroom had a bottle of Mrs. Meyer's geranium hand soap sitting
on the sink, the food would not have enough salt in it. She looked
down at the curried chicken salad sandwich she had ordered. Fourteen dollars it was going to cost her, and yet the kitchen did not
know enough to toast the bread, apparently.

Sylvie, meanwhile, was tucking into a nice big peppery green
salad with gusto, in high spirits today because her latest plan had
given her an adrenaline rush.

"What is it?" asked Cassandra.

"A lemonade stand."

"Huh?"

"A lemonade stand. *For grown-ups.*"

"Oh!" Now this was getting intriguing.

"Brilliant? Right? I am fucking brilliant and I am going to
make so much money."

"Sylvie! I love you. You're brilliant!"

"I've even come up with the perfect location. We'll set up shop on the corner across from the park, where the farmers' market is. So we'll get all the foot traffic, see."

"Do we need a permit or anything?"

"Oh, probably, but this is an illegal operation. We're up to it. Say somebody says something, say a cop comes. We can just pick up and move to another corner. It'll be fun."

A wonderful sense of adventure started to stir in Cassandra, and she felt alive and happy all over. Sylvie was feeling this, too.

"We'll have to make it all pretty," Cassandra said.

"Oh, very."

"Not just pretty, chic."

"Oh, very chic."

"Sophisticated."

"Well, right. That's the whole idea. A sophisticated lemonade stand, crafty yet stylish."

"Cozy but cosmopolitan . . ."

"Right! And of course we'll milk the whole local foods thing for everything it's worth. That's so trendy right now. Like I said! It's brilliant."

"What I especially like about this idea is the whole recaptured innocence angle."

"Hmm. How so?"

"Well, like I was thinking," Cassandra began, "of the time I visited you last year during Halloween weekend. And we were having lunch at that Cuban place in Carroll Gardens, but, like *upscale* Cuban, you know the one? They have those delicious, kind of caramelized coffee drinks. Anyway—remember that outside there was this Halloween parade? *And the parents were all wearing costumes, too.* That was the thing that caught my attention. Actually, I thought it was totally lame, all of those shrimpy little Brooklyn dads looking all smug in their perfectly ironical costumes, I couldn't even catch what the hell most of them were supposed to be."

"Yeah, but what do Halloween costumes have to do with lemonade stands?"

"Oh, Sylvie, everything! Can't you see? It's this whole thing about recaptured childhood, recaptured innocence. It's like, maybe they didn't have cool Halloween costumes when they were kids, so they get to make up for it later. And they make sure their kids have cool costumes, too. It's all a kind of desperate overcompensation for something. And if you think about a lemonade stand—lemonade is, like, the essence of childhood and summertime and happiness. Those same bozos with the Halloween costumes are going to see our lemonade stand and get exactly the same fuzzy, nostalgic feeling."

"You mean those suckers are going to eat this shit up?"

"Exactly. Why do you think cupcakes took over New York City? It has to be because they make people think of bake sales and birthday parties and all of that sentimental bullshit."

"Oh, cupcakes! I make really good cupcakes! And I did used to work at Petunia, remember?"

"I remember." Cassandra laughed, recalling that period of their youth.

"I even totally know how to make those red velvet ones. People *love* those."

"But are cupcakes *still* all the rage in New York? I feel like I've heard rumors that the new big thing is the macaroon. Like maybe I read that recently in the food section or somewhere."

But Sylvie, with her customary shrewdness around the value of a dollar, said that macaroons would be far too expensive to make.

"What do you think we should name it?"

"What?"

"Our business!"

Is it really what you would call a business exactly? Cassandra wondered to herself, and said aloud: "Hmm."

"I was thinking—I'd like to name it after Clementine."

"Oh, I like that! I've always just loved the name Clementine. Let me see. Clementine . . ."

"Clementine and Friends? No."

"Clementine's Party?"

"Clementine's Larder?"

"Clementine's Picnic!"

Sylvie snapped her fingers. "I like that. Clementine's Picnic! It's really pretty. It sounds kind of French, almost."

"It makes me think of a scene out of a Renoir painting or something. Young girls in white pinafores eating bread and cheese on the banks of the river . . ."

The girls she had in mind were Sylvie and herself, their hair in long, thick plaits, Sylvie's black and Cassandra's golden, picnicking on the banks of the Charles back when they were teenagers.

CHAPTER 19

They agreed to test out the lemonade stand the following Saturday and prayed for good weather. And so for the next several days, the girls dashed all around the city buying stuff, Sylvie desperate to turn a profit on their investments as they collected, at Marshalls, more of those white French champagne buckets and blue gingham napkins.

At a cake supply store downtown, they got hopped up sniffing tiny bottled potions of flavorings: lavender, orange, peppermint, rose. Their heads pounding from drinking in all that oozy sweetness, they got hopped up some more on caffeine, their third iced Americanos of the day. They wandered the streets of Manhattan deep in their usual activities: fast walking, fast talking. But today, because they were on a mission, these activities had to them a glitter, an edge.

"So," Sylvie asked. "How much do you think we can get away with charging for cupcakes?"

Cassandra, to whom no subject in the world was worth less consideration than numbers, said, "One-fifty?"

"Under two dollars, no fucking way! The people who live in Fort Greene now are loaded. I should know, I babysit all of their kids, I'm folding laundry for them in their five-story brownstones day after day! These people will think that the more you charge for your product, the more value it has, see. I say two-fifty, to start."

They went to Chinatown to buy teas and herbs because "Chinatown's the cheapest," explained Sylvie.

"You know, these are kind of yummy looking actually," said Cassandra, pointing to a package containing four suspiciously smooth orange-colored custards. All four custards could be had for three dollars.

"Hey! You're right. That kind of soft orange would look great with the blue of the napkins, right? We could buy those and mark them up and say we made them."

"We could say they were—mango pots de crème!"

"Brilliant. Cassandra, that's brilliant. I'm going to decorate them with mint leaves on top."

"If somebody asks you the recipe, do you think you can bullshit?"

"Oh, don't you worry. *I* can bullshit."

They were walking down Grand Street when there appeared, in all her broken, downtown glory, a mythic figure from their pasts. Cassandra spotted her first.

"Oh my God, it's Lanie Tobacco!"

"No!"

But there she was, fabulously, disdainfully nonchalant in a pair of busted black wedges and a leather jacket, dragging with pouty wine-stained lips on a Marlboro Red, to boot.

"Lanie!" called Sylvie.

"Lanie!" called Cassandra.

"Rough night" was all the notorious Lanie Tobacco had to say for herself after all these years; neither of them had seen her since graduation. "I fucked a hippie."

"Jesus." Both girls were immediately sympathetic on principle. So sympathetic was the overimaginative Cassandra that she could practically smell the patchouli.

Lanie tried to undo the zipper of her leather jacket, struggling wildly, hurling ashes everywhere. Finally, after giving up altogether, she said, "Ah well, I guess you get what you deserve when you buy Dolce & Gabbana in Beijing."

Back at the apartment that night, Sylvie tasted one of the orange custards, only to spit it out.

"Oh my God! No way can we sell these. These taste awful. Okay, Cassandra, you owe me three dollars."

Cassandra laughed.

"No, seriously."

"Seriously?" She laughed again, but more weakly this time.

"Well, I wouldn't have bought these things. They were your idea."

"Okay," said Cassandra as, with a twinge of worry, she reached into her wallet and forked over the money.

That Friday, they went to the Marshalls at Atlantic Center to see if they could get more glass pitchers. But Sylvie was annoyed to see that Cassandra went straight for the personal products section. It had long been one of the girls' secrets to stock up on discounted beauty products there. You often could find some nice things.

"Oh my God, look, white almond talcum powder! Smell, Sylvie, smell! I like that, and look, the bottle looks practically Italian."

"We can get products some other day. What I was thinking we need, is—"

"Bluebell and hyacinth hand soap! I love bluebells, just the word *bluebell* is lovely, don't you think?" Cassandra sighed, no doubt remembering some English children's book from her childhood in which bluebells had been mentioned.

"Okay, you stay here. I'm going to go to home goods to look for more pitchers."

"But Sylvie! Look at this stuff. This is a really, really good day at Marshalls, I can tell. You've got to stock up on stuff when they have it. Oh my God! Look at all those Italian soaps." Cassandra's eyes lit on a shelf full of prettily papered soaps. Sylvie, hands on her hips, stormed off. Ten minutes later, she came back to find Cassandra dreamily wheeling a shopping cart of products around the aisles of the personal products section.

"Come on, let's get out of here. There aren't any pitchers."

"Okay, but let me do one more sweep through these Italian soaps. I don't want to miss any really good ones."

"Cassandra! Do you see that line?"

"Yeah, but. It's Marshalls. It moves fast."

"No, it's Marshalls and they have complete and total idiots running the registers. It moves *slow.*"

"But look at all this stuff I found!"

"We'll come back. We'll come back on Monday."

"You want me to leave this stuff here all weekend? Sylvie! These Italian soaps are two dollars each! You want me to just walk away and leave them? Other people will get them!"

"Marshalls gets Italian soaps all the time, Cassandra."

"Not like this, they don't!"

"And anyway. We have to get home and start squeezing the lemons."

Cassandra dreaded the prospect of manual labor, and she felt a queer intensity of loss at the thought of leaving all of those beautiful soaps with their exotic scents (lavender sage, rose peppercorn, lemon mint) behind for other people with lesser taste to collect. But, in spite of her misgivings, she let them go.

Back at the apartment she began to cut and squeeze lemons while Sylvie steeped elaborate floral teas. While she was doing this, she started humming some vague tune to herself. Something French, Cassandra thought. Then it dawned on her that Sylvie was singing: *"Alouette, gentille Alouette / Alouette, je te plumerai / Je te plumerai la tête / Je te plumerai . . ."*

"That song. Cut it out, Sylvie. It gives me the creeps for some reason."

"This song? Why? I sing it all the time to Clementine. She's crazy about it!"

"I shall pluck your feathers, I shall pluck your head . . . Some song to sing to a little girl. I don't know why but there's something about that song. It disturbs me."

Jesus, thought Sylvie, and stopped singing. Then, noticing that Cassandra, who had never been good with her hands, was doing her task rather too slowly for Sylvie's taste, she said, "Oh, here, let me cut you a bunch of them so you can just put them in the juicer and go."

Before Cassandra could say anything, Sylvie took the knife from her hands and started slicing lemon after lemon open in single bold, deep cuts.

And then, "Ow!" she cried. She had cut a thin flap of skin off her thumb. Blood started to gush from it.

"Oh, no!" said Cassandra, and looked for something to give Sylvie to mop up the blood. But there were no paper towels in the kitchen, because Sylvie never spent money on things like paper towels on principle and Cassandra hadn't thought to buy them. And in the bathroom, too, Cassandra couldn't find any toilet paper to spare because they kept on forgetting to steal some. Finally, with a woeful absence of comfort or conviction, she handed her a dirty tea towel. Sylvie stood at the counter weeping, not so much because her thumb hurt, though of course, it did, but because this was getting ridiculous. She was sick of taking care of Cassandra and Cassandra never taking care of her.

Actually, she thought, nobody ever takes care of me. It's not just Cassandra. She had been taking care of herself for years. And then she started bawling even more wildly than before.

"Oh my God, Sylvie," said Cassandra, who winced at the sight of blood and did not fancy herself to be an able nurse, "is it really bad? Should I call an ambulance or something?"

"Don't call an ambulance, goddamn it! Whatever you do, *don't call an ambulance*! Jesus Christ, Cassandra. How the hell could you forget? I don't have any health insurance!"

This sounded, to Cassandra, a dim bell of doom, since for the first time in her life, she didn't have any health insurance either. And then, one year later, just as she was stepping out of Grand Central Terminal and not looking where she was going, she collapsed flat on her hands and knees on the frantic intersection of

East Forty-Second and Lexington. The first thought, though her tights were torn and her knees richly bloodied, was not *It hurts* but *I don't have any health insurance.*

She wanted to tell Sylvie all about it, but by then it was too late for Cassandra to tell Sylvie anything at all.

CHAPTER 20

At six o'clock sharp, the alarm clock rang. Cassandra got out of bed first. Sylvie, sans iced Americano and nursing her now-bandaged thumb, refused to budge. Finally: "You go," she commanded Cassandra. "You go drag the table down to the corner and start setting up. I'll join you."

Drag the table? Drag the table on her own? This was not, so far, a promising start to the day. But I have to do it, she told herself regretfully. I promised Sylvie I would help.

So Cassandra dragged the table all the way down DeKalb Avenue, until she got to the corner of Fort Greene Park. She set up the table and draped one of Sylvie's vintage tablecloths over it. The tablecloth was gray velveteen laced with a pattern of coral-colored roses and, the girls had agreed, very chic.

Some time passed, and Sylvie appeared struggling with untold numbers of Whole Foods tote bags. For such a small person, Cassandra never failed to marvel at how much stuff she could carry.

"Let me decorate," said Sylvie, budging Cassandra out of the way and beginning to readjust the tablecloth. "I have this really specific vision in mind."

"Maybe I'll go get us coffee then," Cassandra suggested, yawning.

Ordinarily this would have appealed to Sylvie, except that she had gotten an iced Americano for herself and polished it off already. So instead it irritated her that this early in the day Cassandra already was asking to take a break and she worried about the quality of her work ethic.

"Yeah, but I was thinking you could make us some signage, like to post around the neighborhood. I brought some paper and

some pastel charcoals. Don't you think that'll be pretty? Here."
And then, much to Cassandra's dismay, she reached into one of the
tote bags and procured arts-and-crafts supplies. Even as a child,
Cassandra had been deathly bored by such things.

"You can draw, like, cupcakes or something. Be creative. Whatever you do, just make sure it's really pretty!"

Glumly Cassandra took a piece of paper and a stick of pink
chalk and tried to draw a cupcake. God, it was all coming back to
her now, she thought, remembering the dusty, dismal art classes of
elementary school. She had always hated getting her hands dirty.
At this rate, her fingers were going to have pink chalk on them
all day.

And Sylvie, glancing down at Cassandra's drawing, thought:
Next time she'd hire some unemployed art school students to
make signs. Clementine can draw a more realistic-looking cupcake
than that. Clementine was two.

"When is Gala coming again?" asked Cassandra. Gala Gubelman also lived in Fort Greene these days and had said that she
would help out.

"Oh God, that reminds me, I have to text her to remind her.
You know how it is with Gala. She'll probably wake up in some
random guy's scuzzy bed out in Bushwick or somewhere and forget all about it."

"Bushwick. Christ! Are people living in Bushwick now, too?"

"Cassandra! People are living everywhere."

"I *guess.*"

"Speaking of Gala, I was doing some calculations in my head,
and if, like, every other guy she's had sex with in Brooklyn bought
a glass of lemonade from us, we'd be making a killing."

"By the way. Is Gala sex-positive or just plain slutty, do you
think? I've never quite gotten a handle on the distinction, myself."

"I think that the idea behind being sex-positive is, you own
being slutty. Like, you reclaim the word."

"Oh. Kind of like black people reclaiming the n-word."

"Uh—kind of."

"But I hate the words *sex-positive*. To me they're not even sexy."

"That's because you don't think anything positive is sexy, Cassandra. You're a fatalist, Cassandra."

"I am a fatalist! I'm a *romantic* fatalist. And I'm proud of it."

"Well, there you have it. And Gala's proud of being a slut, so you two are even."

The morning passed with a discouraging absence of briskness. There were only a handful of sales. Sylvie fretted to Cassandra about "making a return on my investment." Gala, at long last, appeared around noon, and Cassandra was happy to see her because for some reason it seemed to be tough going today, talking to Sylvie. She was acting *so serious* all of a sudden.

"Oh my God," breathed Gala, obviously hungover and wobbling on a pair of red patent-leather platforms, far better suited to Friday night than Saturday morning, "that guy was such an asshole."

"What guy?" asked Cassandra.

"The guy I spent the night with, stupid. I never did catch his name. But he was really bad in bed because I didn't even get off and—"

"And you get off with everybody," supplied Sylvie.

"Really, like everybody! With me, it doesn't take all that much. But this guy! Well, what was I thinking? I let him pick me up on the G train."

"Oh," said Sylvie and Cassandra together, in sympathy, "the G train."

They exchanged a private glance, both of them thinking how much fun it was going to be to gossip and complain about Gala's antics afterward.

"But he was kind of cute in that, like, sensitive Brooklyn way I go for . . ."

"Why do you go for that?" Cassandra wanted to know. "Why do you think that is cute?"

"I just do! I always have."

"That's right. I guess that's why you were one of the few girls who always got laid at Bennington."

"All the time!"

"And she even got off," added Sylvie.

"Yup."

Cassandra asked her: "Did you ever go to bed with Kojo?"

"Who?"

"The black guy. The one who played Mercutio in *Romeo in the Hood.*"

"Oh, no, I didn't go to bed with him. I went to bed with the other one."

"The other what?" asked Sylvie, starting to think that Cassandra and Gala, in tandem, were rather a trying combination. It was not lost on her that the two of them had this in common: both high-strung by nature, they were unusually sensitive to having migraines and multiple orgasms.

"The other black guy at Bennington," Gala said. "There were two of them, remember? The one I had a thing with was called Manu. I think that's a Ghanian name or something, but I don't know, I'm pretty sure he was only from the Bronx. They, like, bussed him and Kojo in. Have either of you ever been with a black guy?"

"No," said Sylvie.

"No," echoed Cassandra.

"Cassandra here only ever goes for sadistic upper-class assholes. All is forgiven assuming they went to Harvard."

"Oh," said Gala sorrowfully, "preppies." And then: "Oh God, where are the cupcakes? Do you think I could have one for break-fast, Sylvie? I'm sooo hungry," she moaned.

And then Cassandra, drinking in the glorious sight of the eas-ily orgasmic Gala eating one of Sylvie's red velvet cupcakes and licking pink frosting from her fingertips, wondered not for the first time why such a piece of woman should be wasted on the skinny lads of this outer borough. This morning she was stuffed into a purple leotard dress from American Apparel. Sylvie, checking out her boobs, seized on the idea that another way to make money might be to hold a wet T-shirt contest with all of her hottest friends in it and charge admission . . .

She handed Gala a piece of paper and some pastels and told her to get to work making signs. Hers would be sure to be better than Cassandra's, at least. But Gala, after a few bored strokes of chalk, crumpled up the piece of paper and turned to Cassandra and said: "So. How many guys do you think you're going to sleep with during your first year in New York? Everybody sleeps with so many new guys their first year in New York."

"Oh. Do they? But I have a boyfriend, remember."

"Whatever, Cassandra," piped in Sylvie. "Listen to you! I thought you didn't believe in monogamy."

"It's never worked out for me. And guys have a way of being, like, so possessive. Remember when I slept with the bass player in Orpheus's band?" Gala asked, tapping Sylvie on the arm. "And he *peed* on my pillow."

"How very animal kingdom," said Cassandra, impressed.

"It was!"

"Well, in theory I don't necessarily believe in monogamy. But in practice . . . Actually there is someone I'm thinking of having an affair with."

"An *affair*? Nobody has affairs anymore."

"They don't?"

"No, they just hook up."

"Oh, so it's just my language you're saying is old-fashioned—"

"I feel like it's the whole idea, too. *Affair* just sounds so formal or something. Sex today is so casual. There's none of that, Oh my darling, let me send you a dozen red roses and meet you in a midtown hotel bullshit. You want someone, you just text them. It's, like, instant."

"You think this development is a good thing, though? I want red roses! I want to meet up in a hotel in midtown!"

"Midtown? Midtown, Cassandra? I was just saying that to make fun of how outdated the whole idea is. I wouldn't be caught dead. Anyway. There're really not that many reasons left to go into Manhattan at all anymore. I'm happier staying in Brooklyn."

"Oh, so you'd be above meeting a man at the Pierre, would you?"

"What the hell is the Pierre?"

"Well. Maybe you've heard of the Plaza?"

"Of course I have, but come on now, Cassandra. How romantic could it be? Everyone knows it's owned by Donald Trump!"

Then Sylvie, ever alert to her surroundings, saw a father and his little boy approaching and whispered, "Oh my God, customers!"

CHAPTER 21

All three young women now rose and straightened their shoulders.

"Hello," said Sylvie firmly.

"Good morning," said Cassandra more firmly still, though it was not, technically, the morning anymore.

"Hey," was all Gala could manage, in a thick, silky purr.

"Do you have sandwiches?" the father asked.

The girls were crestfallen. Sylvie began to run through the other options briskly.

"Daddy, I want a cupcake," whimpered the little boy.

"But, August, it's lunchtime. First I have to find you a sandwich or something. Your mother would kill me."

"Cupcake, cupcake—"

"We'll be back," the father said, scooping the little boy up into his arms. "But hey, I think I'll have one of those iced teas. You have hibiscus? Oh, good."

An impulse buy, thought Sylvie. Good! I was counting on those.

But all Cassandra could think, getting bored with the lemonade stand already, was: What grown man gets so excited about hibiscus?

She was starting to grow weary of Brooklyn, in its present-day faux-folksy incarnation. Since no way could she afford to live in Manhattan, she sure hoped that Edward would propose soon and then she could go and live in Philadelphia, where you could get someplace elegant in Rittenhouse Square for, comparatively speaking, very little money.

After the little boy and his father left, Sylvie turned to her friends and announced: "Well, that was very useful market research."

"What was?" asked Cassandra.

"What he said about coming back later, to get that kid a cupcake. Maybe the problem is we set up shop too early. It's in the afternoon when your blood sugar crashes and you need a pick-me-up. I should have thought of that earlier. I think things are going to pick up after lunch! Now. How are we doing on those signs? *Gala.* You can't just keep crumpling up the paper. Art supplies cost money, you know."

"But I'm not happy with the way my drawings are turning out. I don't think I've done an art project since Bennington."

"I didn't even do them at Bennington," said Cassandra. "I was an English major."

Christ, thought Sylvie, reaching for a piece of paper and starting to make a sign herself. Was she going to have to do absolutely everything around here?

After lunch, the day got hot and business picked up. Sylvie, sniffing a profit, announced: "Okay, you two. I'm going to stay here and watch the lemonade. I want you to go stand at that corner with a tray of cupcakes." She pointed. "I feel like we need to diversify our locations."

"Diversify our locations" was eerie language to Cassandra, to whom business-speak of any kind was utterly foreign. Was Sylvie, like, *serious* about this thing? she wondered. But if that was the case, would she expect her to stand on a street corner in Brooklyn wearing a vintage apron and hawking lemonade every goddamn Saturday? But so many weekends would find her in Philadelphia with Edward, attending black-tie events and concerts on his arm. Didn't Sylvie understand? The lemonade stand was cute and all, and it would be heaven if it brought in a little bit of cash flow. Lingerie money, Cassandra was thinking, remembering Edward.

But nevertheless Cassandra and Gala went and stood on the

corner, clutching trays of cupcakes in their hands with rather frozen-looking smiles on their faces. Sylvie had been right to diversify their locations. Business was good, so good that Gala had to run to get change at a bodega across the street. As it happened, the owner of the bodega had spent the better part of the afternoon taking a smoke break outside and lapping up the pleasant sight of the two buxom girls, especially the brunette in the red patent-leather platforms, standing there with the trays of cupcakes. Now here was a view he could get used to. When he saw the brunette coming, he went inside and got behind the counter.

"Hey, could we have change?" asked Gala, handing him a couple of twenties.

He made change and slowly surveying her deep cleavage asked her: "So. How is business going today?"

"Great!" exclaimed Gala, suddenly excited to be caught up in a rogue operation like the lemonade stand. Plus, the bodega-guy was Guatemalan, and not for nothing had she learned to speak Spanish. She just loved the feeling of hitting it off with people from other cultures. It made her feel like such a nice person. "My friends and I just started this lemonade and cupcake business. I'll bring you a cupcake later on, promise."

Gala left the bodega and joined Cassandra back on the corner. A big rattling old electric blue shit-box of a car drove by and stopped. The girls smelled pot. Gala, being, like Sylvie, a pothead, stopped to breathe it in.

"Hey, those cupcakes you got there?" asked the driver.

"Yes!"

"How much?"

"Two-fifty."

"All right, give me two." He took out his wallet. "No, make that four."

After he was gone, Gala said, "Well, someone has the munchies! God, I really could go for some pot myself."

"We'll have to tell Sylvie. That's a new business angle."

"What?"

"Car sales! Drive-through!"

The girls laughed. There were more sales, mostly to parents with children. Then another car stopped at the curb and the driver rolled down the window, only to call out: "Hey! Do you have a lemonade stand, too?"

"Oh, yes," Cassandra piped up. "It's just down—"

"I was joking," the man said flatly, and drove away.

"Asshole," said Gala, who could always be counted on to get on the bandwagon of hating any man. Hatred was so sexy. That guy had been pretty cute, actually. It occurred to her that the lemonade stand might be a cool way to meet guys. It was getting kind of old, letting them pick her up on the subway.

Business slowed down again, and the girls took the break in activity as the perfect opportunity to start gossiping about their old classmates.

"Oh my God, I forgot to tell you!" announced Cassandra. "Pansy Chapin is getting a boob job. She's engaged to this hedge-fund guy and *he's* paying."

"Well, if he's a hedge-fund guy, he'd better be! Wait—I thought she got engaged our senior year, to that other rich, preppie guy. Did they get divorced already?"

"Oh, him. Oh, no. He broke off the engagement, when he found out she was sleeping with Kojo. There was this big to-do about it. Anyway—I feel like no self-respecting *Bennington girl* should get a boob job. I feel like Bennington girls are supposed to have, like, this natural, bohemian beauty, you know?"

And then Cassandra and Gala, both secure in their own naturally beautiful, naturally generous breasts, god-given full C and D cups respectively, took a moment of silence to contemplate the grave horror that Pansy was inflicting on her own rather more austere body type.

"That sucks," said Gala. "That she doesn't love herself the way she is. And she's so hot, too!"

"Elegant," added Cassandra, her highest word of praise.

"But still. Think of going to bed with a new guy for the very first time and *not having any boobs*. I just feel like you'd get so sick of the guy always being disappointed with what he had to work with. Can you imagine?"

"No," Cassandra admitted. "I can't."

"Oh, hey. Have you been to that really great sex store in SoHo? I was going to go there this week, if you wanted to come along."

"Oh no. I mean, I'm adventurous but not in that way, Gala. I don't like the idea of—toys."

"But wait. Sylvie said you like being tied up. Me, I like tying guys up. Trust me. They go *crazy* . . ."

No wonder she went for those skinny Brooklyn boys, Cassandra was thinking, and said: "Yeah, but being tied up is an expression of, like, ancient hostility. You don't need *toys* for that."

"What do you use, though? I'm curious. To be tied up?"

"Oh, we use—Oh, hello!" Cassandra turned to see a little girl standing there with her mother. "And how are *you* today? My name is Cassandra and this is my friend Gala. What a pretty dress you have on! Would you like a cupcake?"

Why is this lady talking to me in that phony voice? the little girl wondered to herself. And why are she and her friend standing out on the sidewalk and selling cupcakes? They were *grown-ups*.

When the girls went back to check in with Sylvie, she was thrilled to see the fat wad of money they'd made and immediately began to count the twenties.

Cassandra, realizing that she was thirsty after hours of standing out in the sunshine, helped herself to some of the lavender-flavored lemonade.

But Sylvie saw what she was doing and admonished her: "Hey, Cassandra, please don't use the plastic cups! Those things cost money, you know. They're going to add up."

Cassandra just wasn't getting it, Sylvie thought. Getting it about the lemonade stand, and how incredibly important it was to her. Every time someone handed her a dollar bill that day, she felt this warm, safe feeling such as she so seldom felt anymore. Maybe with Clementine. Yeah, with Clementine, but that was it. The touch of dollar bills—the straightforward power of them, the incontestable relief of finally having them after so many lean years—was the next best thing.

"Sorry," said Cassandra rather prissily, stopping in mid-sip. Then she looked at it and thought: What the hell? She'd already used the damn cup, she might as well finish the beverage. She had to hand it to Sylvie, though. The lavender-flavored lemonade was absolutely delicious.

"Oh, Sylvie, that reminds me!" said Gala. "I told the guy at the bodega I'd bring him a cupcake. Do we have any of the red velvet ones left?"

This was the day Sylvie finally came to understand the meaning of the words *a cranberry is a cranberry*. Tish, the woman who first uttered those immortal words, was a grown-up, she thought. Cassandra and Gala were still acting like girls.

That was the difference.

CHAPTER 22

Hey, next time do you think that you could remember to turn your phone off?"

Edward rolled away from Cassandra. His disapproval of her, though she could not recognize it, was starting to be a hallmark of their relationship. They had just finished having sex on the staircase. The whole time, Cassandra's phone had been ringing in her purse, which was downstairs in the living room.

"Sorry." Cassandra rubbed his head and drew him close to her again. "I'd better go and check it, though. It's probably Sylvie."

"Sylvie . . ." muttered Edward. He'd never met her but he didn't much like her. Sylvie would have been most delighted to assure him that the feeling was mutual.

"God, four times she called. I hope everything's all right."

Edward got up and put on his Brooks Brothers boxers, bracing himself for having to listen to Cassandra gab on the phone to a female friend, which was *not* his favorite sound in the world, to tell you the truth. He much preferred her dreamy and docile and murmuring sweet nothings in bed. When he tied her up, she didn't speak *at all* and that was fantastic. She just kind of lay back and moaned.

"So I'm serious," Sylvie began, and from the tone of her voice Cassandra could tell she was hopped up on iced Americanos and that it wouldn't be easy to get off the phone anytime soon. And then Edward would get all annoyed. He didn't like Sylvie; she could tell.

"Cassandra, I'm serious," Sylvie repeated. "I'm starting a business, a real business. How much do you think I should hire people for?"

"Hire people?"

"People to help run the stand and sell stuff. What do you think, ten bucks an hour? Is that too high? Could I get away with eight, do you think? We're in a recession, remember."

"I don't know, Sylvie. Nine? Look. Edward's here and we're about to get dressed to go to the club."

They were totally just fucking right now, Sylvie thought, disgusted. So that's why she didn't pick up the phone when I kept calling! And asked: "Which club?" Cassandra was too self-absorbed to recognize that by asking this question Sylvie was making fun of her. Edward belonged to many different clubs and Sylvie was getting sick of hearing about them.

"Oh, there's this lecture on Degas at the Rittenhouse Club tonight! With a cocktail hour beforehand. You know how I just love Degas! I always have."

Cassandra had been famous at Bennington for her stoical indifference to contemporary art. A striking stance, that.

"So," Sylvie went on. Her voice was snappish. "Here's another thing I wanted to ask you. What do you think about muffins?"

"Muffins?"

"For people to buy in the morning. Like, I make these really good pear-bran ones . . ."

"I don't know, Sylvie. I wouldn't go out of my way to stop for a bran *anything* muffin, but maybe that's just me. I think it has to be something people really can't resist."

Why are they discussing muffins? Edward wondered. What could two grown women possibly have to say to each other about muffins? And would they ever get off the phone?

"But I make amazing muffins!" said Sylvie. She was almost screaming, and Cassandra thought, Goodness, such emotion about a little thing like muffins. "My muffins are amazing. God, this is going to be great, I'm going to make so much money."

Cassandra couldn't help but note the change of the pronoun *we* to the pronoun *I*: *I'm* starting a business. *I'm* going to make so much money. But she was in a magical postsex haze and so none of this mattered.

"Everything you make tastes really good, Sylvie," was all she said. "You're a wonderful cook."

After she got off the phone, she went and lay down in Edward's arms.

"Sorry about that. It's Sylvie. She's starting this little, I don't know, lemonade stand thing."

Bennington girls, Edward thought. They were so hot but so damn flaky! *Sylvie was starting a lemonade stand?* He sure hoped that Cassandra wouldn't get mixed up in a thing like that. How was it that none of her friends ever seemed to have real careers?

When Cassandra got back to Brooklyn, the apartment was in even more of a state of chaos than usual, pitchers of sticky-smelling floral teas steeping on the kitchen counter, spoons crusty with pastel frosting, and a tower of plastic containers filled with dozens and dozens of unfrosted cupcakes. Out in the hallway there were bags and bags full of rotting lemons.

"Are those—cupcakes?" Cassandra asked.

"Yes. But don't have one!" There was panic in Sylvie's voice. "They're for sale."

"When?"

"I'm going to sell them on Saturday."

"It's Tuesday."

"They'll keep," said Sylvie darkly.

CHAPTER 23

The following afternoon, Cassandra accompanied Sylvie while she babysat Imogen. Quinn, meanwhile, had a play-date with a friend of his, Julius, and his nanny, a twenty-four-year-old linguistics major from Smith named Hannah. "That Julius is a bastard," Sylvie remarked to Cassandra, in full view of clever little Imogen, on whom not a single word was lost. "Do you know what he told Hannah, after he met me? He said: 'I wish Quinn's nanny was my nanny. She's so much prettier than you!' Do you believe that?"

"You are prettier than Hannah," chimed in Imogen, not because she wanted to compliment Sylvie but because it was the truth and Imogen was a great believer in speaking the truth. "Hannah's not pretty at all."

"Julius!" said Cassandra. "What kind of parents name their child Julius? It's such a jerky name for a little boy. You know? *Julius.*" She rolled her eyes.

"What are we going to do today?" asked Imogen, getting down to business. If she didn't keep them on track, Sylvie and Cassandra were likely to just sit there for hours *talking* and *talking*. Imogen, not being the introspective type, was big on "doing" things. Cassandra dreaded what might be coming, so before the little girl could suggest something kid-friendly and appropriate, she said, "I have an idea."

"Oh yeah?" said Imogen, prepared not to be impressed.

"How would you like to go lingerie shopping?"

"Cassandra!" said Sylvie.

"Oh, come on, Sylvie, I want to stock up. I feel like Edward's getting sick of all of the stuff I have. I'd like to surprise him with something."

"Who's Edward?" asked Imogen.

"My boyfriend."

"Oh. Well, so what? What does he have to do with it?"

"With what?"

"With lingerie shopping."

"Oh—" Cassandra began. Sylvie cut in to stop her, saying: "Where did you want to go anyway?"

"I got this postcard in the mail saying that Agent Provocateur is having a sample sale. Let's go!"

"Oh my God, a sample sale!" Now Sylvie was persuaded, if bargains were to be had.

"What's a sample sale?"

"Oh, Imogen," said Cassandra, almost with tenderness, "the things I'm going to teach you."

"I think Edward is a stupid name. It sounds old."

"Don't worry," said Sylvie. "He is."

"You think *Edward* is a stupid name? What about Julius?"

Or Quinn for that matter, thought Sylvie grimly.

"I go to school with this kid named Bear."

"Bear?" said Cassandra. "Bear? Does he have a brother named Cub?"

"No, Orlando."

"Orlando? Bear and Orlando? Christ."

"I want to be named Francesca. I have this friend named Francesca. But she's not even that pretty and a Francesca should be pretty. A Francesca should be beautiful! Don't you think so? Will you call me Francesca?"

"Okay, Francesca," said Cassandra.

"Can I call you Cassie?"

"Fuck, no!"

"Cassandra."

"Cassie! Cassie! Over my dead body you'll call me Cassie."

"Okay, Cassie."

"If you call me Cassie ever again, I won't take you lingerie shopping."

"So? I'll get my mother to take me lingerie shopping."

"Oh, no you won't."

"Your mother doesn't wear lingerie. And I should know. I do her laundry." And then Sylvie whispered to Cassandra: "She wears those, you know, passion-killers."

"Oh dear. Those kind of saggy cotton deals with the high waists?"

"Passion what?" asked Imogen.

"Never you mind," said Sylvie.

They got on the train and got off in SoHo. Once they were inside the Agent Provocateur on Mercer Street, Imogen went straight for the whips. She picked up a tiny black feathered one and rubbed it between her hands. She was *in love.* She must own this whip or she *would die.*

"Oh God," said Sylvie, noticing what Imogen was doing. Cassandra was too busy scooping up fistfuls of frothy, candy-colored garter belts.

"Can I get this, Sylvie? Can I, can I? If you buy it for me, my parents will pay you back. I promise."

"Now, Imogen—"

"Francesca! Today I'm Francesca." Assuming this new, splendid identity, she struck a pose with the whip in the mirror. My, but blondes look well in black. The effect was very striking. She'd have to get a whole new wardrobe. She looked down at her peach-colored organic cotton blouse with deepest displeasure.

"What? My parents are rich! Why are you so worried, Sylvie? They'll pay you back."

"No, you're not going to buy anything here, Imogen. But you can look. You can buy stuff here when you're older."

"But Cassandra's buying stuff."

Sylvie turned and there was Cassandra, merrily putting stuff on hold at the register. Sylvie suddenly felt utterly without interest in lingerie. What she wished she could do was go home and bake more cupcakes. She looked down at Imogen, standing there with the whip. Just think. If the lemonade stand took off, she wouldn't have to babysit little brats like this anymore.

Somebody's phone started ringing. "Oh, it's Edward!" Cassandra exclaimed, all aflutter at the thought of him, and stepped outside to take the call. When she returned, she sighed and said, "I'm so disappointed."

"What's the matter?"

"Well, Edward's coming to town this weekend and of course we'll be staying at the Harvard Club, but—"

"This weekend? But I need you to work the lemonade stand, Cassandra."

For ten dollars an hour? Cassandra thought of asking her, knowing full well that Sylvie expected her to do it for free.

"Oh, get Gala to do it. The sight of her is good for foot traffic, right? Just make sure she wears that cheesy American Apparel dress again. I can't stand those dresses! They're, like, the death of elegance, if you ask me."

But nobody did ask you, Sylvie was thinking.

"Gala's hot!" said Imogen.

"I'm not sure," said Cassandra, "that I approve of little girls using words like *hot*. There's something objectifying about it."

"But you approve of taking them to lingerie stores?" Sylvie chimed in.

"Well, you're her babysitter. We didn't have to come here if you suddenly thought it was so inappropriate."

"Can't you get Edward to come another weekend?"

"No, he has some important meeting at the Harvard Club, is the thing. But I'm so upset because, get this! The old rooms are all booked, so we have to stay in one of the modern ones."

"And the problem is . . . ?"

"The old rooms have four-poster beds, see. The modern ones don't."

"So?"

"Well, I just love being tied to a four-poster . . ."

"Oh, Good Lord."

"How does that work?" Imogen wanted to know. "How do you tie someone to a bed? Can you teach me how to do it, Cassandra? Can you? There are a bunch of beds at our house. We have five stories."

"Oh, we just use ties," said Cassandra, not missing a beat. "Edward's ties. They're beautiful. He has very nice clothes. Very classic, you know."

"Like my daddy's ties?"

"I guess." Cassandra now remembered all of a sudden that she was talking to a seven-year-old. "I'm just going to buy these garter belts and then we can get going."

"What's a garden belt?"

"Garter belt, Francesca my friend, garter belt."

"Is it like a garden snake? That would be funny."

"No, it's more like—" Sylvie sighed and held her head in her hands. "Come on, Imogen, let's get out of this place."

"My whip!" wailed Imogen, refusing to let it go. She was having sparkling visions of using it to boss other little girls around on the playground.

"Oh, my God!"

"What now?"

"Would you look at that lavender baby doll! The sheer one, over there! Hold on a second. I think I just *have* to have that."

"You already have—"

"Oh, but Sylvie! Edward just loves me in lavender."

"I would get it in black instead," advised Imogen knowledgeably, putting down the whip with great sorrow and reluctance but figuring that her birthday was coming up and she'd ask her parents to buy it for her then. "Black looks hot on blondes, and anyway, if you get it in black it'll make you look thinner." She smiled. "Cassie."

CHAPTER 24

Three days later.

"Well, would you get a load of this?" Sylvie, on the phone to Cassandra.

"What?" Cassandra was packing her orange suitcase, en route to meet Edward at the Harvard Club in midtown. Gently she folded the lavender baby doll, imagining his capable, manly hands peeling the sheer fabric right off of her helpless, prone body.

"I'm outside, I should go back in soon. But get this. And it's all your fault, too! Megan"—Megan was Quinn and Imogen's mother—"just had this talk with me in the kitchen, because, get this, she walked in on Imogen tying Quinn to the bedpost the other night. And what do you think she was using to tie him up? Her father's ties!"

"That's kind of brilliant, actually."

"Brilliant? This is your reaction?"

"Well, I've never liked the kid. She's a bitch. But you have to admit. She's very precocious."

"Jesus. You can just imagine the conversation I had with Megan. It was hilarious, because you could tell she was horrified but didn't want to act too, too horrified because then it would look like she's uptight about sex and no liberal Brooklyn mother wants that. But actually, I don't think they have that much sex anymore."

"Who?"

"Megan and Dan. I see them, when they get home. I think they're too tired."

"Do you think Clementine's parents still have sex?"

"Not so much."

"Do you think any of the parents you babysit for have sex anymore?"

"Well. Being around kids so much has practically killed my libido, and I'm just the nanny. I get to go home. They don't."

"Hmm."

"I don't know, though. Clementine's parents have only one kid, so that probably makes it a little easier to find time to have sex. But only a little."

"Oh! By the way. I just love what they did with that place in Bed-Stuy."

"Yeah, they bought that when you could get, like, unbelievable deals on some of those amazing old brownstones there. They have great taste, too."

"Megan and Dan, not so much."

"No, not so much. You know, this whole tying-people-up thing reminded me. This one time at a Bennington alumni event—"

"Where was this?" Cassandra was anxious to know, feeling pre-emptively jealous in case she had missed out on it on account of still living in Boston at the time, which was distinctly possible.

"The Salmagundi Club. I went with Gala, I remember. We only went because of the open bar. Also, because of the coke."

"Wait, there was coke there?"

"I don't know. Maybe. It's entirely possible. People could have been doing it in the bathroom, I guess."

"Isn't that always the way?" said Cassandra nostalgically, not that she had ever actually done coke herself, but she had plenty of memories of walking in on people doing it in college and then turning away from them, befuddled.

"Yes, but, I just meant that we went to the event in order to get a coke *connection*. Gala had the name of some dealer who was supposed to have really good stuff."

"Okay, but. Why are you telling me all this?"

"Oh right, because while Gala was talking to the dealer, I was talking to his girlfriend, I remember, and! This is what I wanted to tell you, Cassandra. They graduated in the nineties and after college what she did was move out to LA and work as a dominatrix. She made a ton of money doing that, she said. In fact, between that and what with her boyfriend being a drug dealer, they had enough money saved a couple of years after graduation to buy their own house in Laurel Canyon!"

"And the moral of the story is . . . ?"

"Sex sells! That must be the moral of the story, I guess."

"That's a very old moral, you know. World's oldest profession and all that."

"The point is," said Sylvie, regaining ground, "the point is, there's your plan B, Cassandra. Assuming you have a plan A to speak of, which I'm not convinced you do. You don't even have a job. But that's another story."

Because you're not actually going to marry Edward, Sylvie was thinking. You're going to fuck it up. Our friends know us better than we ourselves do and are capable of predicting our fates accordingly.

"Me? A dominatrix?"

"No, no, not a dominatrix, that would be ridiculous. I think Gala should become a dominatrix and you should become a, what do you call it, submissive."

"Gala already has a job."

"Oh, come on. Would you wish working in a gallery in Dumbo on your worst enemy? It doesn't pay anything and she's pretty much just a receptionist and anyway she's already slept with most of the artists they represent, so she's getting bored."

"Sylvie. You can't be serious."

"Oh, but I am. I've always said you were a natural masochist, Cassandra. And not just sexually either! On all fronts."

"Gee, thanks."

"You ought to think about it. You ought to think about something. Do you have a plan B?"

"I guess not," Cassandra admitted.

"Cassandra."

"Well, I've been thinking. If things get really desperate"—not that she believed they ever would—"I could always pawn my great-grandmother's wedding silver."

Her grandmother had just passed it down to her with great fanfare, now that there was this most respectable man, Edward, in the picture, and drawing the conclusion, as Cassandra herself did, that their engagement would be announced any day now.

"Wedding silver? Wedding silver? That's, like, a practically pre-war concept."

"But Sylvie. This stuff is gorgeous. Trust me. It weighs a ton."

"So what, Cassandra? It's silver. *Silver.* Nobody uses that shit anymore."

"They don't?"

"Do *you?* In case you haven't noticed, we barely have a roll of paper towels in our apartment, let alone silver . . . Silver! I ask you."

"But Sylvie! It's really beautiful."

"This isn't Cambridge, Cassandra. This isn't Brattle Street. You can't just dawdle along. This is New York City! Also, it's the twenty-first century and so far, the twenty-first century sucks. Believe me. Everybody needs a plan B!"

"Well. Louis Hawksworth is in town this week and he's always good for two or three square meals, tops. I always have breakfast with him at that gentleman's club he stays at in the West Fifties, remember, a full, proper breakfast with this really great crispy bacon they have, and then there's this fancy dinner he's taking me to at the American Academy of—"

"Louis Hawksworth? Is he still alive, that guy?" There came a memory of the *War and Peace* course she'd once taken with him, not that she'd actually read it, and how, instead of talking about the book, he'd gone totally silent for long spells at a time while gazing out the windows of the classroom at the deer grazing in the meadows. Dementia setting in, Sylvie had thought at the time.

"Oh, he's blind as a bat, but not dead yet. I don't think. Actually, he gave me this piece of advice I've been thinking about. He said, 'Cassandra, the next time you find yourself in a cab with a man and you want to get out of paying the fare, just ask the driver to stop and get out and then, just before you walk away, lightly tap the palm of your date's hand to your breast and say good night. You'll get out of paying the fare *and* he'll be dreaming about you all night long.' He said some chick did that to him in Greenwich Village in the fifties and he's never gotten over her."

"In the fifties, Cassandra. That could only ever have worked in the fifties. Nowadays, nowadays the guy would expect you to go Dutch and then afterward he'd feel entitled to a blow job, just because!"

"Oh, by the way, Sylvie. Speaking of Bennington people. Pansy Chapin and I are meeting up for drinks at J.G. Melon tomorrow."

"You would have to go uptown, for her." At this point in her life, Sylvie went uptown under no circumstances and into Manhattan under very few.

"Oh, but I just love the Upper East Side. It's so classical."

"You would. Edward must be rubbing off on you, I guess. Has he ever even been to Brooklyn, that guy?"

"Edward? Brooklyn? Probably not. Has Pansy, do you think?"

"No!"

The girls laughed and then Cassandra said: "Actually. It doesn't really matter because I'm not going to do it, but Pansy asked me if I wanted to go in on getting this apartment with her next month. She says she found this amazing place on Seventy-Ninth and Second but can't afford it without a roommate and it's too adorable to pass up."

"Wait, I thought she was engaged to some hedge-fund guy."

"No, another broken engagement, would you believe it? Poor Pansy."

"Oh, poor Pansy me! She'll have another rich boyfriend in, like, two weeks from now."

"It's too bad, though."

"Cassandra! You feel bad for *Pansy Chapin*?"

"Well, I always did like her. I remember how our junior year, she taught me all about these sex positions that *actually work* in the shower. Before I talked to Pansy, I could never get the hang of that."

"Oh, please."

"What I meant was, no offense, but it's kind of too bad I'm living with you already. Pansy has great taste. And some amazing mid-century modern furniture from her grandmother. The last time I saw her, she gave me those really great hand-me-down pillows I have on my bed? The olive green satin ones? Remember? I've always just loved the way that olive green looks with pink . . ."

"Pansy Chapin, Pansy Chapin! I'm sick of the name. This is the girl who once told me that the only good reason to go to Bennington is to have something interesting to talk about at cocktail parties on Fifth Avenue later on."

"So? And what *is* a good reason to go to Bennington? Damned if I know."

Shower sex, Sylvie was thinking as she hung up the phone. When Cassandra said that, there had swept over her a memory of how this boy she had been in love with—was it Jasper or Angus or Bertram or Max?—once hoisted her tiny body in his arms and up against the wall of the shower in order to make love to her. The water pressure in Sylvie's bathroom was weak but the light celestial. Even now, so many years later, she could still recall the lavender-honey softness of that light, not to mention the feel of her silky warm flesh in his arms.

Was this what Cassandra felt with Edward? she wondered. And then, suddenly, it occurred to Sylvie that she couldn't bear to ask her; that she didn't even want to know the answer.

It occurred to her that Cassandra was becoming more and more like a stranger to her these days, and that she didn't even care.

CHAPTER 25

The following weekend, while Cassandra was off at the Harvard Club being tied to a four-poster (one of the old-fashioned rooms had become available to her and Edward at the last moment after all), Sylvie continued to rake in money at the lemonade stand. It was a beautiful, warm Saturday and Fort Greene was full of young couples and parents with children and even Manhattanites, who kept reading in the Styles section that Brooklyn was now paradise on earth and were curious to go and check it out. Sylvie's lemonade stand was just the kind of charming, scrappy little touch they were hoping to see and they were delighted to give her their business. A couple of them even asked Sylvie if they could buy the gray velveteen tablecloth, but Sylvie, realizing that it had value, was determined to hold on to it.

Gala hadn't been able to make it to the lemonade stand either, being too hungover. So Sylvie got Hannah, the nanny of that little boy Julius, to help out. Hannah was plain and therefore unlikely to attract foot traffic like Gala or even Cassandra. But she had something that neither of them did: a work ethic. Sylvie made a note to keep using Hannah as long as she could; even better, she had done it for free and Sylvie saw no reason to bring up the subject of paying her before Hannah did.

On Saturday night, with Edward dozing beside her in the four-poster, Cassandra texted Sylvie:

OMG. PROFESSOR SOBEL JUST INVITED ME TO HAVE DINNER AT
LE BERNARDIN. ACCEPT?

Sylvie to Cassandra:

WHAT THE HELL IS LE BERNARDIN? IS IT EXPENSIVE?

Cassandra to Sylvie:

FAMOUS AND FRENCH. DEFINITELY EXPENSIVE.

Sylvie to Cassandra:

I GUESS YOU CAN LET HIM FUCK YOU IF IT'S REALLY THAT
EXPENSIVE.

Sylvie googled Le Bernardin from her BlackBerry and was
pleased to discover that it was a famous fish restaurant. Sylvie
loved fish and almost never got the chance to eat it because it was
so expensive. She'd have to ask Cassandra to remember to bring
her a doggie bag.

On Monday night, Cassandra was wheeling her orange suitcase
back into the apartment, only to realize that Sylvie was already
in there smoking a joint. Oh dear, thought Cassandra, and it
occurred to her with a pang of guilt that she wished Sylvie weren't
home tonight. She just wanted to take a shower and unpack and
relax. But here was Sylvie, and with a certain zesty sharpness in her
eyes that was getting all too familiar. Not even marijuana could
soften the edges of her, these days.

"Cassandra! Guess what? I got my first investor! Toby is giving
me five thousand dollars!"

"Toby?"

"This kid I know from Cooper Union. He's a green architect.
Maybe you haven't met him yet. Anyway. I know him only because
he used to sleep with Gala, but he has a crush on me now and he's
one of the only people I know who has a real, adult job and any
money at all to speak of. I talked to him today and got him all
excited about Clementine's Picnic."

"What?"

"Clementine's Picnic. We discussed that being the name of the lemonade stand. That's what I'm calling it now! My business. After all! Clementine *is* my good luck charm."

"Yeah, I just didn't realize it was so official all of a sudden. Wait. Did you say he was giving you *five thousand dollars?*"

"Yeah! He's super into the environment, so I think the whole local foods angle got him. And it helped when I said I'd pose for the calendar, I think." Sylvie laughed.

"What calendar?" asked Cassandra, thinking to herself: Local foods? Sylvie bought the ingredients for her cupcakes at the Target at Atlantic Center.

"We got this idea to do a calendar of hot girls in Brooklyn, nude, eating cupcakes from Clementine's Picnic. Cassandra! Just look me in the eyes and tell me that's not brilliant."

"Hmm," Cassandra said, thinking.

"Oh! I have to text Gala to let her know about the calendar. I have to get her to pose, of course."

It was in this fashion that Cassandra first learned that Sylvie had no intention of asking her to pose for the calendar—not that she would have wanted to exactly, because she thought it was lame. But still. It just proved what she had always suspected, ever since they were teenagers, which was that Sylvie didn't think that Cassandra was as hot as she was.

"Oh also, here's another idea I had. Once it takes off, I want to get Clementine's Picnic to start operating at night. You know how you always get late-night cravings for sweets? Like how we always used to go get Nutella? I was thinking, people would totally buy my cupcakes at night. And I feel like there's a real market here, you know? It's about time that somebody provided an alternative to those child molester ice cream trucks!"

"Child molester ice cream trucks?"

"You know! Those greasy white trucks that look like they're

from the seventies that go rattling down the streets at night, with some low-life guy sitting there peddling unwholesome frozen treats to the neighborhood children. Jesus! Those things give me the creeps."

"Oh," said Cassandra, relieved, "Mister Softee."

"Oh, is that what they're called? Anyway. I think I'm really onto something here. I think there's a market."

"Uh-huh."

"Another thing. Did I tell you that *the Italian ice guy* bought a cupcake from us last week? Hannah told me all about it. He was really checking out our operation, Hannah said."

"Oh, good."

"Good! Cassandra, is that all you have to say? Cassandra, it's an incredible compliment, is what it is! He was an immigrant. Those people don't spend their money on stupid shit the way Americans do. They send it back to their families in Nicaragua or wherever. Cassandra! I feel like you're not even listening to me. You seem really out of it tonight."

"If I could just take a shower—"

"Yeah, why don't you? You smell like sex. Dirty sex."

"Well, what of it? This apartment smells like lemons. Dirty lemons."

It came to her in a sickening wave that that's what this scent was, this scent that seemed to have penetrated the whole of the apartment and even her skin: that of rotting, once beautiful, once innocent plump young yellow lemons. Their numbers were mounting and their corpses still decaying in Sylvie's hallway. Oh no, I hope I'm not coming down with a migraine, she thought.

"Before you get in the shower, I just wanted to ask you something, really quickly. No big deal. But I was hoping you could give me a thousand dollars, to start."

"For what?"

"For Clementine's Picnic. Obviously I want you to be one of the first investors," said Sylvie, in a royal tone of voice that suggested that she was doing Cassandra an honor.

"Oh yeah, well, we can talk about that a little later. After I get out of—"

"Oh, but it's kind of time sensitive."

"Time sensitive?"

"It just is. I have so much momentum right now. I don't want to lose it!"

"Well, you won't lose it by letting me get in the shower, I don't think."

"I've made up my mind, Cassandra. I have to be serious about this thing and to do that I need to start getting more investors. The more investors I have, the more it will start to look like I have a legitimate business."

"Oh, okay. Well, that's great, Sylvie. But, since you brought it up, I don't really think I can afford to be an investor right now. Maybe—"

Sylvie panicked. The day had been going so well and she hadn't counted on Cassandra being so difficult. Cassandra was usually so easy where money was concerned. Not for nothing, thought Sylvie, was the phrase *taking candy from a baby* a cliché.

"But Cassandra, you have t—"

"But *Sylvie*. You're doing quite well, it seems to me. You've been doing fine ever since you started babysitting. Good for you! That's fantastic about Toby giving you the five thousand dollars."

"Yeah, but it's not enough, obviously. I'll need to get other investors. And I was counting on getting at least a thousand from you *right now*." In fact, she had been counting on getting much more from Cassandra, over time. "I need to buy an industrial-size refrigerator, see—"

"Sylvie, I really want to get in the shower. I'm desperate to get in the shower."

"Cassandra!" Sylvie was shrieking as Cassandra slammed the bathroom door.

And then Cassandra, trying as best she could to rinse shampoo out of her hair under the anemic water pressure, recalled that Pansy Chapin had asked her to be her roommate. It struck her that she was having the exact same thought Sylvie had had all those years ago when she first moved to New York—a beautiful, dewy, untested young thing just twenty-two years old, and living in Greenwich Village with Rosa Lalage.

Jesus Christ! I've got to get out of this place.

CHAPTER 26

Cassandra stepped out of the shower, wrapped in a plushy pink towel but, due to the state of the water pressure, not quite sufficiently refreshed. Sylvie was crouched on top of the kitchen counter, smoking a joint and trying to chill out. But for some reason it wasn't working tonight. She was *so mad.* She was so mad at Cassandra. She had never been so mad in all her life, and hers was a life that had long been full of indignation. Here we go again, thought Sylvie, and tried once more to convince her.

"The thing is, Cassandra, I've been thinking and you have the money. I know you have it. I know you could afford to give it to me. Come on."

"Do you remember?" Cassandra began, in a different tone of voice, a voice that was melancholy and searching and made Sylvie think that something inconvenient was coming.

"Do I remember what?"

"Sylvie, do you remember that the summer we graduated, when you moved to New York, I gave you the money for the deposit on your apartment? It was a thousand dollars, and up until now I've never mentioned it, but you never paid me back. Remember?"

Fuck, thought Sylvie. She remembers! She could have sworn that Cassandra had forgotten by now. Trying to make her voice sound casual, she decided to say:

"I don't know; I don't remember. Maybe."

"Well, *I* do," Cassandra said. "I have a long memory, and I remember. And I'm not going to give you money again, Sylvie. I'm just not."

Sylvie, now springing off of the kitchen counter and standing before Cassandra with her hands on her hips, was incredulous.

"Seriously?"

"Yes, seriously," Cassandra said simply.

"But—Cassandra!" shrieked Sylvie again.

"Don't Cassandra! me. My mind is made up and my answer is not going to change."

"Edward," Sylvie suggested. She already had a back-up scheme in mind. "Edward has plenty of money."

"So what?"

"Well, I was just thinking—"

"I mean. So what if Edward has plenty of money? He wouldn't give it to you."

"No, obviously not. But he would give it to *you*, wouldn't he? And *then*—"

And then I'd be all set, Sylvie was thinking. She didn't get much past that.

"Sylvie." Cassandra was flabbergasted. "Sylvie, I don't understand. Why are you talking this way? What the hell happened to you?"

There came, out of nowhere, an image of Sylvie, beautiful, brown-armed, twenty-two-year-old Sylvie, appearing in her white peasant dress that lilac-perfumed evening on the Bennington quad. What had happened to *that* Sylvie? Cassandra meant, all of a sudden missing that earlier incarnation keenly. What had happened to *her*?

"*I'm broke*, is what happened to me! *I'm in debt*, is what happened to me! *New York City* is what happened to me!"

"New York City?" echoed Cassandra blankly.

"Yes, New York City!" Sylvie shouted, and now it was her turn to go running into the bathroom and slam the door. Cassandra heard the water running and went and hid in her bedroom. For the first time ever in the history of their friendship, both girls were silent for the rest of the night.

CHAPTER 27

The next morning, Cassandra pretended to sleep in late, waiting to get up until she heard Sylvie leave the apartment. Then she decided to go to Central Park for the day. But by the time she got there, it started to rain and she got a text from Sylvie saying:

IF YOU DON'T WANT TO BE AN INVESTOR, FINE. BUT AT LEAST YOU COULD REIMBURSE ME FOR ALL OF THAT LINGERIE I BOUGHT YOU LAST CHRISTMAS. THAT STUFF COST ME $600.

On reading this, Cassandra called Pansy Chapin immediately. Pansy was at the spa having her toes done for the upcoming weekend in Montauk and happy to pick up. Uncharacteristically for her, Cassandra got straight to the point and asked if she still wanted to be roommates.

"Yes! The move-in date's June first and I don't want to have to call my father for money, in case I don't find someone. I hate him."

By now, it was May 15. Then Pansy remembered something.

"But, wait, I thought you said you were living with Sylvie Furst."

"Yes, but I'd like to get out," said Cassandra simply, and Pansy accepted this without asking any questions because, to her mind, Manhattan was still Manhattan and the boroughs were still the outer boroughs. She didn't care what people said.

"Oh, good! This is so exciting. So you can move in June first. But I hope you can cover your portion of the security deposit? I had to get a broker *just because* and the fee is hideous."

Then Pansy named the fee, and it was. It was such a large sum that Cassandra saw, in one swift moment, that she was going to survive her youth in one way or another but not, perhaps, in New York City.

Nevertheless:

"Guess what? I'm moving to the Upper East Side!" she announced to Edward over the phone. "Seventy-Ninth and Second."

"Well, then!" exclaimed Edward, thinking: Second, huh? That was kind of far over from the park. "I love that neighborhood. My grandmother used to live on Park and Seventy-Seventh, remember. I pointed the building out to you one time."

"Oh, right! I'm moving in with my friend Pansy Chapin. She has all of these great antiques. You'll like her."

"Antiques! That sounds like just the right kind of place for you, sweetie. Is Pansy a Bennington girl?"

"Oh, yes."

"What was her major?"

"Italian. She did a year in Rome. And she was really into art history."

That sounded respectable, Edward thought.

"Actually, it's just possible you might know some of her ex-boyfriends. Pansy's been with a lot of Harvard guys."

The phrase *been with* sounded, somehow, not quite so respectable.

"Can I come see you?" Cassandra asked.

"Anytime."

"How about tonight?"

"Tonight? Wait, but sweetie. We just saw each other a few days ago."

"I miss you."

"And I miss you. But—"

"I could get there tonight," said Cassandra, caressing the last word with her tongue.

"Okay." Edward melted. "It would be nice to see you and—you know."

"I'll get the first train I can."

"Wow. You want it that bad?"

"Yeah, yeah, that's it."

"What's it?"

"Yes—it's just that I miss you so much. I can't wait to see you."

"Sweetie. You're sure that everything's all right with Sylvie and you?" Briefly, he recalled the frantic-sounding conversation he'd overheard the two women having about muffins. "You're just moving because you want to live in a better neighborhood, right?"

"Oh yeah, and Pansy and I will make the place really nice." She almost added *We have great taste* but caught herself. "It will be so much more romantic when you come visit."

"Well, I don't know about you having a roommate, sweetie. I figured we'd still meet up at the Harvard Club."

On the train to Philadelphia, Cassandra received another text message from Sylvie:

HEY, MEGAN JUST ASKED ME WHY IMOGEN WANTS A WHIP FOR HER BIRTHDAY. YOUR FAULT, YOU PERVERT.

And then, just seconds later:

P.S. WHY ARE YOU NOT RESPONDING TO ME ABOUT THE $$ YOU OWE ME FOR THE LINGERIE?

Cassandra stayed with Edward in Philadelphia for the next two weeks. She had sent Sylvie an e-mail stating her intention to move out, to which she received yet another text message saying:

WHEN YOU COME GET YOUR STUFF, BRING ME A CHECK FOR THE
LINGERIE.

And, two days later, when she still had not replied:

ACTUALLY DON'T BRING A CHECK. BRING CASH. I'M TRYING NOT
TO REPORT MY INCOME. DON'T WANT TO HAVE TO PAY TAXES.

The day after that:

IF YOU DON'T WANT TO PAY ME FOR THE LINGERIE, MAYBE
I SHOULD SEND EDWARD AN INVOICE. HE SHOULD GIVE ME
A COMMISSION FOR DOING SO MUCH FOR YOUR SEX LIFE.
WHAT'S HIS ADDRESS?

"Gala, get *this*." Cassandra called Gala immediately and told her
about Sylvie's texts.

"What is it now?"

Gala was exhausted, having heard Sylvie's version of the events
already. But Cassandra proceeded to read her the text messages
word for word.

"You know," Gala eventually said after listening to Cassandra rant and rave. "Sylvie's always having these big blowouts with
roommates. But I didn't think this kind of thing would happen
between Sylvie and you."

But I did think, Gala thought, not without schadenfreude. I
did think that things wouldn't last once they were living together.
Most friendships do not survive such proximity. Nor do most
romances, Gala thought, remembering that time she moved in
with Tess Fox in the studio apartment her parents had bought for
her in the East Village—it had been domestic bliss at first, and then!
Then Tess had accused Gala of stealing her favorite red cardigan
from her Mount Holyoke days without her permission and from

that moment on there was no turning back: everything ruined, everything lost.

Meanwhile, Cassandra was relieved when Pansy said that she could move her stuff into the apartment on May 30, a Saturday. Edward agreed to rent a car and help Cassandra move, and for this she was extraordinarily grateful, because she didn't think that Sylvie would dare try anything in front of him, especially when she'd never met him before and because Edward's smooth male presence was, to her mind, imposing.

She was wrong.

CHAPTER 28

S ylvie opened the door to the apartment wearing a dirty white peasant blouse and a pair of little pale floral underpants. Cassandra figured that she was just waking up and would put some pants on, at least, once she saw Edward, but she didn't. Instead, she stood in front of the door and said: "Cash. Did you bring cash, Cassandra?"

"Let me get my stuff, Sylvie."

But even as she marched into the apartment, all she could think of was the sight of Sylvie's face this morning—it haunted her: it seemed to belong, already, to a stranger. Cassandra imagined her, years later, becoming the kind of rich person who tips badly in restaurants; who during the Christmas season sifts through bargain basements with a pinched, red nose and a bad attitude. She saw her becoming, in short, the kind of person she wanted nothing whatsoever to do with.

Over the years, Cassandra and Sylvie had shared a remarkable degree of physical closeness. They often slept in the same bed. If Cassandra was crashing at her place and had forgotten a toothbrush, she'd use hers. But this morning when she looked at Sylvie, she didn't see that person, that pretty young girl, at all. No. She saw a withered, squirrel-like figure with bags of death under her eyes.

Meanwhile, the apartment looked, to Edward, like something out of a nineteenth-century tenement. What was that smell, that rotting smell? Was it—could it be—*lemons*?

"You two better get out of here fast," Sylvie was saying. "I'm very busy today. I'm having an industrial-sized refrigerator delivered any minute now."

Cassandra thought: The hell you are. How is an industrial refrigerator going to fit in this tiny apartment? Then: Oh, what do I care anymore? She just wanted to get her stuff and get out of here.

Sylvie began to roam around the apartment like a rabid animal on a pair of little scratched naked legs. It was only then that she happened to glance down at them and realize that she had forgotten to put any pants on. Hah! She wasn't going to put them on either. That would serve Cassandra right, in front of Edward. God, did he look like a stiff or what? She noted the judgmental clench of his jaw, the staunchly masculine contempt he exuded. Sylvie could just picture him tying somebody to a bed, that one!

"Did you bring cash? Cassandra? Come on, did you bring the money? You owe me six hundred dollars!"

Six hundred dollars for what? Edward was wondering as he scooped into his arms as many pieces of Cassandra's clothing and bedding as he could carry. He kept his own financial affairs in perfect order and any talk of outstanding debts aroused his suspicions.

"I need that money, Cassandra. I need it for rent."

"Rent? But I paid you for May already and I'm leaving right now."

"If you don't give me that money, I won't be able to pay my rent and Pete will get mad at me again. He tried to evict me once, remember!"

Now they were talking about eviction? thought Edward. Jesus! This was getting serious.

"I remember, Sylvie, but that was ages ago. You've been paying your rent just fine for months now."

"But I still owe him back rent! *Back* rent!"

Cassandra sighed.

"Then that's your back rent, Sylvie, not mine."

Edward was trying to get out the door when Sylvie wrenched an olive green satin pillow out of his hands.

"Hey!" Edward cried out. And it was at this point in the morning's events when he thought: It all must be a dream. Or why would he be engaged in what, to the casual observer, would have appeared to be a pillow fight with his girlfriend's best friend?

"That's mine!" Sylvie insisted.

"It is not, Sylvie! Pansy Chapin gave me that pillow."

"Oh," said Sylvie, letting go. "I thought it looked like something I would have." Pansy has great taste, she thought.

"Sweetie, do you think you could hurry it up here? I've got almost everything now. Why don't you do one more sweep through this place and then—"

"Seven years," muttered Sylvie, to no one in particular. "Seven whole years in New York City I've been paying my own rent, and I just really think someone else should pay it for me for a couple of months. I mean, I just really think I deserve somebody else to pay my rent." She hissed at Cassandra: "Not everybody can just spend their money on pretty dresses! Not everyone has a rich boyfriend who takes them for fancy weekends at the Harvard Club!"

Edward, listening to all of this, thought that explained a lot. Sylvie must be jealous that she didn't have a Harvard boyfriend when, obviously, every woman in the world wanted one.

Cassandra went to collect her products in the bathroom and said: "You know what you've done, Sylvie? I'll tell you what you've done. You have poisoned my natural generosity." She felt that this line struck so cleanly at the heart of the matter that she repeated it: "You have poisoned my natural generosity."

All of their final words to each other took place in Sylvie's bathroom, that lyrical, old-world bathroom, the two of them standing at the foot of the white-painted antique dresser on which were displayed the confections of their many shopping expeditions together: white almond talcum powder. Bluebell and hyacinth hand soap. A stack of elaborately papered soaps from Italy. Cassandra scooped her beauty products into a tote bag, the caramelized light of the spring morning streaming across her face. As she did, she noticed the white French champagne bucket at the foot of the famous claw-foot bathtub. Goddamn it! She'd been counting on taking that with her, too, only to look down and see a pair of Sylvie's tiny blue lace underpants floating in the shallow water.

Nevertheless, the gentleness of the light in the bathroom—the girlishness of it—made her think that what she wanted to do right now more than anything actually was hug Sylvie. She wanted to press that petite body close to hers. And now, gazing into Sylvie's mirror, in front of which the two of them had stood while getting ready to go out so many times, she recalled Sylvie's steady artist's fingers smoothing out Cassandra's eyeliner and trimming her fine blond hair when she used to give her haircuts. She recalled those fingers holding the scissors so close to the nape of her neck with what had been, to Cassandra, unquestioned tenderness.

And now here was Sylvie, staring at her with true, black hatred in her eyes.

Sylvie was, in fact, thinking: Bitch. Bitch. The fucking bitch. Other people! They never fail to disappoint you.

Edward was downstairs by now, waiting with Cassandra's stuff. The two women were left to duke it out alone.

"You want that money so much, Sylvie? I'll give it to you. But before I do, I want you to understand that by you bullying me into giving it to you, this means that I will never be friends with you again. No, let me finish. We have had a long and a rich friendship"— she was thinking of the two of them, golden- and black-haired respectively, sipping raspberry lime rickeys in the Sunken Garden at Radcliffe—"but you make me give you this money and I will never be friends with you again."

And Sylvie, without a moment's hesitation, said: "Cash?"

Sylvie and Cassandra were children of divorce. What did it feel like to get divorced? they used to ask each other. But as of today, Cassandra no longer wondered. Cassandra now knew.

"You like cash so much, Sylvie, I'll make it cash. So let me tell you what I'm going to do. I'm going to go to the ATM, the one at the bodega around the corner. Don't think I'm going to skip out on you; I'm not. Don't think I have any interest in holding on to your keys; I don't. I'm going to come back here and give you the money and the keys, and then it will be over, Sylvie. I will never be friends with you again."

But before Cassandra went to the bodega, she paused at the doorway and said rather grandly: "And another thing. Please go get me my mother's Le Creuset pan."

It was one of those wonderful rustic old omelet pans with a mustard-yellow bottom. Sylvie scrunched up her face as if trying to come up with a way to justify her keeping the pan, but evidently decided against it. She went and got the Le Creuset pan from the kitchen and handed it to Cassandra. The heavy black handle looked almost too heavy for her, brushing against her feeble bare legs. It was the only moment during the whole encounter when she looked the least bit defeated, standing there in her underpants.

CHAPTER 29

t wasn't over yet. Sylvie the petite but indomitable got a second wind. Standing upstairs in her apartment, out of breath from the adrenaline of it all and counting out the six hundred dollars Cassandra had just given her from the ATM, she seized on an idea. Quick, she had to act quick! This was going to be *fun.*

"Hey," she called down the stairwell, just as Cassandra and Edward were struggling with opening the rusty latch of the door. "One more thing!"

She charged down the stairs, hunching her body over the moldering pale blue stairwell. The money was still in her hands—no way would she let it go. Money! It felt so damn good. It wasn't Nutella that was better than sex, Sylvie thought. It was money. Live in New York City long enough, and you'll soon learn that lesson for yourself.

Cassandra, the fool! Cassandra would learn it, too.

Pete the landlord was in his apartment on the first floor playing the piano, the wild, layered notes of the keys lending a delirious cast to the proceedings. By now, he was used to Sylvie having melodramatic scenes with various roommates and so he didn't bother to come out to see what was going on, figuring that this latest unpleasantness, too, would pass.

Why, Cassandra asked herself, should something about the wreckage of this scene, which was, in a weird way, rather beautiful, recall to her now Duchamp's *Nude Descending a Staircase, No. 2*? One's liberal arts education came floating back to one at the strangest of times.

"Did she tell you?" Sylvie demanded of Edward.

"Now, listen you—" Edward was a gentleman, but even a gentleman could not be expected to treat some crazy chick without any pants on like a lady.

"Oh, you stay out of this," said Cassandra. "What is it, Sylvie? And then we're leaving. We're *leaving*," she repeated.

But Sylvie's eyes continued to blaze down on Edward. The lemons collected in the garbage bags stank to the ceiling, clogging the air with decay.

"Did she tell you about Le Bernardin?"

"*Le Bernardin?*" repeated Edward. That fancy French fish restaurant in the West Fifties? He knew it well. His Park Avenue grandmother used to take him there on his birthdays. That might be a nice place to take Cassandra for her birthday next year, he thought. Then stopped himself from going any farther. He and Cassandra were never going to make it as a couple after all. He could see that now. No way could he ever marry a girl like this, a girl who lived in a nineteenth-century tenement teeming with putrid lemon skins in one of the outer boroughs, and who, previous to recent events, had claimed to consider this wretched Sylvie creature her best friend.

"Why don't you ask her who's taking her to Le Bernardin?"

But Edward never did ask Cassandra who was taking her to Le Bernardin, figuring that Sylvie was nuts and the hell with her.

"Oh my God, I forgot the Le Creuset pan!"

Cassandra's voice rang out in the middle of the night, disturbing Edward, who had been sleeping soundly beside her.

"What?"

Can a man ever get any peace? he wondered.

"The Le Creuset pan, the Le Creuset pan! Remember? Sylvie gave it back, but then I left it, I left it. Oh my God, do you think I left it when I went to get the money at the ATM? It would never still be there, if I did . . ."

"Now, now," said Edward tiredly, lifting her nightie.

Cassandra continued to believe for the rest of her life that she must have done just that—left the Le Creuset pan on the floor of the bodega where she had gone to use the ATM. But in fact she had left it at the foot of Sylvie's staircase, where it was with no small satisfaction discovered immediately after she and Edward left and returned to its rightful place upstairs. That night Sylvie had an omelet and a glass of wine. Her omelets were very tasty, Sylvie reflected on taking a bite. Now! If only she could find a way to market them.

PART III

Bitters

Cassandra never forgot the first night she hung out with Pansy Chapin. She was privileged to be a guest in the living room of Gazelle, the house where Pansy and so many of the other superrich girls lived, Bitsy Citron among them. Bitsy was the house ringleader and her dog, Brioche, the mascot. Brioche was a silver Pomeranian, whose coat went nicely with Bitsy's waist-length mane of champagne-blond hair, highlighted on the private beaches and yachts of St. Bart's, where her family was rumored to own fabulous quantities of property.

That night, when Pansy and Cassandra were both eighteen years old and hanging out in the living room of Gazelle, the air was blue with smoke. Everybody smoked in that house, except for Cassandra, who after all was only visiting from one of the tamer, quieter houses across the quad. Some girl had an acid trip while sitting on top of the moss green velvet sofa, beginning to shake uncontrollably and slide down the cushions. Nobody did anything. Eventually Bitsy stormed out of her dorm room, stalked by her boyfriend, the Bulgarian sculptor guy, who was lushly showering her with a fistful of euros. This move had great cachet because the dollar was said to be losing its value even back then. Pansy Chapin turned to Cassandra and asked her:

"Have you ever had an STD before?"

"No," said Cassandra, who, it being only her freshman year, was still technically a virgin. This crisis was remedied over the course of the following summer, under the deft tutelage of a much older gentleman and family friend. Sylvie, always pragmatic, had gotten it over with back when they were still in high school by crashing a party at MIT one Saturday night and going home with the first guy she found there who looked like he might actually know what the hell he was doing and not turn out to be a virgin himself; with MIT guys, anything was possible. Still, Sylvie preferred them to Harvard guys because Harvard guys were not merely nerds, they were assholes.

"Ugh, yeah, well, I guess you don't really look the type. But! You never know. *I think I might have one,*" Pansy whispered.

"Oh, no," said Cassandra, shocked.

"Tell me about it! Because if I do, it's going to be a disaster."

"Oh my God, you don't think you have—"

"AIDS? Of course not. Nobody gets that anymore. But I think I might have, like, maybe chlamydia or something."

"I had chlamydia once," Bitsy Citron volunteered.

"You did?" Pansy Chapin squealed.

"Uh-huh. If you have chlamydia, it's like this . . ."

Her boyfriend, the Bulgarian sculptor guy, was now sucking her toes in front of everybody. Everybody was used to this: they had sex everywhere, even in the kiddie pool outside of Gazelle in which Brioche was prone to taking a piss. Bitsy had beautiful feet. You could thank St. Bart's for those, too. The sand made the bottoms all soft.

"My vagina has something *black* coming out of it," Pansy Chapin wailed. Pansy Chapin was wearing tennis whites. "Black, I said, black! Oh my God, this is going to be a disaster," she repeated.

"Why?" asked Bitsy idly.

Pansy Chapin related how that very weekend she was supposed to be going to New York City for a sex-crazed weekend with her fiancé at his duplex on Central Park South, and how he was going to kill her if he found out that she had an STD, because it would mean that she'd been cheating on him again.

"Have you been?" asked Cassandra. Not to be judgmental; just because she was genuinely curious.

Pansy and Bitsy both looked at her blankly. The Bulgarian sculptor guy finished sucking Bitsy's toes to his personal satisfaction and got up to go back to his studio. Bitsy French-kissed him good-bye.

"The thing is: I can't fuck this relationship up. I've got to marry this guy! My trust fund," Pansy Chapin now confessed to Cassandra, "you see. It's one of those small, tasteful ones. Nothing to write home about."

"Are you from Boston, by any chance?" Cassandra had pegged her as being from one of those old Brahmin families, having grown up on some tony side street of Beacon Hill, maybe.

"Maine. Bar Harbor."

Better and better, Cassandra thought. Bar Harbor sounded very tony indeed.

"Oh, well. I'm from Boston. Cambridge," she clarified.

"You know? I think we have things in common," promised Pansy.

Cassandra's heart leapt. Bitsy, never having stepped foot in New England before visiting Bennington, wasn't interested in any of this. Why hadn't she gone to Bard? she sometimes wondered, say on the dead of a Sunday evening. It would have been just that much closer to the city to make a difference. She changed the subject by complaining about this absolutely humongous diamond ring she had lost at the bottom of Julian Schnabel's swimming pool while she was fucking some guy whose name she couldn't even remember: "I think he was maybe, like, one of the art *handlers* or something . . ."

"Oh poor Bitsy, just ask your family to get you another," Pansy said. "They *own* diamond mines, don't they?"

"Yeah, but."

Brioche then waddled into the living room, wagging her tail and drooling, because one of Bitsy's friends had just fed her some of her antidepressants.

"You're in love with Pansy Chapin," Sylvie accused Cassandra later on that term. It was spring term of their freshman year; the lilacs at the End of the World were flowering outside their window in mad profusion, and Bitsy and the Bulgarian sculptor guy could be found wildly rutting in a ditch of broken daffodils. Every weekend that marvelous season Pansy Chapin vanished to a duplex on Central Park South and she took two weeks off of classes—nobody called her out on it, nobody cared—to be flown to Paris by her fiancé and feted like a kept woman at the Plaza Athénée. For Cassandra, she brought back from Paris a pink umbrella. She used it for years, years after college, Cassandra did, until it was just like the daffodils, that pink umbrella, bought by one Pansy Chapin in Paris for one Cassandra Puffin in Bennington, Vermont: its neck broke. Gala Gubelman was in love that spring, Penelope Entenmann, Vicky Lalage, and Angelica Rocky-Divine, too. If the notorious Lanie Tobacco out of all of the girls wasn't, it was only because Lanie Tobacco wasn't sentimental, Lanie Tobacco wasn't a fool, though she was arrested right around this time by the Bennington Police for "bicycling under the influence." Chelsea Hayden-Smith and Beverly Tinker-Jones, younger even than Cassandra and Sylvie were then, younger than any of them, had not yet plunged to their deaths through the wide glass windows of the fifth-floor dance studio of the college's performing arts building; they had not yet applied to Bennington, had not even heard of it or the purported excellence of its modern dance program, perhaps. Sylvie's hair was black. Cassandra's, still golden. They were lying in bed when Sylvie made her accusation about Cassandra being in love with Pansy Chapin. Twin beds they had then, the type of beds they would never after college sleep in ever again.

"Am not!" Cassandra protested.

"Are too! You're fascinated by her. Bewitched by Pansy Chapin! That bitch. Also! That apple green cashmere sweater she gave you? The hand-me-down. If I were you, Cassandra, I'd stop wearing it. It's *way* too tight on you."

"I can pull off a tight sweater, thank you!"

"Yeah, but, I don't know. Not that one, somehow."

"Oh yeah, well, you're in love with Gala Gubelman, so there!"

"Am not!"

"Are too! I bet, why, I bet that you want to *make out* with Gala Gubelman!"

"Whatever, Cassandra, everybody on campus has already made out with *her*."

And now, years later, Sylvie was living just blocks away from Gala Gubelman in Fort Greene and Cassandra, meanwhile, had crossed the river—the River Styx, maybe—to worship at the devilish altar of Pansy Chapin on the Upper East Side.

CHAPTER 31

Bitters, I thought. Bitters and soda. You know. I first got into these when I did my year abroad in Italy."

Pansy reached for the brilliant orange bottle of Campari and began mixing her and Cassandra cocktails. If they both happened to be home on any given evening, that was what they did. They made a ritual out of it. Orange, as it happened, was one of Pansy Chapin's favorite colors—and all the more striking a predilection, that, because so few people could pull it off; but Pansy, with her deep, moneyed tan and streaky blond hair, could. It was right after the Fourth of July. Pansy had just gotten back to the city from the Hamptons, and Cassandra from a weekend spent at a horse show in the Pennsylvania countryside with Edward. The orange of the bottle of Campari matched exactly the orange of the silk scarf that Pansy was flaunting, jet set–style, in her hair.

That Pansy dressed like this even in the privacy of her own home was only confirmation of her supreme glamour to Cassandra.

"Do you remember . . ." she began, accepting Pansy's cocktail. "Cheers."

"Cheers! Do I remember what?"

"When you used to make martinis for us?"

"Hmm . . . ?"

"At Bennington. Sylvie and I were living in the Pine Room then. Remember! I think it was our sophomore year. We had a fireplace, remember, and Alphie the security guard used to come and bring the logs and build the fire and everything. You would come over, and you'd make us dinner in the kitchen. You'd make us steak and Caesar salad and double-stuffed potatoes and real martinis."

"As opposed to fake martinis?" Pansy yawned.

"Well. I guess what I mean is—real, adult martinis. It all seemed terribly adult to me anyway. When you used to come over and cook for us."

Imagine cooking a group of girls dinner, Pansy thought, when everybody knew that the reason one learned to cook in the first place was to please a man.

"Are you ever going to learn how to cook, Cassandra?"

"Oh! That. Well, yes. I'm hoping to—now that we're settled into the apartment."

"Oh good. Feel free to use any of my cookbooks if you want."

"Thanks! And, oh! That reminds me. If I learn to cook one of these days, then I can start using my great-grandmother's wedding silver."

On the very night they'd moved into the apartment, Cassandra had been positively giddy to show Pansy the silver, unfurling from the blue velvet depths of the box the long-stemmed scalloped oyster forks and ice cream spoons, to Pansy's squeals of delight and approval.

"What *I* recommend is: learning a signature dish."

"Yeah. Like what?"

"Steak, to start," mused Pansy.

"Yeah. I think I can get the hang of steak. I *hope*."

"*My* signature dishes are veal scallopini and Chicken Marbella."

But I want those to be my signature dishes! Cassandra thought, with a wholly illogical sense of betrayal and indignation. Those are the perfect signature dishes for a girl to have.

"Fish, too. You ought to know how to do something with fish if you're with a guy who prefers it. Some guys do. Sole Véronique, maybe . . ." Pansy was lost in thought. "That's the one with the grapes."

"Pansy." Cassandra got up the courage to ask, for she had a certain grave matter on her mind. "What are your thoughts on monogamy?"

"*Monogamy?*" Pansy merely laughed.

"Oh, I thought so," said Cassandra, relieved.

"Thought what?" asked Pansy suspiciously.

That you were a complete and total slut, Cassandra knew better than to say out loud.

"Oh, just that you would be—understanding."

"What's going on? Is there a guy? A new guy?"

"Well"—Cassandra hesitated—"kind of. Did you ever take a class with Professor Sobel?"

"Professor Sobel! The opera guy? Yeah, come to think of it I *did*. For one day! But he made us sit outside in the meadow just so he could smoke his precious cigarettes and I just couldn't bear it anymore. It was *February*."

"Yeah, he was famous for making his classes do that. Well, anyway. I was kind of a favorite of his back at Bennington, and then I ran into him earlier this year in New York, at this concert I went to with Edward. When I first moved to the city, he invited me to lunch at La Grenouille, to celebrate . . ."

"La Grenouille!" shrieked Pansy. La Grenouille was *her favorite*. She was jealous, suddenly, of a man taking Cassandra to La Grenouille, because Cassandra wasn't as hot as she was, and girls who weren't as hot as she was were, generally speaking, undeserving of the finer things in life.

"Oh, it was so much fun. I got the cheese soufflé. Have you had their cheese soufflé?" But of course Pansy Chapin had had the cheese soufflé; Pansy Chapin knew how to make cheese soufflé. "Well, and then after that he invited me to Le Bernardin." Cassandra paused importantly. "For dinner."

"But in a way, lunch is more chic than dinner, I think." Pansy was recalling with a pang the reckless afternoon assignations, the gorgeous champagne breakfasts, of her youth. "Dinner is more obvious."

"I think so, too! That's exactly what I thought. But still, dinner is more . . ."

"Of a clear-cut invitation," filled in Pansy. "From the man's point of view."

"Yeah, so . . . I'm attracted to Professor Sobel, *but*. The thing is, I'm not that into monogamy, actually, but Edward is."

"Oh no, he isn't," Pansy assured her.

"Pansy."

"No man is. Not really!"

"That's a little cynical of you, don't you think?"

"When you've been with as many guys as I have . . ." Pansy trailed off, reminding herself that Cassandra was something of a late bloomer, compared to herself. At age fourteen Pansy had lost her virginity on a private beach in Bar Harbor to a brutish Dartmouth senior who was summering there and had never looked back: thus began her storied romantic career. So how did you lose your virginity? was a bottomless subject at Bennington. An unusually large number of the girls there had scintillating stories to tell; Lanie Tobacco, for one, had been dismantled of her maidenhood on a pool table by the drummer of a band called "Leftover Crack."

"I like older men myself," Pansy said, changing the subject. "I mean, I like the *idea* of older men. I think I'd go quite nicely with one." She paused, picturing herself, quite without qualms, as the ultimate accessory; a gold pocket watch, a vintage Jaguar in a snazzy color. "But the thing is, I've tried before, and I just can't get into their bodies!"

"I've never been all that hung up on bodies, though. I just feel like physical attraction can be based on so many different things. You know?"

But Pansy didn't know. She said: "As a matter of fact. What I really go for are black guys. Did I ever tell you about the time I dated this incredibly hot Cuban guy who turned out to be a crystal meth dealer? Oops! Did I say Cuban? I meant Haitian!"

"No!"

"Well—" Pansy began, but Cassandra interrupted.

"Is it true what they say about black guys?"

"What they say about their cocks?"

But Cassandra didn't even have the patience to listen for Pansy's answer, jumping in just to make clear: "Sex is a really intellectual thing with me."

"Oh," said Pansy Chapin, getting up to make herself another cocktail. The bottle of Campari was now half-empty. She would have to replace it; Pansy hated half-empty or tarnished things; they upset her love of physical perfection. "Oh, Cassandra, Cassandra! You'll get over that."

CHAPTER 32

P ansy!" Cassandra called, later on that night.

There was no answer.

"Pansy!" Cassandra moaned again, from her bedroom.

But still, Pansy refused to answer, because she was in the midst of her elaborate beauty preparations, rubbing her entire body with a concoction of brown sugar and baby oil, in the exact same ritual she had done ever since her days at Bennington and that Cassandra did now, too. Because for Pansy, at least, there was a new guy in the picture—a new hedge-fund manager, in fact; it hadn't taken her long to nab another one since the breakup of her most recent engagement. What Cassandra didn't know yet, poor thing, was that Pansy was planning on moving into this new guy's loft in TriBeCa, just as soon as he gave her a ring. He was thirty-five and, to Pansy's mind, on the fast track to marriage. Like Cassandra, she would be turning twenty-nine next year and was starting to get nervous. Even in this day and age, a girl could afford only so many broken engagements.

"Pansy!"

Jesus, what could possibly be the matter? Pansy wondered. It wasn't a fire, at least, because she would have smelled it. So obviously, short of a fire, there was no reason to get out of the bathroom before she was ready; Cassandra could wait. Pansy surveyed her sleek, freshly oiled brown body with a cool appraiser's eye; what good fortune it was, to be so beautiful.

Eventually she swaddled herself in an oversize white terry-cloth robe—stolen from the Westin Excelsior in Rome; Pansy, much like Gala Gubelman, had a touch of the kleptomaniac about her when the occasion called for it—and went into the living room, where she fixed two martinis, *strong*, before carrying them to Cassandra's bedroom. The door was ajar, and Cassandra was sprawled face-down on her bed, shuddering with tears.

"Here," said Pansy, handing her a martini. "It looks like you could use this! What's the matter?"

"It's—Edward!"

So he dumped her at last, Pansy thought. She, like Sylvie, had suspected that Cassandra and Edward's relationship would not be long for this world.

"Oh, no! What happened?"

"He—he dumped me."

"Oh, you poor thing . . ." began Pansy, wondering if she was on the right track here, for she was not, by nature, the heart-to-heart type.

"And he did it over e-mail, too! Look!"

Pansy read the e-mail, which was not all that interesting or revealing unto itself, though she knew that Cassandra would be hell-bent on discussing its finer points. It was gentlemanly and brief—with a coldness at the heart of it that the illusionless Pansy identified as being absolutely final.

"But our relationship wasn't like that!"

"Like what?"

"Well. We didn't really do things over e-mail."

"Oh."

"Our relationship was—classy."

"Well, count your blessings, in this day and age. At least he didn't do it over text message. Or on Facebook."

"Pansy! I'm not *on* Facebook!"

"Oh right. Of course not." Pansy was on it herself only because if you were as photogenic as she was, why not?

The loneliness of her life—without Sylvie, without Edward—suddenly struck Cassandra in that moment. Oh my God, she thought, undone. I'm *single*.

"Pansy, may I ask you a question?"

"What is it, Cassandra?"

Valiantly Cassandra tried to frame her thoughts.

"Do you believe all that stuff about how single women can still love themselves and have self-respect and inner strength, blah blah blah?"

"No," said Pansy Chapin. "I do not."

"Me neither."

"Being single is like shopping at Trader Joe's."

Cassandra understood at once where Pansy was coming from.

"It's a sign of a compromised existence," Pansy continued. "Have you ever gone to a party where they actually served frozen hors d'oeuvres from Trader Joe's? Those dreadful slimy potstickers and so on? I *have*. I wanted to *die*."

"I hate Trader Joe's!"

"Of course you do."

"I don't want to end up as one of those sad-sack girls you see around who shop at Trader Joe's and have Tuesday night book clubs and are proud of their banana bread recipes . . ."

"Oh right, those girls all own cutesy oven mitts from Anthropologie, don't they? They own oven mitts with *poodles* on them. *Poodles* or *reindeer*."

"Yes! Ugh. You know something else? I've never liked Anthropologie either."

Cassandra sat on her bed, pondering her future. But all thoughts led back to the past and to Edward.

"I know. I'll write him a letter."

Please don't, Pansy was thinking, with the ruthlessness of one who has loved and lost many a time. If only women knew how unattractive the spectacle of having a bad breakup made them. The cozy "nights in" with the dreaded ice cream and lumpy socks, the recurrent tears and all of the wasted months of emotional "processing" and ever-spiraling conversations about a situation that could never ever change—Pansy hoped that Cassandra didn't think that any of that was going to be going on around here!

But already, Cassandra was blathering on about her choice of notepaper. She reached for her letter box, from which spilled sheets and sheets of French stationery.

"And I'll stain it with my scent ... Or, I know! Can I borrow that vanilla Santa Maria Novella perfume of yours? I keep meaning to go to the store downtown and buy a bottle for myself ..."

Then why don't you already? thought Pansy, who, ever since grade school, had blanched at the thought of sharing things.

Cassandra, meanwhile, was getting so caught up in the specifics of this imaginary letter to Edward that she almost forgot that he had broken up with her.

"You know, I just remembered something," said Pansy, trying to steer Cassandra away from the notion of the letter. "I just remembered how much I liked your first boyfriend. The one you had who used to come and visit at Bennington."

"Oh, really? I liked *your* first boyfriend, too." Cassandra was thinking of the one Pansy used to go visit at his duplex on Central Park South.

"Oh, but he was hardly my *first—*" Pansy, with her epic list of lovers, was temporarily flummoxed.

"No, of course not. But I mean, the guy you were with while we were at Bennington."

"Well," Pansy admitted. "He was the first of my fiancés." And the only one of them I ever loved, she thought, and was surprised by the swell of true emotion she felt in that moment. She heard herself suddenly saying: "You know, Cassandra, don't take it so hard with Edward. I think there can only ever be one true love anyway."

"What true love?" Cassandra asked.

Pansy Chapin sighed.

"The first one."

. . .

Edward, sitting at his broad oak desk in his apartment in Rittenhouse Square, poured himself a good stiff drink before opening
Cassandra's letter. He found himself irritated at first, and then—
was it on account of the lingering scent of Santa Maria Novella
vanilla perfume on the envelope?—subtly, mysteriously aroused by
the prospect of hearing from her again. Since he'd sent her that
e-mail nearly a week ago now, there'd been no response. Finally,
he'd texted her a couple of times just to check up on her, and still
no word. Not that he was worried. After all, she was living with
Pansy Chapin now—a girl of whom, unlike Sylvie, he had every reason to approve—and surely Pansy would be there in the apartment
to comfort her; that's what girlfriends were for.

Once he finally read the letter, though, he smiled. The main
thing he took away from its contents was that she would let him
fuck her again. But that could wait, he told himself, because in the
meantime, to recover from Cassandra and her emotional excesses,
he had taken up with a nice girl from his rowing club who wore
Lily Pulitzer and had graduated from Wellesley.

CHAPTER 33

Gala Gubelman rolled over in bed. Cassandra was calling.

"Oh my God, so! What happened?" Gala asked.

It was the morning after Cassandra's much-trumpeted dinner at Le Bernardin with Professor Sobel. Blissfully she ran through descriptions of warm poached lobster, oysters, and pink champagne, but none of this was what Gala had picked up the phone for.

"But *then* what happened? I mean at the end of the night."

"Oh, well. He said he just *had* to get back to his place to listen to the complete string quartets of Elliott Carter on his new speaker system."

"So music, he mentioned listening to music together. They always say that!"

"No, *not* together, is the thing. When I said, Oh how wonderful, or whatever, he said that for him, listening to music in the privacy of his own apartment was a serious business, and he preferred to do it alone and uninterrupted by the babble of precocious coeds."

"Sylvie *said* he was an asshole."

"Gala! You promised you wouldn't mention *her*. She's Sicilian dead to me."

"Oh yeah? That's exactly what she says about you, too!" Gala, ever since the girls' breakup, had been "in the middle" of Sylvie and Cassandra, and, as is only natural where triangles of three women are concerned, had relished every minute.

"But seriously," said Gala now. "What is it about him anyway?"
"Who?"

"Professor Sobel, silly. He looks just like a giant pirate!"

"But Gala, pirates are sexy. Pirates are an iconic masculine archetype."

"Hmm." Gala had to concede that Cassandra might be onto something there, but nevertheless shared with the fastidious Pansy Chapin a distaste for the aged male body on principle.

"You know what else I think it has to do with—" Cassandra said.

"What?"

"He's a smoker, you know. He smells like cigarettes."

"Ugh. As bad as Lanie Tobacco?" The notorious Lanie had acquired her campus nickname on account of the clotted stench that accompanied her tiny dark person at all times.

"But I *like* the smell of nicotine on a man."

"Well, *I* don't."

"My father was a smoker."

"Your father's dead."

"Exactly."

"Is it just that you don't want to be alone?" Gala persisted.

"Uh-huh," said Cassandra cheerfully, thinking of how she had admitted just the same thing to Pansy. Self-respect, inner strength, blah blah blah, be damned.

"*Cassandra.*"

"Oh, what, and you do want to be alone?"

"Uh, no."

The very suggestion was outrageous. The one dismal week at Bennington in which Gala Gubelman had been between admirers, she had arranged a trip to the town bowling alley with her girlfriends that Saturday night, not knowing what else to do with herself. Never again, she had decided, and by the following week she was screwing a freshman. Just to get her mojo back, she said. That had made Orpheus jealous and for the rest of the term they were boyfriend and girlfriend again.

"Well then, don't tell me that I have to be."

"But New York City is full of guys, Cassandra."

"I don't want *a guy*, I want *a man*, thank you very much."

"Oh, I get it, somebody older."

"Well"—Cassandra thought about this—"somebody who can take me out to dinner, to start . . ."

"Yeah, nobody takes anybody out to dinner anymore. That's true."

"That's what Sylvie said. Sylvie said that guys today go Dutch."

"It's go Dutch or die, pretty much," Gala Gubelman conceded, wondering if, what with the crummy state that modern dating was in, she shouldn't be on the lookout for a Professor Sobel type herself.

Meanwhile, Professor Sobel had found himself with an extra ticket to *Tristan und Isolde* at the Met and had decided to extend another invitation to Cassandra. He got this idea because his ex-wife was a great opera lover as well, and he had a long history of running into her at performances there. When faced with the possibility of confronting one's ex-wife, it always did a man's ego good to have a comely former student on his arm. Cassandra would do, he felt.

"You think the crowd's old *here*," he remarked to Cassandra, once they were seated. "You ought to go check out the people who still go to chamber music concerts."

"I love chamber music!" swooned Cassandra, jumping ahead and imagining Professor Sobel paying to take her to other concerts in the future; she could get used to this.

It was predictable, Professor Sobel thought, Cassandra liking chamber music. Everything about her—just like every other Bennington girl he'd had a crush on before her—was getting predictable. He asked himself: Would it be worth it to go through with the whole silly charade of seducing her? After all, a poor fatherless girl like Cassandra might get clingy afterward. Originally—back when she was not so predictable—her rather orphanlike air had been a major part of what had attracted him to her. It could be great fun destroying a girl like that if you were in the mood for drama; but Professor Sobel realized that he wasn't, anymore.

"About love . . ." He groaned, and sighed. Taking a girl to go see *Tristan und Isolde* was a natural segue to talking about love, and why not toy with her expectations a little? "How much do you know about it, anyway? Hmm? A girl like you?"

"Enough," said Cassandra smiling, though in fact she was thinking of Edward. It had been over a month now, and there'd been no response to her letter, in spite of her noble efforts with the Santa Maria Novella vanilla perfume on the underside of the envelope. Evidently the breakup had been for real. The only thing that would help her to get over one man was to go to bed with another. She was looking forward to testing this theory with Professor Sobel at the end of the night.

"It's overrated."

"It's *what*?" said Cassandra, incredulous.

"Overrated, I said. Love is overrated. Also it's repetitive. It's so goddamned repetitive! So you don't know that much about it, do you, or you would know that for yourself."

"But love makes the world anew! At least, the great thing about it is that it has the *capacity* to do that, don't you think?"

"All I can tell you, kiddo, is: passions weaken in your sixties. That's the one thing that Proust never lived long enough to understand."

"Proust! What's Proust got to do with anything?" I thought we were on *Wagner* tonight, she said to herself, momentarily thrown by these ever-shifting cultural references.

"Oh. I used to teach him. He's my other great love. Didn't you know that? Maybe it was before your time."

"But you're on the *music* faculty," Cassandra protested.

"Doesn't matter. Bennington is—interdisciplinary! They pride themselves on mixing things up."

"Actually, I kind of hated that it was so interdisciplinary. I don't think I got a good, solid education at that place *at all*. Actually, I thought a lot of the curriculum at Bennington was stupid."

"A lot of things are stupid," said Professor Sobel pleasantly; on this, at least, they could agree. "And not just at Bennington, either, more's the pity."

They sat there brooding—not even pretending that they were connecting—until the curtain came up. By intermission, Professor Sobel was thrashing to take a smoke break. Cassandra followed him outdoors. See, this is what I mean about her being clingy, he thought to himself as they stood next to the fountain getting dirty looks from all of the smoke-free spectators. There was nothing like the self-righteousness of nonsmokers, the idiots, to put him in a wrathful mood and suddenly he announced:

"Let's blow this joint."

"This joint, you're calling it now? *This joint?* It's the Met!"

"So what? It isn't a very good production."

Actually, it was. And Professor Sobel knew it, too. But he was bored with *Tristan und Isolde,* tonight. He was bored with everything.

"But . . ." Cassandra, unable to accept the crummy turn of events that was taking place before her eyes, tried to appeal to his paternalistic side, a technique that never failed, or so she imagined, with men. "But what about my education?"

"Your education? Jesus, I thought we already covered that. I thought we agreed it was a total fucking waste."

"But I mean my *cultural* education. Just because I might have graduated a while ago doesn't mean that my education stopped! I feel like the whole point of living in New York City is to do things like go to the opera . . ." The thought occurred to Professor Sobel that there must have been thousands upon thousands of young women in New York City believing this drivel and at the starkness of this revelation he didn't know whether to laugh or to weep. So he did what he did all of those years ago on learning that the modern dancers had died, and lit another cigarette and never thought about it ever again.

"I mean," Cassandra was now saying, "what if I go to a cocktail party next week and this production of *Tristan und Isolde* comes up and I want to have something intelligent to say about it?"

"Intelligent! You don't need to be able to say something intelligent about anything, ever."

"What are you talking about?"

"What I'm talking about is: all right, so say you're at a cocktail party. *You* shouldn't be the one to say something intelligent about this production of *Tristan und Isolde*, you should ask somebody else, preferably a man, what *he* thought about it, and preferably with an alluringly air-headed question mark in your voice."

"Really?"

"*Yes*, really."

"You mean it comes to *this*?"

"*What* comes to this?"

"Why"—Cassandra threw up her hands—"you might as well say—a woman's whole life!"

"And to think, I thought you were so interested in continuing your education. You ought to thank me. This has been an extremely educational evening for you."

"But it's—horrible, horrible! What you're telling me."

"Well, what did I tell you? Don't you ever remember anything?" Professor Sobel was thinking back to the first meal he'd had with Cassandra, that lunch at La Grenouille, that April afternoon, the deepening, thrilling roses in Cassandra's cheeks, the superb, velvety taste of his frogs' legs Provençale. "Childhood is ending all the time."

CHAPTER 34

And so it is, thought Cassandra, walking down Central Park South alone after the opera. She had gone and watched the rest of it by herself, not that she had been able to concentrate. It had seemed too much of a confession of failure to leave when Professor Sobel did—that is, if they were not leaving to go home together. She couldn't have borne to humiliate herself in front of him that way—just what would he have thought, that she was going to go home and watch Netflix or something degrading like that? *Being single is like shopping at Trader Joe's*, as Pansy Chapin in all her wisdom had said. Cassandra flinched, recognizing that Pansy Chapin was right. Still, she told herself, certain standards of behavior must be upheld: another humiliation that could not be borne, obviously, was taking the crosstown bus on a night like this. And there was the inconvenience of it being too late to walk across the park. This accounted for her decision to amble down toward Central Park South, where she was hoping to be able to pick up a cab. Sylvie hated this part of town, Cassandra knew, but she loved it. Especially at nighttime, she loved it. Also, it helped being in a part of town where there were so many hotels. It meant that you could count on two important things: being able to use a decent bathroom and getting a cab. After all, if you were an attractive young woman and you were well dressed, Cassandra had found, one of the bell captains was sure to assume you were a guest and hail one for you. She didn't have the strength, right now, to hail one herself.

Once she was inside the cab she took out her phone and cradled it in her hand, wondering who she could call to complain about Professor Sobel right now. But it was late and anyway, all of her friends that she could think of had boyfriends and would probably be with them right now: it was a beastly hour to be alone. As the cab turned down Madison, she observed a cool, impassive blonde in a brief black dress on the arm of a businessman. Maybe she's a high-class Russian prostitute, Cassandra thought to herself, excited. The Carlyle, for instance, was full of them: Edward had taken her there for martinis once. At the thought of Edward, Cassandra felt discouraged again, and thinking about Edward led naturally enough to thinking about Sylvie, from whom she was also now totally estranged. Never before, it occurred to her, had she been without a boyfriend *and*, even worse, without a best friend.

Still, one of the well-known advantages of living in New York City is that if it's late at night and you don't want to be alone, you don't have to be. You can go to a bar or a diner. Cassandra, upon realizing that Professor Sobel, that bastard, hadn't even taken her out to dinner this time, decided to go eat. There was a twenty-four-hour diner just around the corner from her apartment, over on Second Avenue. She flinched and almost decided not to proceed when the first person she saw in there was a middle-aged man with hairy arms wearing pea green hospital scrubs and wolfing down a burger. His hunger seemed immense, his lonesomeness palpable. Are these my people? Cassandra wondered. By this she meant the people who hang out in diners, the people who have nowhere else to go. But she stayed and slid into a booth anyway. She made up her mind to order black coffee and a fried egg sandwich. The coffee arrived, bracing, medicinal. Cassandra took a few life-giving sips and heard somebody asking her:

"Excuse me. Did you go to Sarah Lawrence by any chance?"

"No," Cassandra said, startled that a stranger should have spoken to her here. She looked up to see a faded blonde in a black leotard sitting at the counter eating French fries.

"They have feta on them," the stranger said, pointing. "Want to try? Feta and oregano, I think. They're Greek French fries. They're good!"

"No, thank you."

"Were you ever in the theater, then? Costume design? I feel like maybe I know you from back when I did costume design . . ."

"Nope."

"Window dressing? Did you ever work in window dressing? I used to do the windows at Bergdorf Goodman. I did the holiday windows and everything!"

"Oh, really? They're beautiful. But no, I never did anything having to do with window dressing or costume design or anything like that. So, sorry. I don't think we've met before."

"Wait, Bennington. You went to Bennington."

Cassandra laughed.

"Lucky guess. You're right, I went to Bennington."

"Orpheus. Do you have a friend named Orpheus?"

"Orpheus McCloud?"

And then she remembered. She remembered where she had met the blonde in the leotard before. Of course. It was on that night, that snowy night, when she and Gala and Sylvie had gone out to his apartment in Astoria together.

"Wait, you used to date Orpheus, right?"

"If that's what you want to call it, sure."

Cassandra blushed, feeling that further intimacies were coming. They were. Lee, it came back to her. The stranger's name was Lee.

"I used to go all the way out to Queens to fuck Orpheus," Lee said now. "That was back when I still thought having casual sex was actually exciting. Now I'm used to it. It's boring. It's as boring as everything else. Anyhow, I remember I would stop at that taco truck they had, the one right under the train tracks. I wonder if it's still there. He never fed me, Orpheus. What was I expecting, I wonder? Younger guys don't. I cooked for him sometimes, but that got kind of pathetic, so I stopped. That must have been years ago, come to think of it. *Years!*"

"Oh yes, I remember now. You were making a lamb roast."

Now it was Lee's turn to laugh. Caustically, Cassandra noticed.

"Can you honestly tell me you don't want any French fries?"

"All right," Cassandra admitted, and took one. "Hey! You're right. These are good."

She helped herself to another, as her sandwich arrived.

"I told you so. But all that oregano makes your breath stink. So it's the kind of food you really have to eat after you get laid, not before."

"Hmm. Is that so?"

"Wait, so did you or didn't you get laid tonight? When I saw you walk in here, I thought you did."

"No," Cassandra confessed, thinking with shame of her date with Professor Sobel.

"Oh." Lee seemed disappointed. "I just figured you had. And you must have left right afterward because the guy was an asshole: that happens to me all the time. It's just the way you're dressed and everything. You didn't get all dressed up to come to a diner on Second Avenue, did you? That's a very pretty dress you have on. I noticed it right away. I know fabric," she added, rather ominously, Cassandra thought.

"Oh right, costume design. Are you still doing that?"

"Oh, no. I'm not doing anything with my life right now, actually. I have a problem with the morning," Lee said, as if this explained everything, which, to Cassandra, it did. She translated it to mean: *I have a problem with life itself.*

"Are you an insomniac?" she asked her.

Lee nodded.

"That's why I hang out at diners, see. Diners are good for that. Also, the Apple store. The Apple store is the best thing that ever happened to insomniacs in this town, if you ask me."

"The Apple store?"

"Yeah, the main one right across from the Plaza. It's open twenty-four hours! It always has really good music playing, too."

"I see," said Cassandra slowly. She did see—she saw the crazed and sleepless and lovesick and abandoned denizens of New York City all converging upon the Apple store, say around three a.m., and pacing back and forth, till morning came, in its glacial white depths. Maybe I should get a job, she thought, sobered. Or I might end up like one of them.

What she failed to observe, however, was that she bore something of a resemblance to Lee already. Somebody else could have seen it—Sylvie, for instance, or even Gala. But we can seldom see such things for ourselves. Lee, also, saw it and asked her now:

"How old are you?"

"Twenty-eight."

This, too, felt like a confession.

"But you're not married."

"No . . ."

Lee hailed the waiter and ordered an egg cream. "Want one? Please don't say, Oh no, I'll just have some of yours. I hate it when women do that."

"Me, too. But no thanks, I don't want an egg cream. I do want more coffee though."

She made eye contact with the waiter to get him to come over.

"You're pretty," Lee said, assessing Cassandra. "But you'd be even prettier, you could be absolutely stunning as a matter of fact, if only you had darker eyebrows. I know! You should have *raven black* eyebrows!"

"But I don't have raven black *hair*," Cassandra protested, reasonably enough. "Why should I have raven black *eyebrows*?"

"It's the contrast, silly! The contrast on you would be fabulous."

"Would it?"

"I used to be a makeup artist once; that's the problem with being a blonde, and I should know! Blondes are pretty and some men may prefer them, but. Brunettes have better eyebrows."

"Do they?"

"Always," said Lee remorselessly. "And any blonde you can think of who does have good eyebrows pencils them in. Your eyebrows are a good shape but you really, really need to start penciling them in."

"My roommate . . ." began Cassandra, trying to picture Pansy's eyebrows, which she was certain were just devastating, if only she could remember them. "My roommate is a natural blonde, and I assure you that there is nothing second-rate about her eyebrows. Her name is Pansy Chapin and she was one of the top two or three most beautiful girls at Bennington. The other two were my friend Gala Gubelman—oh! You met her that night at Orpheus's—and this modern dancer with very red hair called Angelica Rocky-Divine."

"She sounds like a bitch," said Lee, of Pansy.

"She is," Cassandra replied, not without affection.

CHAPTER 35

One night about a week later, Pansy and Cassandra were making spaghetti carbonara together when Cassandra noticed, all of a sudden, that Pansy was wearing a diamond ring. It sparkled on her delicate brown finger, for Pansy Chapin was tanned all over. Even at Bennington she had been legendary for her audacity to frequent the tanning booths in town, rather than go flabby and blanched, like lesser mortals, over the course of the New England winter.

"Oh, that's so pretty!" Cassandra exclaimed. "Is it your grandmother's?"

Cassandra had one quite similar to it, from *her* grandmother. It had been passed down, along with the wedding silver and some other pieces of jewelry: an amethyst drop necklace on a fine gold chain, long jade earrings, several gold charm bracelets, and a handsome gold signet ring that Cassandra thought was very chic and just the sort of thing that Pansy herself might wear. The diamond ring of her grandmother's was something that she used to wear to black-tie events with Edward, she reflected, and all of a sudden regretted that the spaghetti carbonara she was making was not for him.

"No, actually," Pansy admitted. Since it was already the middle of August by now and she intended to move out of the apartment by September 1, she might as well go ahead and break the news to Cassandra. "It's—from Jock! We're *engaged*," she clarified, seeing that Cassandra appeared to be a little slow on the uptake.

But this was madness, Cassandra thought. Just how many broken engagements did Pansy think a girl could afford to have? Nevertheless, in the spirit of hypocritical female friendships that make the world go round, she turned off the kitchen faucet so that she could come over to Pansy and better admire the ring.

"Congratulations! It's beautiful!"

"Well, yes." Pansy shrugged. As a matter of fact, her last ring had been even better, she thought, but perhaps there was no one in the whole world to voice such an ungrateful observation to right now, and suddenly Pansy Chapin, standing in their kitchen, glass of vino in hand, felt a lush, plaintive pull toward the wilds of memory and fiancés past. "It's lucky that I happen to actually look good in diamonds. Anyway, it's going to be a Jewish ceremony. Jock insisted on that. Thank God, though, I won't have to convert. And his last name is only Kaplan, which isn't too, too bad. I won't even have to change my monogram!"

"Well, isn't that convenient?"

"So, this means that I'll be moving out, of course."

"Oh, right, of course—" But we just moved in, Cassandra was thinking. *And* they had signed a yearlong lease.

"In September. Jock's loft *is* fabulous, but we'll want to start looking to buy in the suburbs. Not Greenwich!" Pansy clarified. "I think Greenwich is tacky! I'd like to be more in horse country . . ."

"Do you ride?" Cassandra couldn't remember.

"Oh, no. Horses *smell.* I just like the clothing."

Equestrienne wear would look good on her, Cassandra agreed, and in no time got so mesmerized by the image of Pansy sporting dark jodhpurs and a Hermès scarf that she forgot their immediate predicament about the apartment.

"Anyway, I'm sure you can find a roommate for September first. Some person, some Bennington girl . . ." Pansy yawned.

"I guess," said Cassandra wistfully, not feeling convinced.

CHAPTER 36

Cassandra's solution to looking for a roommate was to call up Gala Gubelman and offer to buy her dinner.

"With booze or without booze?" Gala wanted to know.

My, but everyone is anxious about being taken advantage of in this city, Cassandra thought, but said:

"With booze. My treat."

"All right then," Gala decided.

They picked a night when Gala was free and agreed to meet at J.G. Melon.

"Ugh, there are guys in pink shirts all over the place here," Gala muttered before flashing her dimpled smile at the bartender and saying sweetly: "I'll have a Corona."

It was a steamy night at the very end of August. Cassandra had on an angelic white cotton dress and was sipping a gin and tonic.

"Yeah, well, I used to come here with Pansy," she said.

"So *that* explains it."

"Thanks for coming all the way up here, anyway."

"Speaking of which!" Gala sighed, accepting her Corona from the bartender and asking him for extra limes. Gala Gubelman loved "extra" anything: limes, mayonnaise, hot sauce. "Do you know how long it took me to get here? First, the G train was down. Go figure! So I had to walk all the way to Atlantic Center. And then! Even when I finally got on the express . . ."

Cassandra thought sometimes that the only thing she missed about living in Boston was that people talked a lot less about the subway there. One's commute was not a continual conversational pitfall, as it was in New York. She cut Gala off to ask her:

"Do you know anyone who's looking for an apartment? I don't want to live with a stranger. Pansy said to look for other Bennington girls, to start..."

"Bennington girls! They wouldn't be caught *dead*."

"What?"

"Uptown."

With some defensiveness Cassandra began to enumerate the many subtle charms of the available apartment and its location. Gala dismissed every one of them as unlikely to be of sufficient interest. Also, she said, all of the girls from their year who she could think of already had their own places. No one was looking.

"What are you getting to eat, anyway? I'm *famished*. The burger is good here, right?"

"Yes. I always get the burger. But Pansy was fond of the Cornish hen, I remember."

"Cornish hen? Who besides little old ladies would order the Cornish hen? Are you fucking kidding me, Cassandra?"

"Not at all."

"Pansy always *was* pretentious. I don't know why you were ever friends with her. Sylvie and I weren't. Fuck it, I'll have the burger."

"Well, what about younger Bennington grads? Do you know any younger Bennington grads?"

"Yeah, but. There's a whole community of younger Bennington grads living in group houses in Red Hook. Red Hook is really big with them right now. Or! They can't even afford to live anywhere in New York City at all and so they're all decamping to Philly or Baltimore. Detroit could be next, at this rate."

Gala shrugged, indifferent. The bartender informed them that two guys in pink shirts had just sent them a round of drinks.

"You know something? That never happens to me in Brooklyn," she admitted to Cassandra.

"It doesn't?"

But Gala was so beautiful! That's outrageous! she was thinking. She told her so.

"Yeah, but, you must be forgetting, Cassandra. It doesn't matter if you're beautiful or not. Chivalry is dead."

"Are you going to go home with one of them, then?"

"I don't know, maybe. Are you?"

Her relationship with Edward over, her dreams of having an affair with Professor Sobel dashed, Cassandra thought: Why not? Why the hell not?

"They look like they went to Williams," Gala said. "Remember at Bennington when we used to go and crash frat parties at Williams?"

As a matter of fact the answer turned out to be Amherst—the two guys who had sent them drinks had gone to Amherst. As Gala and Cassandra soon learned in the course of going home with them that evening, and forgetting to look for a roommate.

The following morning Cassandra, hungover and doing the walk of shame in punishing late summer sunlight down Lexington Avenue, texted Pansy:

JUST A REMINDER THAT TOMORROW IS SEPTEMBER 1. RENT IS DUE.

Pansy to Cassandra:

IT WAS YOUR RESPONSIBILITY TO FIND A ROOMMATE, CASSANDRA. I'M LIVING IN TRIBECA NOW.

Cassandra to Pansy:

IT'S JUST FOR SEPTEMBER. I'LL HAVE SOMEONE BY OCTOBER 1. PROMISE!

Pansy to Cassandra:

> JOCK WOULD DIE IF HE KNEW, BUT I DON'T EVEN HAVE THE
> MONEY THIS MONTH. I'M BROKE.

Cassandra to Pansy:

> SPEAKING OF JOCK: GET HIM TO PAY IT, WHY DON'T YOU?

Pansy to Cassandra:

> I CAN'T GET HIM INVOLVED. IT WOULD MAKE IT LOOK LIKE I'M
> MARRYING HIM FOR HIS MONEY.

Cassandra to Pansy:

> AREN'T YOU???

And when there was no response, Cassandra to Pansy again:

> WHAT'S IT TO HIM, ANYWAY? HE'S A GODDAMN HEDGE FUND
> MANAGER.

Pansy to Cassandra:

> PLEASE STOP BOTHERING US, CASSANDRA. WE'RE IN THE
> HAMPTONS AND ABOUT TO LOSE RECEPTION.

Bullshit! thought Cassandra. Would all of those hordes of
bloodless yuppies in the Hamptons with their precious iPhones
really stand for them losing reception? Could Pansy possibly be
telling the truth? But Cassandra didn't know, because among the
numerous failures of her life in New York so far was the fact that

she had not been able to nab any invitations to the Hamptons or anywhere else this summer. The only time she'd ever been to that corner of the world at all was once, in her Bennington days, as the guest of Angelica Rocky-Divine at the family estate in Sag Harbor: it had been off-season then and Angelica had run about playing the flute and wearing a long red silk kimono in the majestic, wind-swept apple orchards.

After getting Pansy's text messages, Cassandra endured a lack-luster afternoon, spent killing time at various coffee shops up and down Lexington Avenue. How many iced coffees could a grown woman drink in a single afternoon? she had good reason to ask herself. Also, it was a Saturday, and Saturdays that are spent in the city in the summertime are always depressing. So is the day after you've had casual sex, usually. Almost inevitably by about three o'clock in the afternoon, any residual animal glow has worn off and you start to feel desperate. The consolations of the flesh are merely temporary. This is why some people are driven to become promiscuous: they need to recharge that early, excited feeling again and again. Around dinnertime, sitting disconsolately on a bench in front of one of the boutiques on Madison Avenue and watching the European tourists go by, one of whom was a louche young man in lavender suede loafers walking a poodle, Cassandra texted:

GALA, WHERE ARE YOU?? CALL ME!

"Oh God, she's texting me again," moaned Gala. "She wants me to actually *call* her. Should I?"

"I don't care," said Sylvie, who went back to squeezing lem-ons. Tomorrow it would be Sunday, and she was expecting a brisk crowd at the lemonade stand.

The air was stifling in Sylvie's non-air-conditioned apartment, and Gala undid the halter-neck of her ratty plum-colored vintage 1940s sundress—a garment she'd had as long ago as Bennington, and associated many exciting, libidinal memories with—and let her bare boobs spread out luxuriously as she flopped down on the floor. The floor struck her in that moment as the coolest place to be in the whole apartment.

"Do you mind?" she asked Sylvie.

"That you're still friends with Cassandra?" She *did* mind, in fact.

"No." Gala motioned to her chest. "That I took my top off. I'm *dying* here."

"Suit yourself."

Gala wiggled around on the floor to make herself more comfortable, propping one of Sylvie's miniature flowered silk cushions underneath her belly. Then she called Cassandra, who without further ado started to blather on about the indignity of what Pansy had done and how she still hadn't found another roommate.

"I *never* liked that Pansy Chapin!" Gala announced.

"But, wait. Then why did you have a threesome with her?"

"That wasn't Pansy Chapin, that was Bitsy Citron, and anyway, Cassandra, liking the other girl in a threesome has nothing to do with it."

"Oh." Cassandra stood corrected.

"This one time I was in the dining hall at Bennington and I happened to see Pansy having this, like, really intense-looking conversation with Orpheus—"

"Wait, were you two dating then?"

"Well, we were hooking up, anyway. We were involved, is the point. So! I went and eavesdropped on them. And then I heard Orpheus saying"—here, Gala, who was a very good mimic, did a Kentucky drawl—"*Listen, Pansy, I am not saying that you are an evil person . . . And do you know what Pansy Chapin just sat there and said, without missing a beat? *But, Orpheus, I am an evil person.*"

"Jesus!"

"Yup, so don't say I never told you so."

"But you told me so *too late!*"

"Actually—speaking of Orpheus. He's looking for a new room-mate, he said."

"In Queens." Cassandra pouted.

"Cassandra will never move to Queens," said Sylvie knowledge-ably, as soon as Gala got off the phone.

"Yeah, but." Gala went into the details of Cassandra having to cover Pansy's portion of the rent this month, and the two of them deciding to break the lease come October. "I think she's looking for an exit strategy."

"An exit strategy! But I thought that Pansy Chapin was supposed to be her exit strategy."

"Well—tough luck for her, then. I ask you! Depending on Pansy Chapin!"

"That's the thing about life," mused Sylvie.

"What is?"

"Well, you come up with an exit strategy, see. But then some-times that's not good enough. Sometimes you find out that what you really need is *an exit strategy for your exit strategy.*"

ilver? *Silver?* No, I'm afraid we don't take silver. We already
have a surplus of it in stock, and I'm sorry to say, it's just
not moving for us anymore."

"What *is* moving, these days?"

"Anything mid-century modern right now. Mid-century's all
the rage."

Like what Pansy Chapin has, Cassandra thought. That bitch.

"What about jewelry? Do you take jewelry?"

"Well . . ." The salesgirl in her black sheath dress and period-
appropriate red lipstick paused and looked over Cassandra from
head to toe, as if trying to assess what the value of the jewelry of
somebody like her might be worth. Not much, was her conclusion.
She probably just has some piddling sentimental little hand-me-
downs of her grandmother's she's hoping to cash in. My, but the
world was a rough place out there right now, the salesgirl reflected,
and not for the first time. Cassandra looked to her like a nice, genteel young woman who in another age could have gotten a decent
job no problem, rather than being reduced to the absurd adventure of trying to pawn off her finery up and down the antique
stores of East Sixty-First Street. The spectacles you saw, living in
New York City! Any number of them could break your heart. That
is, if you let them get to you, which the salesgirl, for one, had no
intention of doing.

"Oh all right, all right!" Cassandra exclaimed. It was the sixth
store she had tried that afternoon and she was finally getting the
picture. "You don't have to go into it all, I already know what you're
going to say. Thank you for your time, anyway."

"You know. You might try the Diamond District, that part of town," advised the salesgirl, watching Cassandra and her camel-hair coat. It was a beautiful coat, too, but the hem was unraveling. Cassandra, unlike the adroit Sylvie, was never at her best with a needle and thread and was going to seed on all fronts. She needed cash, and she needed it fast.

The very next day, she found herself waiting in line in a dim, dusty establishment on the fourth floor of an undistinguished office building on the far reaches of West Forty-Seventh Street. The silver was so heavy that she'd had no choice but to take it in a cab. Cassandra was sent into a tiny room with a thick Plexiglas window. The jeweler sat on the other side of the window, his desk littered with greasy black wrenches and tweezers and scales. He weighed and accepted the glorious haul of wedding silver first, then tackled the jewelry.

Picking up a pair of tweezers, he announced to Cassandra: "I have to take them out."

"Take *what* out?"

"The stones." He gestured to the diamond ring, the amethyst necklace. "To weigh them."

Oh well, diamonds don't suit me anyway, thought Cassandra, but nevertheless found herself wincing as he pried it out of the scalloped rose gold setting, dating back to the Edwardian era: that ring had been in her mother's family for generations.

"Nice," he said of the amethyst. It was a big one apparently.

Next up to be dismantled were the charm bracelets. The individual charms, as well as the gold link bracelets, had to be weighed separately to determine their value. At the sight of these poor cast-off charms, the tears welled up and began to flicker on Cassandra's eyelashes.

"Look," said the jeweler, stopping what he was doing to draw her attention to a charm in the shape of a seahorse. "Look, its eyes."

Its eyes were studded with two dainty emeralds. With an expert, single twist, he pried them out and then they, too, bounced up and down on the dingy scale.

That did it. She let out a long, wounded wail. Thank God, though, she did leave there with cash; the jeweler, entirely unfazed by the sight of his down-and-out clientele bursting into tears, accepted everything. Outside on West Forty-Seventh Street it was raining and Cassandra's mascara ran down her face in long, weepy, blackish violet streaks. She decided to walk back uptown. Meanwhile, it rained and rained. Soon she heard thunder. This catastrophic aspect of the weather suited her sense of personal devastation. At the Korean flower stands, dahlias were nodding their battered heads, pink and orange and purple, too, and mixed in with the sound of a man hawking sleazy plastic umbrellas—"Umbrellas! Five dollar! Umbrellas!"—were the rich, yearning chords of a man playing the violin. Life in the arts! Cassandra thought, with a momentary swell of pity for her fellow man. It's a bitch. That guy's pretty talented actually.

By the time she had walked all the way over to the East Side—collapsing, to regain her strength, on a bench outside the entrance to Central Park—the weather had cleared. Two middle-aged women strode right past her, one of them puffing on a cigarette. They were just exiting the park.

"If you want my opinion," said the woman smoking the cigarette to her friend. *"It's time to get rid of the horses!"*

My sentiments exactly, thought Cassandra, and at that very moment she decided to call up Orpheus McCloud, who happened to be in bed, just for old time's sake, with Gala. When old lovers are together, they will often discuss old times. Just as the phone rang, Gala was imploring him: "I'm sorry! I'm still, like, totally sorry about that STD I picked up from that guy Christophe I was sleeping with in Paris . . ."

"Hey, why would Cassandra Puffin be calling me?"

"Oh! I bet because I told her you had a room in your apartment that was available. She was living on the Upper East Side with Pansy Chapin, that frigid little bitch, and—"

"*Frigid* is not the word," said Orpheus, who, unbeknownst to Gala, had been unable to resist being swept into bed by the evil, luminescent, streaky-blond Pansy himself. "Well, I guess I might as well pick up. The only other person who's interested in the room is Chase Raven."

"Chase Raven? But, wait! I thought he was *dead*. I thought he *OD'd*."

"No, he just took a term off to go dry out in Bali and never came back."

"Oh." So that explained it.

Orpheus picked up his phone. Cassandra got straight to the point.

"Well, I just wanted to know: Is the room in your apartment still available?"

It was; but when Orpheus got off the phone, Gala snuggled up next to him and said, "You know, Orpheus. I don't know if you really want Cassandra for your roommate. She still doesn't have a job yet."

"But Gala," said Orpheus, whose family had, indeed, once founded the state of Kentucky and to whom practicalities were of less than urgent concern. "Who do we know who does?"

Good point, thought Gala, having recently bailed on her gallery job in the absence of any other employment opportunities because she just couldn't fucking take it anymore. But she'd done this, in a fit of satisfying pique, only to discover that Sylvie was right. Sometimes what you really need after all is an exit strategy for your exit strategy.

PART IV

Forget-Me-Not

CHAPTER 38

Cassandra stopped at the taco truck. She didn't get a taco, though, she got a salted tongue empanada. After much experimentation, she'd decided that that was the best thing the taco truck had going for it. A buck twenty-five a pop; Sylvie would have been impressed by just how cheaply Cassandra was eating these days. If only she could have told her.

By now, it was the Wednesday before Thanksgiving. Not that you could tell that Thanksgiving was upon us, because in Astoria, where Cassandra was now living with Orpheus McCloud, the streets were full of immigrants, blissfully unencumbered by the obligations of this most American of holidays. The taco cart, not to mention the hookah lounges over on Steinway Street, or Little Egypt as people called it, would be open all day tomorrow. Cassandra was relieved, for she was spending the holiday alone this year, the first time she had ever done such a thing in her whole life. Every other year she'd spent it with her mother in Cambridge, the spinsterish bleakness of which was lifted only by the sweet relief of Syvie coming home to see her family for a few days' time: Sylvie, arriving in a black minidress and white lace tights, shaking snowflakes from her cap of dark hair. But that, all that, was many years ago now.

Cassandra walked home through the trash-clogged streets. Her furnished room at Orpheus's had been the crash pad of many a rootless Bennington grad over the years. Should she stop to think of the shenanigans that had occurred on that unlovely, lumpy bed before it was hers, she would feel a faint disgust. The boy who'd lived there just before her, a caddish, overrated painter, used to lure girls to his studio at Bennington by promising to fuck them on top of crusty, wrinkled sheets of canvas. The notorious Lanie Tobacco had just recently hurled a lit cigarette in his face outside of a dive bar in Bushwick. That was the latest in alumni news.

Cassandra went into the kitchen and unpacked her empanadas. So greasy and delicious, and with those nice little sprinkles of radish and lime on top: when you are poor, broke to the bone as Cassandra now was, even the smallest of things can give you pleasure. Stuffing one's face with empanadas was a pastime best indulged in alone, she felt. But just at that very moment her solitude was disturbed by the appearance of Fern Morgenthal coming into the apartment.

"Hey," said Fern to Cassandra, pausing to slip off her moccasins. Other than her moccasins she had on a black leotard and a pair of dangerously tatty black lace tights. No pants.

"Hey," said Cassandra right back.

Fern was subletting Orpheus's room while he was on tour in Europe for the next couple of months. She herself had graduated from Bennington just that June and had spent the summer bumming around with friends, expatriate-style, in the cafés and underground art spaces of Berlin. As of that September, she was newly arrived in New York, where the rest of her classmates were, and looking forward to building some kind of a life for herself.

She was twenty-two years old.

Was Fern pretty? Cassandra, squinting at her over the dirty foil of her empanada wrapper, considered this most crucial of questions carefully. She didn't think so, really. Or, at least, Fern's style of prettiness—vague and underdeveloped and elfin, with soft brownish bangs falling into her eyes—was not to Cassandra's more flamboyant taste. To her mind, the greatest beauty of her era at Bennington was still Angelica Rocky-Divine, whose long, indolent white body Cassandra recalled unclothed in all its plush splendor while doing cartwheels at the End of the World. But what Fern had was youth. Cassandra, who would be turning twenty-nine in February, could see that now. She could practically smell it: the spring white freshness coming off Fern's skin. It was a blood scent, to Cassandra; it stirred up something predatory in her, and she felt, not unpleasantly, more like an older man than like a former Bennington girl herself.

(Fern, for her part, considered Cassandra so ancient that on determining that she had graduated in the year 2003, had been stirred to ask her: "Oh my God, so were you there the year the dancers died?"

"Yes," Cassandra said simply, thinking it becoming to assume a melancholy tone.

"Oh my God, those poor girls! That must have been *rough*."

"Believe me. It *was*.")

"So . . . do we want to job-hunt later tonight like we talked about?" Fern asked brightly.

"Not really," said Cassandra, equally brightly.

"But I said I would help you, remember? I said how I was going to help you write your bio?"

As a member of the younger, ceaselessly self-promoting genera-tion, Fern was up on the ways to network, and was not ashamed.

"Bio? Remind me again why is a bio supposed to be better to have nowadays than a résumé?"

"Oh, because résumés take way too long to read, for one thing," replied Fern, once again in the spirit of her generation.

"Oh, is that it?"

"Uh-huh. And! I could take your photo if you wanted," Fern offered, thinking: But not tonight. For one thing, Cassandra would have to wash her hair first. With blond hair, you can always tell when it's dirty, as Cassandra's clearly was tonight. Also, she would have to be sure to put on some eyeliner or something; Fern herself never posed for photographs without first doing a flawless cat eye. But Cassandra did not seem to recognize the value of controlling one's image in a digital world. She was not even on Facebook, Fern had been stunned to learn, and did not do online dating either, even though, right now, she was obviously single. "Photos can be a real selling point to prospective employers."

"What, am I supposed to put a head shot on my résumé now, too? Or is it my bio? Anyway, what possible difference could it make? I'm not an *actress*."

"No, no, head shots aren't just for actresses anymore, that's what I'm trying to tell you. Everybody has one! Like, even if people just look you up on LinkedIn—"

"Linked in to what, is what I'd like to know," Cassandra muttered. "That is the question."

"No, no, really, my friend Dorian Frazier, she got a job at Sotheby's right after Bennington because some guy looked her up on LinkedIn and said he liked her cheekbones."

"He actually said that?"

"Yeah, well, I mean he said it later on once they started sleeping together. He was her boss. He was married. You can thank your cheekbones, is what he said to her once it was over. He wanted to make clear to her, see, that she didn't know shit about art. He said that, too: You don't know shit about art. There was this big to-do afterward and she had a nervous breakdown and had to move back home to Connecticut. But, whatever. The point is, she never would have gotten that job at Sotheby's in the first place if he hadn't seen her photograph!"

"But if she had a nervous breakdown and had to go home, what good did the job at Sotheby's do her? For instance. Did she ever go back to New York?"

"Oh, no, never. Never again, Dorian says!"

What a waste, Cassandra thought. Of youthful promise and youthful cheekbones. After all that, to just end up back home in Connecticut. Connecticut! Which was probably the most boring state in the union, after Vermont.

"By the way. Remind me again what you're doing for Thanksgiving?"

"Oh, that. Staying in, I guess."

"Oh no, that's so—" Fern thought of saying *sad*, which was what the situation deserved, but then decided against it because she had noticed that Cassandra could get touchy so easily.

"I hate Thanksgiving. I've *always* hated Thanksgiving." There rolled over her assorted memories from childhood, the tragic efforts to which her mother, a widow, would go to make things festive for just the two of them, showering Cassandra with pretty trinkets that would have had much more meaning if only they had been bought by a man. "And another thing is, I hate, I have absolutely no use for, turkey. Turkey! Who the hell came up with turkey? The Puritans, that's who! I'm from Boston and take it from me, those people, the Puritans, the WASPs, they don't know food."

"I wouldn't know. I'm from Portland," said Fern, contributing nothing worthwhile to the conversation, Cassandra felt.

"Which Portland?"

"Which? Oh, Portland, Oregon."

But I already knew that, Cassandra was thinking, congratulating herself on her powers of deduction, which so seldom failed her. I could have told you that.

"I'm from, like, right outside of Portland," Fern went on, unpacking, to Cassandra's grave displeasure, several enormous cans of pumpkin puree from the cavernous depths of her Trader Joe's tote bag. "I'm from—"

"Everybody loves Portland."

"Portland is awesome, it's—"

"I wouldn't."

"Wouldn't what?"

"I wouldn't love Portland. I just know that the entire Pacific Northwest is not for me."

"But, wait. Have you ever even been there?"

"No."

"Then how do you *know*?"

"I didn't like San Francisco all that much either, to tell you the truth," Cassandra went on, ignoring Fern's more fact-based train of thought. "Everybody says: San Francisco, San Francisco! You know what San Francisco is to me?"

"What?"

"San Francisco is like one great big cashmere yoga hoodie."

"Huh?" Fern had studied sculpture at Bennington, not English. She hadn't even taken the occasional creative writing workshop; she wasn't as swift as Cassandra to pick up on metaphors.

"Cashmere yoga hoodies. *Cashmere yoga hoodies.* If you don't see for yourself what's offensive about that concept, then honestly, I can't help you."

"So," said Fern eventually, "I was going to bake a pumpkin pie."

"What, for Thanksgiving?"

"Of course for Thanksgiving. It isn't Thanksgiving without pumpkin pie."

"Who says so? The Puritans again, is it? I've told you and told you: those people don't know food. You know what I'll be having for Thanksgiving?"

"What?"

"A liver and black olive sandwich."

Fern, who had lived off-campus in the vegetarian co-op at Bennington, chose to ignore this by looking preoccupied as she turned on the oven.

"There's this liver and black olive sandwich I like to get from the Halal Sandwich Shop, down on Steinway. Ever been there? It's where all of the Egyptian cab drivers go. It's great!"

"Hmm. Speaking of restaurants. I'm so excited, this guy I'm seeing, this artist, he's renting out Momofuku next week, for his after-party. It's going to be awesome."

"Momofuku. Momofuku. Momofuku is like the cashmere yoga hoodie of restaurants; Momofuku is for fools!"

"Hey . . ."

"I've been to Momofuku, too, you know. I was once taken there by this guy I was seeing." She tried to imitate the dreamy emphasis that Fern's tongue put on the word *guy*; that all Bennington girls did whenever there was one in the picture, so long were they used to living without them. "He was paying, thank God, so I ordered this duck entrée. Afterward we left and I was still so hungry, I didn't even have the energy to go back to his place, which of course was what he was expecting after this supposedly grand gesture of taking me to *Momofuku*. All I could think was: If only we'd gotten Peking duck in Chinatown!"

"Chinatown! But that's totally different, Cassandra. I'm seeing this guy who's a sous chef at this place in Williamsburg and he says that David Chang's technique is really amaz—"

"A sous chef. So now you're seeing a sous chef. I thought you were seeing an artist."

"Well." Fern sighed, promising loads of dramatic narration to come. "It's really complicated with me and the artist. He's older than me and he's just starting to get really, really big in the art world. I met him my senior year at Bennington, when I was doing this archiving internship at this gallery in Chelsea. Things moved really fast! It was just so incredibly passionate. I think he'd like to marry me but—"

"But what?"

"Well, I've noticed something. I've noticed that he isn't any good with money. He's so preoccupied with making art, I pay the bills and keep track of all the practical stuff. I know that when people see us together at openings they must think that I'm so much younger than him and he's the powerful one in the relationship, but what they don't know is—I'm the powerful one! Sometimes I even lend *him* money. I call the shots."

"Uh-huh."

"It's just, going forward. I couldn't marry a man who wasn't any good at managing his money. He's *thirty-six*. I feel like by the time you're thirty-six, you ought to have figured out how to manage your money."

"Have you figured it out?"

"What?"

"How to manage your money."

"Yeah, I'm really good at it actually. When I was waitressing and saving up to go to Berlin—"

"I used to be good at managing my money," said Cassandra. "When I was twenty-two. Do you want to hear the story of my life ever since?"

CHAPTER 39

Not really, Fern thought, but Cassandra persisted: "I was living with this girl Pansy Chapin on East Seventy-Ninth. It was a beautiful apartment, totally *chic*, totally *just so*; Pansy has all of these really great antiques. Then, just after I'd moved in, and I had to pay this absolutely enormous security deposit, she upped and got engaged to another hedge-fund manager."

"What do you mean, another?"

"Oh, Pansy's always had these fabulously rich boyfriends. She's gorgeous, even if she did just have to get a boob job. Like, even when we were at Bennington, the rest of us would be sitting around all weekend eating apple cider doughnuts, whatever, and *she'd* have some guy flying her to Paris for a rendezvous at the Plaza Athénée. She brought me back this umbrella once. A pink umbrella. From Paris—"

"Well, that was nice of her, anyway," Fern interrupted.

"No, it wasn't. It broke! It broke, Fern, it broke!"

"Well, I mean, um, *yeah*. Umbrellas will do that. I guess."

"Be that as it may, I am prepared to take the loss of the umbrella that Pansy Chapin gave me entirely personally. So! Where was I? Oh, right. So it's years later and there I am living with her and she meets this guy and she gets engaged and she moves into his place in TriBeCa. And then, get this, she decides she doesn't want to pay rent at our place anymore. I was like 'Pansy, just get your boyfriend to pay it for you, what's it to him? He's a goddamn hedge-fund manager' but *no*. Anyhow. We ended up having to break the lease in the end. It was this big fucking ordeal. I lost a ton of money. *I had to pawn my great-grandmother's wedding silver,*" she added threat-eningly, as if to let Fern know to what depths she, a fellow Ben-nington girl, might one day have to stoop on the godless streets of New York City.

Wedding silver? thought Fern. Who cared about wedding silver anymore? What she and everybody else she knew thought was cute was arranging things in mason jars.

"I pawned my signet ring," Cassandra went on, in a torrent of high emotion. "An amethyst necklace, all of these gold charm bracelets I had. One of them even had real emeralds . . ."

But mentions of signet rings and charm bracelets were falling, like so much else, on Fern's deaf ears.

"And now, now I'm through with stuff like silver. I don't pre-tend anymore. I've just given up on all fronts, I moved out to Queens with Orpheus and I eat from the taco truck. But, when I first moved in with Pansy Chapin, I thought we'd have dinner parties! I thought I was going to learn how to make—sole Véro-nique! Chicken Marbella! I only ever got as far as spaghetti car-bonara, though." Cassandra laughed, a crazy, reeling laugh. "I used to imagine myself using my great-grandmother's silver. I had this rich boyfriend, too, back then, I thought I'd have him over and he'd see the table set with my great-grandmother's silver and he'd ask me to marry me . . . I thought I'd have this whole other life."

There rolled over her another memory, this one of the lemon chiffon cocktail dress hanging on her bedroom door, crystallized in the lavender-honey light of Sylvie's apartment.

"Jesus. What happened?" It was to Fern the disappearance of the man and not the silver that was the more foreboding detail, and for the first time the woeful saga of Cassandra was starting to make her worry about her own prospects as a woman.

"Oh, him. He dumped me. I had this friend Sylvie, Sylvie Furst. Sylvie was right about—everything. As a matter of fact, Fern, since you like to date artists, this story might come in handy sometime. About a million years ago now Sylvie used to date this guy, Ludo Citron—"

"Oh my God." Fern stirred delicately with the reverence of one who still believed in art. "I know him."

"Yeah, he's supposed to have turned into this really big deal in the art world, I guess."

"I mean. I don't just know who he *is*. I actually *love* his work. I actually *own* a pair of his Pumas."

You would, thought Cassandra, and resumed:

"Well, once it was all over between them, what Sylvie did was, she threw a roast chicken at him! It landed on his lap."

"But Cassandra, that's terrible! I would never do something like that. Never, never, never," vowed Fern.

"Not now, maybe. But you might, someday."

Fern elected to ignore this. Somehow the story of some crazy chick throwing a roast chicken was not in keeping with the dignity of art.

"Wait, what happened to your boyfriend you were telling me about? Did you throw a roast chicken at him, too, or what?"

"No, but— If only I had listened to Sylvie! See, she used to say I wasn't really the kind of girl he was going to marry. He went to Harvard and I think he was just into me because I was this slutty, bohemian Bennington girl; I don't think that sexually speaking he was all that into preppy girls and can you blame him? They're homely! Also, I'm fatherless. Did I ever tell you that? That means I have no self-esteem to speak of around men. Absolutely none! Sylvie was right about that, too. Where was I again?"

"Hey, I'm sorry your boyfriend dumped you and that you have daddy issues and all, but what are you talking about? You're actually saying that a Harvard guy will be into a Bennington girl for sex but that he won't marry her? Maybe in, like, 1962 we had that reputation but now—"

"You don't think that Bennington girls are *still* complete and total sluts? Because I sure do."

"You have some kind of dated ideas about female sexuality, if you ask me. If a girl happens to enjoy sex"—the girl Fern was thinking of was herself—"it doesn't mean that she's a slut."

"Okay, but if she's desperate for it?"

"Desperate? I'm not—"

"Right, because you're so powerful because this older male artist wants to marry you. You were a sculpture student, you said? Done any of your own work lately?"

"Well, I mean I just graduated, Cassandra. And then I was in Berlin—"

"See, see! You haven't. You haven't done any of your own work and neither have I. I wasted my twenties on men and buying stupid French lingerie I couldn't afford and I don't know what the hell else. So did most of my friends who went to Bennington. None of us have one goddamn thing to show for it."

"You really hate that place."

"Oh God, it's a total fucking racket. And the worst part! Speaking of money. I'm still paying off my student loans."

"You are?" But Cassandra had graduated, like, ages ago, Fern was thinking.

"Well, come to think of it I'm not exactly paying them off at the moment, but . . ."

Fern was silent, and Cassandra, frustrated to no end by her low affect, thought: Sculpture students were not apt to be perceptive. Their average intelligence was only a cut above that of the modern dancers.

"So! Did I tell you I started a new job today?"

Fern thought it wise, at this point, to change the subject.

In *that?* Cassandra was thinking—meaning the dangerously tatty black lace tights. No pants.

"Uh-huh. It's on the Upper East Side. Fifth Avenue, way, way up there, past the Met, even . . ."

"Carnegie Hill," shot back Cassandra, not to be outdone.

"Carnegie *what*?"

"Carnegie Hill. That's what it's called. That neighborhood."

"Oh, cool. It's super fucking fancy, whatever you want to call it. Actually, I got this job through Bennington!"

"Do tell."

"Well—do you remember that girl Jude St. James? Oh, I forgot, you're so much older than me, she wasn't your year. She was my year to begin with, except she took all this time off to go to Africa. I don't think she's graduated yet, or maybe she's not even planning to anytime soon. She's a lesbian and she's passionate about Africa," added Fern, as if these two facts added up to a third.

"Africa . . ." muttered Cassandra, wondering why the hell it was that rich people always wanted to go there; she sure didn't.

"Well, anyway, she totally grew up at this humongous place on the Upper East Side. Only—get this—she's always going round and telling people she's from East Harlem instead. *Whatever.* I actually went to East Harlem once! I met this guy, on the subway platform at Union Square. We made eye contact. Before we knew it, I was back at his mother's place in East Harlem. Now *that* was weird. His mother made us dinner afterward. Goat stew or something sketchy like that, and I'm a *vegetarian*. Where was I again . . . ?"

"You were telling me about how you got your new job through Bennington."

"Oh, right, thanks. I'm working for Jude's *father.* That's whose apartment it is on Fifth Avenue. That's where I was earlier today. He's so loaded, he doesn't have to do anything anymore except look after his money and fuss over his art collection. That's what he hired me for. He asked Jude: Do you know any Bennington girls who would be interested in helping me to organize my art collection? So Jude, she suggested me!"

"Ah!"

"It's kind of an awkward setup, though, because Jude really hates him, she says."

Cassandra, of course, did not have a father, but had long observed that girls who did, especially rich ones, often hated theirs and was not surprised.

"And! Turns out, some of the stuff he collects is really, really incredibly filthy, too."

"Really?" Cassandra was titillated.

"Uh-huh. I was surprised because, you know, nothing really seems filthy *nowadays*, right? I think maybe it's because I'm more used to seeing porn online, you know? It seems dirtier somehow in paintings or drawings. It seems dirtier when you see it on *paper*, somehow."

"I disagree, Fern. I disagree with the thrust of your premise completely. Everything online—everything online is not only anti-erotic, if you ask me, but *banal*, as well."

"Oh my God, that is so not true, Cassandra! I think that technology and everything has really made the world a better place."

"*How*, though? And don't say, Oh, it's made things so much more convenient! I hate that word—*convenient*. Convenient, expedient! So go ahead, tell me! How has it actually made the world a better place?"

Fern responded by listing a number of apparently rather pithy celebrities whom she suggested that Cassandra could follow on Twitter. And that was the end of that.

ver since moving out of Sylvie's nearly a year ago now, Cassandra had shown a positive genius for ending up in the wrong boroughs. The right borough, obviously, was Brooklyn. But to get to, say, Williamsburg from Astoria, it took three train transfers, and Cassandra, not caring for Williamsburg in the first place, couldn't be bothered. She started turning down invitations, and before too long people knew better than to invite her, because if the event was in Williamsburg, no way would she come. Greenpoint was okay according to Cassandra on something like a once-every-six-weeks basis, but only if you went out for Polish food, and that was just because she happened to be fond of borscht. None of her other friends gave a damn about borscht; they were all raring to go try the latest, distinctly non-Polish places that were cropping up along the avenues. But soon, Cassandra had stopped venturing to Greenpoint either. She had vowed to never walk the scenic streets of Fort Greene ever again, and this included all of its outskirts, which she claimed were also Sylvie-haunted. Cassandra had never even been to Bushwick and she intended to keep it that way, thank you very much. Bed-Stuy had jumbo rats. Park Slope? You did not invite Cassandra there, no, not even if you lived there, not even if you were throwing a housewarming party; everything about it put her in a cantankerous mood and was subject to relentless commentary the minute she got off the subway. People kept telling her that she could find no objection to Brooklyn Heights, at least; Brooklyn Heights was so beautiful. Boston is beautiful! Cassandra shouted at them. And Boston is boring. Brooklyn Heights, it is so beautiful and so boring, you might as well just be in Boston. This was the last straw, people felt: *comparing New York to Boston.*

Her friends all found her behavior increasingly exasperating. It might have worried them, if only they had been interested, but the fact of the matter was they weren't anymore. They were women going on thirty now and they were always busy. Meanwhile, Cassandra had become just like Pansy Chapin before her: the one Bennington girl for whom you had to go into Manhattan if you ever wanted to see her.

"Do you ever actually *see* Cassandra anymore?" Sylvie asked Gala at brunch in Fort Greene one afternoon. Sylvie had just ordered: Sweet-and-Salty French Toast ($14). Gala: Lettuce-and-Watercress Salad with Marcona Almonds ($12, Hardboiled Egg $2.50 extra).

"No," Gala had said, thinking that she really should have gone with the French toast instead and counting on Sylvie giving her a bite. "Does anybody?"

The absence left by one's female friends is best filled with—what else?—a man. Thank God for Cassandra, then, that Edward had resurfaced. Just that fall, the two of them had started sleeping together again, although, as he so frequently reminded her, taking on his old paternalistic tone, "we aren't actually together." Actually, the situation worked out well for both of them, for no longer having much to say to each other as human beings, perhaps having not had that much to say even in the beginning, their bodies now said the man-to-woman essentials. Cassandra even showed a savage absence of sentimentality in visiting Philadelphia again, where, instead of enjoying the fruits of Edward's tony social life as a girlfriend, she waited for him in his apartment like a mistress, creamy, stockinged legs in the air. This was a relief actually. By now she knew that she would have gotten sick of all of those Christmas concerts and horse races, had life with Edward ever shed its glamorous unreality and become real.

"Oh my God! You look so pretty. Where are you going all dressed up, Cassandra?"

It was Fenna Luxe, Orpheus's latest girlfriend. She was a wil-

lowy blonde who played the guitar and did Reiki and presently she
was standing in the hallway of their apartment naked. After many
failed attempts at being more respectable, Orpheus and Cassandra had decided to run a clothing-optional household. She spent
so much time getting in and out of the bathtub that finally she
figured why get dressed at all, and Orpheus didn't mind, because
Cassandra had very nice boobs and he enjoyed looking at them
and this meant that Fenna, who was utterly lovely, now could also
flounce freely out of the confines of his bedroom au naturel. Cassandra didn't mind Fenna being naked either and, being lonely
these days, enjoyed her company very much. Fenna had been a Bennington girl but after Cassandra's time and only very briefly; she'd
dropped out after getting a record deal and because she hated the
weather.

"The Upper East Side," said Orpheus. "She's going to the
Upper East Side. Cassandra is the only person we know who ever
goes uptown."

"Cool," said Fenna, who was from Malibu and not inclined to
be judgmental, except about the weather.

"Midtown. I'm going to midtown. The Harvard Club is in midtown."

Cassandra stood in front of the mirror studying her features
and darkening her eyebrows, as had been recommended to her by
Lee, that night at the diner. Lee, it turned out, had been correct:
emphasizing her eyebrows gave Cassandra's peaches-and-cream
countenance a sense of distinction it had not had previously. It
also, although she did not know this, made her look older. Which
she most certainly was, and felt.

"Oh," said Fenna, "it's that guy Edward again!"

"Uh-huh," said Cassandra, spraying perfume. L'air du Temps,
her favorite. Sylvie used to wear it, too, though in her case not since
high school, probably. The girls used to pick up deeply discounted
bottles of it at Marshalls. I bet she wears something organic or arti-

sinal now, Cassandra thought, something made in small batches in Brooklyn. Fenna wore rose oil, plain and undiluted; Cassandra even borrowed it from her sometimes, which was just another plus of living in a clothing-optional household, because under one's clothing or even a bathrobe rose oil can get sticky.

After leaving the apartment that night, Cassandra splurged on a cab to midtown; it doesn't take too long to get there from Astoria, and so for once she could afford it. She swayed into the well-appointed lobby of the Harvard Club on a pair of hot pink suede d'Orsay stilettos that were the sexiest shoes she owned. After a series of days of subsisting on salted tongue empanadas, she was very much looking forward to ordering shrimp cocktail and filet mignon. She and Edward kissed. Once they were seated, he looked serious, but then he always looked serious. This, too, was one of his charms. Another one was that he didn't care for Brooklyn either: or, even more gratifying, he scarcely knew that it existed.

"Cassandra . . ." said Edward. Why doesn't she wear color anymore? he found himself wondering, for her dress tonight was striking and black. There was this one yellow dress he had been fond of her in—some soft, nearly see-through material—he'd always wanted to get close to her and touch it whenever she was wearing it. What had become of the girl in that dress? Like most heterosexual men, he was not observant enough, however, to guess that the change in her appearance had anything to do with the darkening of her eyebrows. It was more of a general impression that he gathered, staring at her across the table right now.

"Yes?" Much fluttering of her lashes, while eating a shrimp.

"Cassandra . . . Cassandra." Edward cleared his throat and resumed his professorial tone. He was not a professor actually, though Sylvie had once proclaimed that he looked like one. "Cassandra, we are going to have a nice dinner tonight, a nice long dinner, we can have dessert and coffee and everything, and then at the end of the evening I am going to put you in a cab and I will give you money for it and you are going to go home."

"Oh, so you don't want me to spend the night?" She was fine with that, not spending the night.

"No. I mean that I am going to make you go home immediately after dinner. I didn't reserve a room for us tonight."

"You didn't?"

"No, I didn't. This is a platonic dinner, except, except that after it we are not going to be friends. It would be inappropriate, given the circumstances."

"Are you engaged?"

"Hey!" Edward was disappointed. "How did you guess?"

"You used to say how very, very *emotional* I am; how very *passionate*; how very, very *intuitive*."

"Well, then," said Edward, grateful that the waiter was now clearing his oyster shells and that soon they'd be onto their entrées.

"Who is she? Did she go to Wellesley? No, Harvard. Are you marrying somebody else who went to Harvard?"

"Duke, actually. She was the captain of the tennis team." He was too much of a gentleman to add that she had graduated much later than either of them; she was twenty-five, or nearly a decade his junior. But there was such a big smile on his face when he said the part about the tennis team that Cassandra had to accept that he was actually in love with her.

"What's her name?"

"Keller. Keller Houghton."

"You are engaged to a woman named Keller? *Keller?* Repugnant fucking name."

"It's her middle name she goes by. Her real name is Cynthia."

"Of course it is, of course it is! I could have told you that if only you had asked me, I'm intuitive, after all."

By the time the entrées arrived, Edward was thinking to himself that Keller was rather less intuitive than Cassandra, and wasn't that a blessing, because marriage to one of these self-confessed *very, very emotional, passionate, intuitive* women was apt to get tiring. As a matter of fact though, he would have preferred that she go by Cynthia. He thought that once they were married he might try calling her that. Cynthia, sweet Cynthia. Her real name, which might become to him alone a nickname—a catcall of husbandly possession. To tell you the truth, Keller wasn't as beautiful as Cassandra either. Strictly speaking, most people looking at her would have said she and Cassandra were quite similar—Keller was even blond, with some of the same general rosy and pleasing characteristics. But Keller wasn't romantic. For instance, Keller: Keller wore sensible underwear. She had only one sexy set for when they dressed up to go to black-tie events and that was that.

"How is your filet mignon?"

"Good, good. I mean: *excellent*," said Cassandra, trying to list all of the eligible or even not-so-eligible men she knew in New York City who might be persuaded to take her out for luxurious red meat suppers in place of Edward. She was getting to be more like Sylvie in her calculations, although unlike Sylvie, she would have preferred to get protein *and* get laid in the course of the same evening.

"I'm glad, sweetie." Edward was content with digging into his diver scallops.

"Did you just call me sweetie?"

"Oh, I'm sorry, I shouldn't ha—" He was thinking of Keller and what she would say if she could see him right now dining at the Harvard Club with a woman like Cassandra. Keller may have been less emotional, but she also had less of a sense of humor, and a sense of humor in a wife might count for something, it occurred to him now.

"Oh, it's fine, Edward. I like it when you say it, actually. Only I guess that now when you say it, it has to be platonic."

Bennington girls, Edward thought, while proceeding to make deft small-talk with Cassandra over the entrée portion of the evening: they were romantic. Tragic, even. That ex-friend of Cassandra's, Sylvie, the crazy wild black-eyed chick with the apartment full of rotten lemons: tragic. Still, there was something kind of romantic about the apartment full of rotten lemons; neither Keller nor any of her friends would have been capable of such majesty of ruin, such an artistic statement that would connote in one image the desolation of their lives. They didn't have it in them! Cassandra in those hot pink, obviously, heartbreakingly Parisian pumps of hers now looking forward to being sent back to Queens in a cab was also a little bit tragic. He recalled her lingerie, things called teddies and garters and basques, beautiful, silly, soon-to-be-broken things that she begged you to ply apart. He still desired her, but you didn't want to marry somebody tragic unless you wanted to blow up your life, and no way did Edward want to blow up his. He would be married in a royal fashion in Rittenhouse Square and move to the Main Line, and Keller would bear him two fine and able young children. But he never forgot her. *Cassandra.* Or Sylvie either. The stench of rotten lemons. Sometimes when he was sitting alone at the breakfast table or when he scooped up his children, especially his daughter, into his arms the memory of it would drift into his brain, perfuming and permeating his otherwise untroubled life.

"Do you remember Harvard-Yale weekend?" he asked her.

Cassandra replayed the words: *Harvard-Yale weekend.* She had still been living in Boston then, that weekend she took the train to meet him in New Haven. She had been wearing her camel-hair coat, the hem of which was not yet coming undone. On the train she had fancied herself playing the Franny part in *Franny and Zooey*—that Zooey went stark raving insane after that weekend was entirely lost on her at the time, though Sylvie had pointed it out. Anyway, that weekend felt like a lifetime ago. And now Cassandra, not Sylvie, was the one thinking: *I was so young then.*

"Yes" was all Cassandra said now.

"Well, right before we went to the Harvard-Yale game, that morning we met up in the hotel, do you remember that you begged me *not* to make us go?"

"Vaguely."

"Well, and you were squeezing me so tight you wouldn't let me get out of bed and you said, 'I like sex so much better than football.' You just wouldn't get dressed and go to the game. It was then I knew that I'd never be able to marry you."

"Because I don't like football?" This was getting ridiculous! Edward was an intellectual. He didn't like football either, unless it concerned the Harvard-Yale game, and then it was apparently sacred.

"See, but Keller. Keller has a good attitude about things. Keller likes sex *and* she likes football."

"Because her name is Keller! Keller! She sounds like a dyke."

"Hey now! All I'm saying is that a wife, a wife has to be able to have sex with you and then get out of bed and go to the football game, or whatever the occasion is. I have a big social life in Philadelphia, Cassandra; I have things to go to. I like to be with people. You like to be either in bed alone with a man, or you like to go gab to your girlfriends, and you don't know how to do anything in between."

If Cassandra had been interested in what is known as "personal growth"—and who, pray tell, is honestly interested in that?—she might have taken Edward's words to heart. She might have thought: *My next serious relationship, I will remember that. My next serious relationship, I will do better!* Instead, she decided that clearly she was much better cut out to be a mistress and that was just fine with her. Exciting, even. A relief quite frankly, if being a wife meant you had to act all into football. They chewed the rest of their entrées in a fine and nasty silence.

"Port!" she heard Edward saying with that combination of gusto and good manners that she now despised in him, and would forever afterward. "Remember how sometimes at my apartment in Philadelphia we used to drink port?"

But now it was Cassandra who asked: "Do you remember . . . ?"

"What?"

"Do you remember what else happened the weekend of the Harvard-Yale game? Do you remember that woman who harassed us?"

"Where are you going with this?"

"That woman. The black woman. Maybe *that* helps to narrow it down for you?" She smiled at him wickedly, and Edward got a sinking feeling about what was coming.

"Remember after we got out of the game, that black woman who was driving down the street in a nasty beat-up old car and rolled down her window just to shout *Fuck you!* at us. Remember her?"

"Some people, because of their histories, feel so disenfranchised . . ." Edward began, preferring to take a sociological tone.

"You know why she did that, Edward?"

"All right, Cassandra. Why?"

"Because she knew. She knew we were a really fucking annoying couple. *Smug.* We were *smug.*"

I am not so smug anymore, she was thinking; smugness being the divine privilege of youth, and she was not, as had just dawned on her here at the Harvard Club, quite so young anymore.

"Hey—"

"By the way, Edward, that black woman, that woman in her nasty old car, I think I can kind of begin to understand her rage. Can you? No, no way, you're way too one percent."

(Just the previous fall in downtown Manhattan there had been the tumult, and finally the anticlimax, of the Occupy Wall Street movement, from which Cassandra had cadged this phrase and during which Gala was to remark to Sylvie on another occasion when the two of them met up for brunch in Fort Greene: "You know something funny? In the old days I would have gone over to Occupy Wall Street to meet guys, but now that just seems *dirty.* Now it just seems so much cleaner to meet them online." "Totally, totally," Sylvie had agreed, lunging at an elderberry cocktail.)

"Hey," Edward attempted to soothe Cassandra, "let's not get carried away here."

"Oh, please. Where more relevant to bring up the one percent than at the Harvard Club, I ask you?"

She could sympathize with it, she felt. The viewpoint of that so-called disenfranchised black woman on the decayed streets of New Haven that day. (Could New Haven possibly have been so decayed when Franny voyaged there? It did not seem possible.) She believed it because she was a fallen woman, not from virtue, which nobody took seriously anymore, but from class, which people did.

"This is just *another* reason I'm going to marry Keller. She doesn't go around making scenes at the Harvard Club."

"Where better to make them, though? The masses ought to storm these places, they ought to—"

"Jesus."

"Oh forget it. I don't like you, Edward, I've never liked you, and I can't believe I ever fucked a Republican, but! That reminds me. Are you sure you wouldn't like to get a room?"

Edward didn't. That was for Cassandra the last straw. She got up from the table and, in doing so, even skipped dessert, a tactical error that later on, in the cab, she regretted. But d'Orsay heels are great for an exit like that and her hips swayed deliciously. Plus! She gave all of the more compatible, but bored, couples dining at the Harvard Club that night something interesting to talk about after she had gone.

CHAPTER 41

Gala, Gala, do you believe the part about the *port*?"

This was Cassandra the next morning, on the phone. Although she and Gala couldn't be bothered to make the effort to see each other in person all that much anymore, the two of them still did G-chat and sometimes even talked on the phone; Gala was still for Cassandra a Sylvie stand-in, the girlfriend on whom she liked to download her woes. "He thought I'd be all placated if he offered me some *port*. Who the hell drinks port anymore anyway? And! He said we could have dessert and everything, like I was this little girl who needed to be offered an éclair from the dessert cart, or I would throw a tantrum. Do you think that's the way he sees me?"

That's the way everybody sees you, Gala thought, but said: "That's rough, the part about the tennis. This reminds me, I had this really cool thing last summer with this guy who was a washed-up tennis pro but still pretty hot. He picked me up at McCarren Park one Saturday. Didn't you meet him? No, I guess that must have been Sylvie."

"Oh?" Cassandra tried but failed to make her tone of voice sound casual. "Is Sylvie dating anybody these days?"

"I thought she was Sicilian dead to you."

"Yeah, but."

"Sylvie just works all the time and you already knew that. Just like she already knew that you would still be sleeping with Edward even after he broke up with you. You're onto each other. Friendships like yours: you can't get rid of that shit."

"Can't you?"

"Well, maybe you can or maybe you can't. *I don't know.* Oh my

God, Cassandra, you're making me late to work again!" Gala had a new job now, with decent benefits even, at an up-and-coming social media think tank in Chelsea. Her supervisors were guys and they all had crushes on her and she had already gotten a raise. Gala Gubelman was moving on with her life. Most nights after work she went out for OKCupid dates on the High Line. Gone were the carefree days of letting guys pick her up on the subway, or even in the more salubrious setting of McCarren Park. Gala knew what wise women approaching the age of thirty all know, which is not to leave the master plan of their lives up to fate. "I have to go, Cassandra. But next time, Jesus, Cassandra, text me, that's what the ladies are doing with each other these days."

"Ladies? Ladies, you say? I thought that texting was for men. I thought that women still wanted to talk to each other."

"Not so much, I don't think."

"Why not?"

"*Because they're busy.*"

"Does Cassandra even have a job, or what?" Sylvie wanted to know.

This was later on that evening, when she and Gala were having dinner at her place. They had a standing Wednesday night date in which they agreed to stay in and cook and smoke pot together. Outside it was snowing. Inside Sylvie's Chinese paper lantern cast a homey pink glow on the surroundings. The radiator hissed. Before answering, Gala peeled off her mittens. Red mittens, old ones, hand-knit by some girl who had been in love with her at Bennington. Every time it snowed Gala Gubelman wore those mittens and every time she wore them she thought not of that girl, whose name she could not even remember, but of that time and place and of being young and desired. In the years since Bennington she had had many lovers, but at some point in her mid-twenties she had stopped going to bed with other girls and made the pursuit of men—stolid, not so interesting as other girls usually were, preferable only for the width of their shoulders or the remarkable feats of their cocks—her focus. Something of the poetry of sex had gone out of it right around this time, Gala had noticed. That girl, whoever she was, had threatened to throw herself into the lake in North Bennington after Gala had rejected her. Nothing had come of the threat but the high romanticism of it had been enough to make on Gala an enduring impression.

"Uh, she job-hunts, I think."

"Doesn't everybody?"

"Good point."

"I mean, seriously!"

Sylvie was indignant. But then, Sylvie was always indignant. That had not changed.

Gala pushed a lock of hair behind her ear, concentrating. She was in the middle of unpacking groceries: toothsome produce she had picked up after work at the Union Square Farmers Market. Now that they were almost thirty, she and Sylvie were not so painfully broke anymore. They could afford such indulgences from time to time. They had even started to give dinner parties and to go to them. The plan tonight was to make a very ambitious, multi-layered frittata. Sylvie had gone so far as to buy an expensive cheese around the corner at the Greene Grape, something she would not have seen fit to do in the old days.

"Wait, she's not working right now, I don't think, but she *was* working recently. Fern Morgenthal set her up with something— something at this restaurant she was working at, I think . . ."

"Cassandra *waitressing*?"

"No, no, I think she was just a hostess actually. That was it."

"Oh well, is that all? If she quit then, I really can't blame her. You don't make any money doing that."

"Yeah, but. I don't think she *quit*, I think Fern said she was *fired*, eventually. I forget why."

"Oh."

Sylvie would have liked to blame her for this but couldn't, not when you considered how many times she and Gala had been fired from various jobs in New York City themselves. There was something kind of exhilarating about the experience of being fired, Sylvie thought, remembering. She could still recall one fabulous, fiery exit she had made, storming out of the office of that fashion agency where she had briefly worked in a pair of white leather short shorts that she knew she looked totally hot in. The middle-aged fashion editors had all glared at her, enraged. They must have imagined that with her youth and her beauty and the unblemished golden backs of her thighs she had it all. And I never even knew, Sylvie thought. I never even knew how lucky I was. Then, too, she remembered, there had been the early, frantically sexual love affair with Bitsy Citron's older brother, Ludo. The collapsed cardboard boxes and unfinished canvases of his studio; the immortal occasion of their final parting in which she had hurled a roast chicken from FreshDirect onto his lap, the grease splattering his expensive Swedish jeans. Artists, Sylvie fumed to herself. Artists were the worst. She took it as a personal affront sometimes to think that they alone might have managed to preserve some of the youthful idealism and high-mindedness that she had lost since college, and would never get back again.

"Hey, do you have a Le Creuset pan or anything like that?" Gala asked all of a sudden, getting sick of talking about Cassandra. They were always talking about Cassandra, it seemed. "I'm wondering what I should cook the frittata in."

"Sure, sure," said Sylvie smoothly, and reached for a wonderful old mustard yellow one hanging from a hook on the wall.

"Oh my God! This is *great*. This is *gorgeous*. I've been wanting to get one just like it." They had reached the age, also, when buying new cooking appliances was even more exciting to them than buying new clothes. "Where did you get it?"

"My grandmother," Sylvie lied, and no more was said about the Le Creuset pan or Cassandra for the rest of the evening.

CHAPTER 42

S ome months later, when she was so broke she'd resorted to stealing rolls of toilet paper out of the bathrooms of the restaurants in her neighborhood, Cassandra got a job at an upscale baby boutique, with locations in SoHo and Williamsburg. The store was called Forget-Me-Not. All of the girls who worked there liked to give dinner parties and had French names: Nanette, Claire, Rosabel, Therese. No doubt grim old Tish, still rotting away in Harvard Square behind the counter at Black Currant, would never have approved of these names, or of the girls themselves and their outlandish expectations.

In her free time, Claire was a platinum-haired, raven-lashed aspiring pop star, who enjoyed the flexibility of working at the boutique because it allowed her to go on tour in Europe twice a year. Therese and her fiancé owned an organic soul food truck and recently had gotten a cookbook deal. Rosabel had delicate jet-black eyebrows and was a ballet dancer. Nanette was, fresh from Bard, a painting major, and the youngest of them all. Cassandra, now thirty, was the oldest.

The owner's six-year-old son was named Sheridan. Her husband was a sculptor and high-end carpenter, who had installed a magical play station made out of silver-birch bark in the back of the store, so that parents could browse the color-coded racks of organic cotton clothing in peace. The domed ceiling was the perfect shade of Botticelli blue, tender yet unisex. So this was what New York City had come to in the twenty-first century, Cassandra thought. Galleries for toddlers.

At the SoHo location, the clientele consisted of European and

Japanese tourists turned out in bright scarves and buttery driving loafers. Or stylists would drop in from *Martha Stewart* or *Lucky*, hoping to borrow a handmade "soft sculpture" cloud mobile for a photo shoot. Childless gay couples bought the white shag footstools that had been designed specially for Forget-Me-Not and intended for nurseries. Cassandra could handle all of this; she could meet these people's gazes head on.

But at the Williamsburg location, where she worked, none too willingly, on occasion, it was another story. She would begin the day on the unfashionable streets of Astoria and about an hour later get off the L train on Bedford Avenue, where the universe exploded into a flurry of black tights, fluffy jackets, and rakish, rock-star-style hats worn with curious aplomb on members of both sexes. And not infrequently, Cassandra couldn't even tell the difference between them.

At the store, too, gender continued to pose a conundrum for Cassandra in these dubious modern times. The owner, whose name was Mavis Asher, boasted to customers of Sheridan's wardrobe, "Don't worry, I put my boy in tights." Cassandra would hang some exquisitely distressed rose-colored henley T-shirts on the girls' rack, only to have Mavis up and move them to the boys', as though it should have been perfectly obvious that antique rose was *the* color for little boys this season.

The floors in the Williamsburg store had been handmade from rustic, sloping wood by Mavis's husband, and even more than little Sheridan and his tights, those floors were her pride and joy. The first thing you did if you opened the Williamsburg store was mop the floor with a terrifying, to Cassandra, combination of boiling water and Mop & Glo. She had made the mistake of asking Mavis, the first time, "But is the teakettle a fire hazard?" It was old and creaky, sputtering at a perilous angle on top of the toilet.

"Of course it's a fire hazard," said Mavis, adding, without further ado: "The trick is, the water has to be boiling. Hot, hot, hot.

And you rinse out the mop in the sink, you don't ever put it back in the bucket. Four times minimum, rinse, rinse, rinse. Mop & Glo in the bucket, *and* you sprinkle it on the floor as you go along. You put some muscle into it, see."

And then Mavis did a demonstration, spinning her small, yogic body round and round and swishing the mop back and forth with demonic vigor.

Mavis, like all Brooklyn women in their indeterminate late thirties who own their own brownstones, spent boundless amounts of energy exerting the superiority of her opinion on the subject of all earthly comforts. She "only" used certain brands of paper towels or toilet paper (neither of them, Cassandra noted, organic, for organic paper goods were often thin and Mavis preferred fluffy). The hand soap in the bathroom had to be geranium, and the slender, amber diffusers arranged in the store bergamot.

The specter of that hissing teakettle, meanwhile, loomed large in Cassandra's imagination, for she still didn't have any health insurance. So, in the event of an accident, she would have to add the emergency room bill to her other woes.

Another task—also involving Cassandra's least favored element, fire, heat—was steaming every single piece of clothing before it went out on the floor. Everything, from Finnish ski parkas to French sun hats, had to be crisp. One afternoon while steaming a pair of eighty-eight-dollar skinny black Parisian jeans for a twelve-to-eighteen-month-old, it came to Cassandra that what she felt like was Lily Bart, near the end of *The House of Mirth*, when having run up ruinous debts and cast off from society, she is reduced to taking a job in a millinery shop. That settled it, Cassandra thought. She had not become an English major for nothing.

A naturally vivacious personality, Cassandra was an excellent salesperson. She swiftly memorized all of the brand names and where their clothes and toys were made and the things to tell customers about them—the tunics and bloomers that had been "designed in Paris and woven in Nepal"; the German building blocks, dense as the Black Forest itself; the Spanish brand that was very "fashion forward" and the French one that was like "A.P.C. for babies." And then there were the rubber duckies, one of the store's best sellers. Not ordinary, cuddly-type rubber duckies, but instead rather architectural-looking and special, fashioned by some "green" Japanese design company.

But retail—not a line of work she had ever had to stoop to before—also required a certain physical swiftness she sorely lacked. It wasn't only the teakettle and the steamer. It was also—and much more relentlessly—gift wrapping. In Cassandra's universe, there existed no right angles; she couldn't see them and she certainly couldn't shape them. Gifts at Forget-Me-Not were wrapped in gray tissue paper and tied with mushroom-colored silk ribbons, colors like blue and pink being far too vulgar. The Forget-Me-Not stamp—the logo of merry bluebirds and tiny, curling flowers had been designed by Mavis's husband; was there a thing that man could not do?—was to be pressed firmly in the lower right-hand corner of the gift box. Unless it was Cassandra doing the gift wrapping, and then the stamp might end up in any of the four corners, for to her they were all the same.

Cassandra would never forget the sight of the sheer animal panic in the formerly gentle eyes of Therese, the girl with the organic soul food truck and a bosomy, maternal soul, the day she first saw Cassandra try to gift wrap. Before moving to New York, Therese had been an art teacher at a progressive middle school in Los Angeles, and like all teachers, she prided herself on being able to address different learning styles. But *this*. When she, Therese, tried to demonstrate how to smooth the corners, Cassandra attempted the same motion, or rather, pretended to be attempting it, only to have the tissue paper rustle up and out in all directions as if singed by electricity—really, it was a most extraordinary sight.

And Mavis, the first time she saw Cassandra gift wrap, though she had already heard dark murmurs of this travesty sweeping among the other girls, thought: Is the new girl handicapped, in some subtle, creepy way I failed to detect during the interview? You never knew with people, these days. There were so many free-floating afflictions and conditions out there. But just what was the name for this one? she wondered.

She'd liked the idea of having a Bennington grad on the staff. Also, Cassandra had interviewed so beautifully. Little could she have known that interviewing would turn out to be her only skill! And if the girl couldn't gift wrap or mop the damn floor that well either, come to think of it, then maybe she'd better stick with hiring underemployed art students. English majors were probably better off in offices, although everybody knew those types of jobs barely existed anymore. Oh well, figured Mavis. That's just too bad for them.

And meanwhile, there remained Cassandra, struck dumb at the foot of the gift wrap station, a haunted expression in her big blue eyes.

CHAPTER 43

Now ordinarily, Sylvie wouldn't have been caught dead in the likes of Williamsburg, having woken up there too many mornings in random, scuzzy lofts from one-night stands in her early twenties. But this afternoon she was there on business. It was a gentle, thawing, pale-yellow day at the beginning of April, one of those days at the turning of a season when people feel at their best, full of lightness and possibility, and even being in Williamsburg couldn't put Sylvie in a bad mood. A new gourmet foods store, named Shallot, had just opened up on Bedford Avenue, with a made-in-Brooklyn theme, and wouldn't you know, it was carrying Sylvie's brand of homemade syrups and jams. She was going there today to drop off her new flavors for spring, for naturally, at Shallot everything had to be seasonal.

With this in mind, Sylvie was replacing the winter's jars of brandied-cherry marmalade with bottles of rhubarb-rosewater syrup. The store's owners, Annie and Laurel, were going to use it as a mix in their homemade ginger ale, as well as sell the individual bottles on their peeling white-painted wooden shelves. Shallot had been designed to look like a country store, and the fully restored, fat-bellied, blue-trimmed vintage refrigerator to the right of the door even had its own name, Lucien.

The girls behind the counter all wore chambray aprons and vintage scarves in their hair, and to Sylvie they all seemed extraordinarily young. Imagine being one of those girls, she thought. Imagine still working for somebody else. She shuddered, thinking back to the crummy jobs and tyrannical, idiot bosses of her youth.

See, she had been correct all along. She could run her own business and she could do better; she was a born entrepreneur. Sylvie's business—named Clementine's Picnic—was doing splendidly. Those suckers—among them Sylvie's former employers—lapped this shit up: the joke never got old, with Sylvie. The corners of her quick black eyes crinkled in laughter, just to think of it. She'd shown them! She and her lemonade stand. She'd been right about everything. She'd said those morons would pay two-fifty a cupcake, and they did.

Come May, she planned to set up the lemonade stand again, hiring other people to work it so that she could focus on the big-picture business operations. Her plan was to hire only really hot girls, because they'd be sure to attract foot traffic, then regular male customers, who would come to buy lemonade and cupcakes as an excuse to flirt with them. Sylvie glanced again at the girls behind the Shallot counter. Were any of *them* hot enough? She wouldn't be above poaching them from Annie and Laurel, if they were. But no. These girls were cute but, on the whole, too wholesome-looking, and Clementine's Picnic had use for only complete and total babes. She'd make them wear, like, gingham hot pants or something . . . Yeah, gingham would go well with the whole "picnic" theme. Maybe she'd look into getting gingham tablecloths this year. A classic blue and white, maybe, or that soft, sherbetlike orange . . .

Sylvie still dearly loved a bargain and never saw any reason to spend more than she had to, but it was so nice, for the first time in her life, to be able to afford things. Not only for the good of the business, but for herself; ever since she'd started to make such a success of Clementine's Picnic, she'd been able to pay off all of her back rent to Pete the landlord, and was even starting to build up her credit again.

And she was making enough money to pay for her own health insurance.

This was Sylvie's dream come true.

Annie and Laurel greeted her with pleasing fanfare, proclaiming her rhubarb-rosewater syrup "absolutely amazing." They also had a check for her based on sales of her brandied-cherry marmalade, which they told her had been "a huge hit" around Valentine's Day. So, wonder of wonders, the check was even bigger than expected.

"Excuse me," said one of the girls behind the counter, for all the world as if Sylvie were a celebrity and she was about to ask for her autograph, "are you Sylvie Furst?"

"Yup."

"*The* Sylvie Furst? The girl who started the lemonade stand?"

"Yup."

"Like, *the* lemonade stand, the one that was on the corner of Fort Greene Park?"

"Yup. That's the one."

"God, we'd love to be able to afford to live in Fort Greene," the girl said, gesturing to the other girl behind the counter. "This is my roommate, Ellie. And I'm Abigail." Shyly, both girls put out their hands. "But we looked and looked, and we just couldn't afford it, so now we live in Bed-Stuy."

The poor things, thought Sylvie: girls named Ellie and Abigail in Bed-Stuy. What a racket New York City was, when you really thought about it.

"Oh, but lots of people are living there now," said Sylvie, for clearly the people who had lived there before, for generations and generations, did not count. "The fact is, I got in on the Fort Greene wave years ago. Really, I was one of the first. Just lucky, I guess."

"That's so cool," said Ellie, "the way you just started a lemonade stand on the corner, just like that. And now—now, you're like, this really cool businesswoman!"

Both of them had noted Sylvie's products flying off the shelves at Shallot, and the sight had filled them with a wonderful, swelling feeling of hope they had seldom enjoyed since moving to the city after graduation last June.

"We love to bake," said Abigail. "At Mount Holyoke, we had this cook club we used to host in our dorm every Friday night. Actually, Ellie's gingerbread used to be sold at the South Hadley farmers' market. We used to go and volunteer there on Saturday mornings. It was really cool."

Mount Holyoke, thought Sylvie grimly to herself. So that explained it. They might have been a lesbian couple, these two, or maybe they just hadn't gotten laid by a real man in a while, which was so frequently, and tragically, the case in Brooklyn, that she really couldn't blame them for that. Perhaps that was what accounted for the rather neutered, folksy quality the two of them had, standing there in those silly chambray aprons. She bet they had a hell of a work ethic, so maybe she'd hire them to make jams or bottle the syrups or something. Why—a glorious inspiration struck her—girls like this were so desperate and dumb, maybe they'd even do it *for free*.

Now that Sylvie herself was higher up on the New York City food chain, owning her own business, she was absolutely delighted that the economy made it so easy to exploit the young and willing workforce.

Sylvie left Shallot, promising to stay in touch with Ellie and Abigail. Afterward, Abigail turned to Ellie and said: "Oh my God, she's so cool. Do you think maybe she'd ever hire us?"

"You know, she has such a great local business model, I think I'd even work for her for free."

"Oh, totally," said Abigail, and then she and Ellie, their futures now all aglitter with limitless opportunities, went back to restocking the orange-and-white-striped biodegradable paper straws made by a fashionable Brooklyn-based design company that also made cute stationery.

Sylvie had been planning to go back to Fort Greene after finishing up her errands at Shallot, but then she remembered that there was this really great baby boutique on one of the side streets.

Clementine's birthday was coming up in the first week of April. Maybe she'd stop by that store and pick her up a present.

Clementine was turning four years old and speaking in full, melodic sentences in her soap-bubble voice. Sylvie adored her as much as ever, and really did consider the little girl for whom she had named her business to be her good luck charm. Sometimes it seemed that her fortunes had turned around not only with meeting Clementine but—more recently—with getting rid of that bitch, Cassandra.

Sylvie turned down a side street off Bedford Avenue, walking toward where she remembered the baby boutique being. Oh yes, there it was, she recognized it by the pink tutu hanging in the window. Forget-Me-Not! Oh, Sylvie thought, her heart warming up at all things child-related, what a cute name for a store.

Sylvie, forever business-savvy, was wondering if Forget-Me-Not might be interested in stocking some of her products. Her syrups would go over so well at little girls' birthday parties, or might even be enjoyed by grown women at baby showers: there was a potential market here. She made a note to herself to get the name of the store's owner before she left.

It was Sylvie who recognized Cassandra first, for Cassandra, preoccupied with steaming a tiny cerise-colored pinafore with white rickrack trim, was too flustered to pay attention to customers at the same time, which was what the job description required. As a matter of fact, it was Cassandra's inexpert style of steaming the pinafore that gave her away for certain. Otherwise, there were many other shopgirls in Williamsburg whom Cassandra in some general sense resembled. But no one but Cassandra would stare at the handle of the steamer from which the heat was escaping with such naked terror in her eyes, and furthermore, she was steaming the poor pinafore not with the firm, up-and-down motion Sylvie would have used but with desperate, random jerks. Sylvie stared, and stared, Cassandra still failing to look up at her. God, Sylvie thought to herself, it would be fun watching Cassandra steam clothing, if only it weren't also so frightening. Since Cassandra wasn't looking at her yet, Sylvie now took a second to slyly text Gala Gubelman:

OMG CASSANDRA!!! I RAN INTO CASSANDRA.

Gala was on the pulse and from her cubicle texted right back:

OMG. TELL, TELL!!! XOXO

Then Cassandra, apparently finished with the pinafore, took it off the hook of the steamer and put it on a clothing rack, though Sylvie and her gimlet eye could tell that it was still wrinkled. It was then that Cassandra, hanging the steamer handle on the hook at what was clearly the wrong angle, glanced up and saw her.

Sylvie.

CHAPTER 44

W ell. Cassandra had been expecting this encounter for some time. So had Sylvie, though never could she have predicted these particular circumstances. She'd gotten off too easy, Cassandra figured, not having run into Sylvie yet, since that morning at the apartment. So this comeuppance was only her due. After all, neither she nor Sylvie had ever believed in life letting them off the hook; they believed in worst-case scenarios, small and large humiliations, consequences. In their own words: *This would happen to us!*

But they were no longer an us, and hadn't been for quite some time. They might never use that word quite so casually ever again, though Sylvie still felt a kind of transcendent connection with Clementine that Cassandra, these days, had accepted no longer feeling with anyone.

Sylvie studied Cassandra. She had on a rather beatnik-style ensemble of black leotard and cigarette pants, unrelieved by any color or cutesy touches to speak of. But, Sylvie thought to herself with a twinge of betrayal, Cassandra wears dresses! It was unfair, her going beyond the bounds of what Sylvie would have predicted. Indeed, once Cassandra laid to rest the steamer and regained, relatively speaking, her composure, Sylvie noticed something altered about her appearance altogether. And then it came to her: she was no longer a genteel Cambridge girl who seldom strayed far from the outskirts of Brattle Street. She had gotten that look, that look that people had when they moved to New York and which Sylvie herself had had for years, the one that had to do with a certain fearless way of carrying yourself. Cassandra no longer looked like a girl, period. She looked like a woman and a woman who lived in New York City, at that.

And also: she'd gained a little bit of weight, Sylvie, who used to have her exact measurements memorized, couldn't help but notice. Which must mean that she was single, because Cassandra wasn't the type to let her figure go if she had a man.

Sylvie stood up straight and started to approach Cassandra with the indefatigable confidence so surprising in a woman of her petite stature. But then just as she did, Cassandra put out her hand and said hello first, even going so far as to say *Hello, Sylvie*, which was actually—Sylvie had to admit—a pretty classy move. She'd just been planning on saying *Hey*, and even that had seemed to her a far more gracious overture than the situation required.

But then hey, Cassandra was working! Sylvie was a customer. Cassandra had to be polite to her. Except, wait a minute—Cassandra was working in a baby boutique? *Cassandra hated babies. Cassandra had always hated babies.* If she had to stoop to a retail job, and in this economy even Sylvie couldn't blame her for doing that, how did she end up here? Shouldn't she be working at a store that sold French soaps and perfumes, or one of those pretentious downtown lingerie shops selling satin cat-eye sleeping masks and vibrators that looked like tiny, precious pieces of modern art and went by Italian names? She could definitely be a crazy lady in a vintage clothing shop. She could work at a bookstore. Anything but *this*. Sylvie was of the opinion that Cassandra, that lunatic, shouldn't even be allowed near children. As if the girl's sheer damaged nature could have contaminated the precious threads of gently rumpled fair-trade Indian cotton.

Here in Forget-Me-Not, a silence having clotted between the two women, Sylvie looked down at a display case and absently stroked the rounded toe of a red ballet slipper (handmade in Munich, Cassandra could have informed her, if only she'd asked). But instead Cassandra said the one magical word that was left in the English language, the one word that briefly, for Sylvie, erased years of disappointment and betrayal. That word was Cassandra gently asking: "Clementine?"

At this very moment, Gala was texting her:

SYLVIE, WHERE ARE YOU? I'M DYING TO HEAR EVERYTHING!
HAPPY HOUR TONIGHT, YES?

But Sylvie ignored this and answered Cassandra: "Of course. Her birthday's coming up. She's going to be four."

Like she's her mother, thought Cassandra with the old, easy scorn, bragging about birthdays. So nothing had changed. Except that Sylvie did look older—more settled, less savage and hungry perhaps; hard to believe that this same woman who was now a stranger and must be treated like a customer once had chased her around an apartment littered with cupcake wrappers in her underwear. Funny. She rather missed that girl in her underwear, the sweet, pungent wildness of her; the white-hot intensity of her conviction.

Cassandra gestured to the red ballet slipper, and said, "I remembered that Clementine always liked deep pinks and reds."

"And shoes, remember."

"Oh, right. Shoes, too."

They remembered other things, too, and might even have said them, but face-to-face, nothing came naturally. So Cassandra suggested that what Clementine would really like for her birthday was a pair of similar red ballet slippers with pink grosgrain bows on them (these shoes were made in Paris, which was far "more chic" in Cassandra's mind than Munich). Sylvie was dying not to accept Cassandra's recommendation, but had to admit she always did have great taste. Those shoes were just perfect for Clementine, and even Sylvie didn't want to allow her spite toward Cassandra to get in the way of a gift for a child. Cassandra felt the same way, which said something, however small, for the moral development of these two young women.

Cassandra rang up the sale in silence. Sylvie, fishing through a porcelain candy dish of star barrettes next to the register, picked out a red one for Clementine and added it to her purchase. She loved styling Clementine's hair, which was getting thicker now and soon would be long enough for Sylvie to do up in a French braid.

She wanted to tell Cassandra all about Clementine's Picnic; she wanted Cassandra, more than anyone in the world, to know what a success she'd made of the lemonade stand that had come between them. It should have been so easy, letting it drop. But somehow—even Sylvie, whose native quickness was the defining quality of her personality—couldn't pull this off.

And if Cassandra had been able to tell Sylvie things anymore, if on this beautiful, champagnelike afternoon they had let go of old resentments and loathing and if golden words had poured forth between them, if they had dashed out of the store, girls again, looping arms down the sun-kissed avenue, she might have told her all about the abortion she'd had not long after she started working at Forget-Me-Not. The child might have been Edward's, or it might have been somebody else's, somebody who didn't matter. Gala's prophecy had come true: *Everybody sleeps with so many new guys their first year in New York.* She had now been there for two, and had slept with many.

And in the end none of it had mattered, for she'd gone by herself to a clinic far out in some blasted, treeless nameless section of Queens, where the operation was performed by a harried woman speaking butchered English in that least melodic of accents, Chinese. Cassandra to Sylvie, so many years ago: *What if Chinese becomes the universal language?*

The night she discovered that she was pregnant, Cassandra had gone to an art opening in TriBeCa at which she'd run into none other than Angelica Rocky-Divine, just back in the States after years of dancing for a burlesque troupe in Vienna and sporting a black velvet *le smoking* jacket with peacock blue satin tails.

"The doctors all say I'll never dance again," sighed Angelica in the moonlight. Cassandra had joined her outside on the stoop of the gallery for a smoke break. Apparently she'd brought back from Europe assorted injuries—fractures and such. "So fuck it, I might just have to become a *yoga instructor* like everybody else."

"Oh, no," said Cassandra, recalling Angelica's bright, unshackled beauty and the way she used to spin naked at the End of the World.

"But enough about me!" Angelica stubbed out her cigarette with a spike heel, gorgeous and predatory all over again. In spite of the injuries she still refused to submit to practical footwear. "How are *you*, Cassandra?"

"Pregnant."

"Oh, is that all? Well, not to worry! I know this *dear, dear man* who's an abortionist on Park Avenue. My senior year at Nightingale-Bamford, I don't know what I would have done without him! Did I ever tell you? I was having this totally torrid affair with *our beekeeper*."

"Hey, wait, *Nightingale-Bamford*, did you just say? I always thought you went to Spence!"

"Oh no, you must be confusing me with Bitsy Citron. Vicky Lalage, she went to Chapin."

"Oh, right."

Cassandra still had an outsider's eagerness to place these things.

But even with Angelica's referral the Park Avenue abortionist turned out to be far too expensive. Cassandra had thought of calling Gala for advice, then decided against it because she'd remained friends with Sylvie and Cassandra hadn't wanted Gala to gossip. It was Fern Morgenthal, of all people, who'd directed Cassandra to the place in Queens; Fern had been knocked up by the older artist she was sleeping with, her first winter in New York. The artist kept the abortionist on retainer, not that this meant that he ever paid for his services of course. The girls he bedded were perfectly willing to pay for other things, he couldn't help but notice, so why not expect them to pay for their own abortions, too?

But now, she realized, there were so many things that Cassandra might have discussed for hours and hours about the abortion with Sylvie: how, if the child had been Edward's, she was most certainly the only woman in *that* waiting room who had been knocked up by a Harvard graduate; how, because she still didn't have any health insurance, she hadn't gotten a checkup since then, and because the Chinese woman had been so brutal, she feared that she might now never be able to bear children—not that she wanted them exactly, but still. But still, she could picture herself saying to Sylvie, over pieces of burned toast slathered with Nutella, I'd still like to think I had a choice in the matter.

Breeding condition, she sometimes wondered, thinking back to that queer phrase of Sylvie's. Was she still in breeding condition?

She would have told Sylvie the story of what had happened to her just days after she'd had the abortion and found herself back behind the counter at Forget-Me-Not. It was a Sunday afternoon and the store was full of young mothers and babies in strollers, so full of strollers, in fact, that they kept on knocking into one another. Cassandra, first feeling self-pity and melancholy, then felt—rage! And, thus compelled, spoke right up to one of the mothers.

"Why don't you leave your baby on the stoop? Nobody's going to take it."

That was the exact moment she got over the abortion, she realized later on, because one can draw strength from rage but almost never from sadness alone.

But no, Sylvie and Cassandra didn't say any of this to each other; they didn't succumb to the languor of the weather. Cassandra finished ringing up the sale and handed Sylvie Clementine's birthday presents in a Forget-Me-Not bag. She thought of saying "Good-bye," but then decided against it, for it occurred to her that they had already said that word to each other in no uncertain terms. So all she volunteered was:

"Well, anyway. I hope that Clementine likes the shoes."

"She will," Sylvie said, and turned to walk toward the door.

Crushing some numbers in her head, she thought: So Cassandra must *not* have given me her employee discount. Oh, well, fuck it. She could afford things now, and anyway, this was just further proof that neither of them owed each other anything anymore.

But then, just as she was about to leave, the sight of that pink tutu swaying in the window and shimmering in the April light filled her with a sudden, splintering sadness. Why, on such a lovely afternoon, things going well, bills paid, credit restored, the check from Shallot snug in her pocket, *her dreams come true*, damn it, should Sylvie feel nothing but smallness and ingratitude? Why should it take a toddler's tutu to make her see a kind of innocence—a capacity for dazzlement—that had long gone missing from her life, and that no sense of earthly security could compensate for?

It wasn't that she missed Cassandra. No. She still believed that she was well rid of her, and she was proud, too, of all that she'd accomplished in the last year on her own. So it must be something else that she missed, something else that was lost.

Suddenly, she remembered herself that first year in New York City, the girl with the glamorous Italian haircut and the expertly applied wings of silver eyeliner, wheeling down some street flashing with lights late at night. She still went into Manhattan then; she went everywhere. She was up for anything. What struck her was the same revelation she'd had on running into Vicky Lalage that day on the sidewalk of Fort Greene: *I was so young then.* She was so young and so beautiful. She could say that now with perfect composure, without even sounding conceited, because that girl was a stranger to her and she knew that now.

Something funny had happened to Sylvie ever since she'd gotten health insurance. Although she was grateful to finally have it, she couldn't help but notice: the world didn't seem quite so jagged and wild anymore, once you were insured, which also meant that it didn't seem quite so alive. When you had health insurance, and after so many years of fending for yourself without it, the blades of knives had all turned dull, the taxis didn't hurtle down the streets quite so fast. Why, they weren't even quite so yellow anymore, that gorgeous, iconic yellow one associates, almost more than any other color, with the streets of New York City.

She wanted that feeling back, that rounded softness in the eyes, dew in the pores, hope in the soul—all those telltale signs that those Mount Holyoke girls, Ellie and Abigail, had not yet lost. This was the same virgin quality that Cassandra had sniffed and found so provoking in Fern and the same quality that those other young women, the modern dancers, Chelsea Hayden-Smith and Beverly Tinker-Jones, in plummeting to their early deaths from the windows of the dance studio of the performing arts building, would never, ever have stolen from them. They flew, quite literally, out of this world with it intact.

Sylvie, remembering that she prided herself on being a realist, rallied to her senses. To hell with this droopy, mournful feeling, she thought. Aha! She got an idea . . .

(Also, she decided, she would text Gala back and say yes to happy hour tonight. She would regale Gala with how pitiful Cassandra was, and she would get drunk and be light and witty and cruel.)

What she was picturing, now, was not her younger self in New York but in Cambridge, the sweet, dreary hamlet of her vanished girlhood, that place that in its curious, cobwebby mixture of intellectualism and innocence was so remote to her that she seldom even thought of it anymore, in Cambridge one purplish gray winter morning with Cassandra beside her: standing at the counter of Black Currant and tormenting poor, hobbled Tish, aslant on that mysterious pair of crutches, by asking her with a big smile on her face for extra cranberries on her oatmeal. That girl! That girl with the beautiful, clear skin, beautiful, compact body, black leggings, and motorcycle boots! That girl, with the glittering callousness of youth upon her! That was the girl who she wanted, for the purposes of today's encounter, to pretend to continue to be.

Sylvie straightened her spine and pivoted her body back toward the register.

"Hey, Cassandra," she announced. "I'm so sorry, I must have forgotten to ask! Do you think that I could have this gift-wrapped?"

CHAPTER 45

n later years it sometimes seemed to Cassandra that her life as a grown woman had only officially commenced with leaving Sylvie's apartment that fateful Saturday morning and with moving into Pansy Chapin's. It also seemed that it was much easier, in her life as a grown woman, to fall in love than it was to make friends. This was one of the revelations of adult life that most surprised her; others were more easily accepted. And yet after Edward, she met somebody else. Then, when that fell apart, too, she met somebody after him, eventually. But she never did dare to call any other woman in her life by those words, so blameless on the surface, but so dangerous underneath, *my best friend.*

Pansy Chapin, too, evaporated: she eloped with her latest fiancé in Torcello, surrounded by a canopy of fruit trees, oleander, and roses in the exact same spot where she had been proposed to by the first of her fiancés, and the only one of them she ever truly loved, her senior year at Bennington. For even Pansy Chapin, when she was young, had had a heart. Even Pansy Chapin, when she was young, had had it broken. And then one night Pansy Chapin made her husband the perfect duck a l'orange and the perfect vermouth and water with the perfect lemon twist for his dinner and looked around her perfect house and at her perfect antiques and wept and wept. She and Cassandra were never to speak again after that fiasco they had over breaking the lease on that place on Seventy-Ninth and Second, which had resulted in the catastrophe of Cassandra having to pawn her great-grandmother's wedding silver, the lowest point of her life, lower even than that horrible day she had to schlep out to the end of the 7 train in Queens to go and get an abortion.

But still, Pansy Chapin had taught her things. It was Pansy, after all, who first had opened Cassandra's more virgin eyes to the rapture of sex positions that actually work in the shower, it was Pansy who had passed down to her the narcotic beauty ritual of rubbing one's entire body with a mixture of brown sugar and baby oil just before a rendezvous with a lover: something that Cassandra was to do throughout her life and the very scent of which stirred in her all of the agonies of desire.

And it was Pansy, too, silky, calculating little Pansy, out from such a tender age to nab a rich husband, who had possessed the wisdom to recognize that the only good reason to go to Bennington is to have something interesting to talk about at cocktail parties on Fifth Avenue later on. Even when she was long past the age when she should have dared to flaunt black leotards without a bra underneath but insisted nevertheless on doing exactly that, Cassandra noticed that she had only to mention having gone to Bennington in order to tickle in the average male animal of a certain generation and social class a reliable quickening of interest. This was the only legacy of her education that could be put to any practical use to speak of.

"Cassandra is a prostitute."

Thus spoke Gala Gubelman to Sylvie Furst. This was some years later at brunch.

"Not really!"

"Well, all right, not really. Not exactly. But I thought that word would get your attention."

"What now?"

"Well! She doesn't pay her own rent. Some old guy's been paying it for her. Also! He gives her jewelry. Sapphire earrings. She had them on. The last time I saw her."

"Hmph!"

"Big sapphires, too. Jumbo. Swaying. Absolutely fucking huge."

Sylvie was thinking, as she had the morning she bulldozed

down the flaking blue staircase of her apartment in her tiny floral underpants, bringing to Cassandra's mind Duchamp's *Nude Descending a Staircase, No. 2*, for one's liberal arts education comes floating back to one at the strangest of times, that money is better than sex. But this was interesting, commendable, even, what Cassandra had done, in apparently combining the two. At this period in her life, Sylvie was beginning to seek an exit strategy from her exit strategy, because Clementine's Picnic was struggling. The market for artisanal syrups was glutted, the "made in Brooklyn" model was getting overexposed. Sylvie had seen the future and it was in rooftop gardening. Her very first client was Vicky's mother, Rosa Lalage. And from there she was launched on another wondrous career, Sylvie Furst, Urban Landscaper. Right around this time, she also took up self-care and returned to Zumba dancing.

"Also!" Gala relished being up on all the alumni news. "Pansy Chapin is pregnant."

"*No!*"

"Yes!"

"That bitch."

They clinked glasses and asked for the check.

"Fuck," Gala fumed, tapping her forehead. "*Fuck!* Is this place cash only?"

"Yup," said Sylvie complacently, but did not offer to cover for her. Better not to, Sylvie had decided as a matter of principle. People ought to be able to look out for themselves. Dependency got sticky.

This meant that Gala had to run, huffing and puffing, to the nearest ATM. Bennington girls were not the cross-country type, and furthermore, now that she was in her thirties Gala had to watch her figure; she had started to get a little out of shape around the middle and was no longer as ripely, lavishly beautiful as she had been in college. None of them were.

When she got back from the ATM, she put cash down on the table and announced:

"Do you know that we've been out of college now for ten years?"

"Jesus. Ten years! Seriously?"

"Yes, seriously! Didn't you get the postcard in the mail about the ten-year reunion?"

"Oh, you know what? Probably not. I bet they have my old address on file."

"Oh, right, right. That explains it."

Sylvie no longer lived in the apartment in Fort Greene. The previous year Pete the landlord had sold the building for millions. The new owners had fixed it right up. She never went back. Though sometimes, sometimes that apartment and especially its bathroom, that old-world bathroom with its terra-cotta sink and its lavender-honey light, floated back to her in dreams, as it sometimes floated, unbeknownst to her, into Cassandra's. Both Sylvie and Cassandra went on to live in places with far better and certainly more comfortable bathrooms than that one, bathrooms that had decent water pressure, not to mention other modern amenities. And yet they missed it. That bathroom, ornamental, outdated, practically useless for the unromantic purposes a bathroom is meant to serve, was the one that they missed.

"I wouldn't go anyway," Sylvie said, of the reunion. "Are you going?"

"I don't know, honestly. Orpheus went back there to play a show last year and he said it's not the same."

"What's not the same?"

"Well, for one thing"—Gala revealed the following bombshell in a conspiratorial whisper—"Bennington is now *a non-smoking* campus."

"Get out!"

"I know! Outrageous! That's what Orpheus and I thought."

"This entire conversation is making me feel old."

"Me, too. And you know what else Orpheus said? He said he didn't even think that the girls they're letting in now are as hot as they used to be, either. He said they're just letting in, like, these boring preppy girls who weren't smart enough to get into Middlebury. They don't wear *leotards*. They don't do *art* . . ."

Neither Gala nor Sylvie had done anything resembling art in quite some time either, but this went unremarked. One didn't after college. Or only the very lucky or the very disciplined or, failing that, the very delusional ones still did. You had to grow up and accept this.

"The Bennington girl is a dying breed," said Sylvie sadly.

"I know! And we're the last of the species," Gala agreed with her, as, going Dutch, they settled the check.

CHAPTER 46

I t was not altogether untrue what Gala had said. Cassandra did
live off this man for a time until one day she didn't, anymore,
and she had to go and pawn those sapphire earrings. Worse than
that, much worse, she had to *get a job*. This was how she eventually
ended up as a coat-check girl at a steakhouse in midtown. One
night she checked the coat of Pansy Chapin's husband, Jock, who
was dining there on business but did not have any reason to recognize her or to know that this member of the subservient classes
and his cosseted wife had once been girls together on a hilltop in
Vermont.

But before this, long before, Cassandra had come to meet the
man she lived off one fine April evening at a party on Fifth Avenue,
to which she had been invited by Fern Morgenthal as her plus one.
What Fern had not bargained for, however, was Cassandra getting
propositioned by the host in the middle of said party.

"But you can't do that, Cassandra!" she wailed. "You can't just,
like, drop everything and run away to the Hamptons in the middle
of the night with *Jude St. James's father*!"

The two of them were hiding out in the bathroom of his apartment on the night of the party, gossiping and conspiring in high-
pitched voices, because Bennington girls are, in addition to being
easy, hysterical.

"Why ever not?"

"Because, for one thing, his own daughter *won't even speak to him*."

"So?"

Fern went wildly on:

"This one time, she told me, he bribed her to give him her
puppy . . ."

"Bribed her with what?"

"*A building in her own name on Park Avenue.* Somebody else manages it, obviously, and rents it out and all that. But! Don't tell anyone but that's the income she lives on while she's in Africa. She lives off a building on Park Avenue."

"That's kind of genius actually."

"What is?"

"Bribing her with a building on Park Avenue to get the puppy."

"No it isn't, it's manipulative! And *then*! He didn't even keep the puppy. He just took it from her and gave it to some bimbo he was seeing, Jude says. He just wanted to give her a lesson. Like, that she wasn't above money after all. That nobody is, Jude said."

I hope he never gives me a puppy, Cassandra was thinking. I'd prefer jewelry.

"And another thing. How are you going to get there, anyway? Will you take the Chutney? The one time I went to the Hamptons, I took the Ch—"

"The Chutney, what the hell is that, the Indian bus?"

The idea only seemed like common sense to Cassandra: she was imagining that there might be a Japanese bus called the Wasabi, a Mexican one called the Tamale, and so on—the possibilities were endless. But the Fung Wah, in fact, no longer existed. It had been shut down by the Feds. This was yet another thing about the world as Sylvie and Cassandra had known it that had changed.

"The Jitney, the Jitney! The bus that goes to the Hamptons is called the Jitney."

"Whatever, Fern. We're not exactly going to be taking *the bus*, I don't think." Cassandra opened her clutch and fished around for her lipstick. But one did not want to put on a fresh coat of Yves Saint Laurent lipstick, costing thirty-four dollars per gilded tube, with one's breath stinking of those very excellent oysters she had cadged from the hors d'oeuvres table, she felt. "Oh my God. I wasn't prepared for this! Do you by any chance have a breath mint on you?"

"No!"

"No, no? Then what are you good for?" Cassandra screamed at Fern, her handmaiden. She faced the mirror, fluffing her hair; the Yves Saint Laurent lipstick now cradled in the palm of her hand like a grenade. "I'll tell you what you're going to do right now; I promise I'll make it up to you later. Run down to the nearest bodega and get me some breath mints. And then I'll distract him until you come back."

Fern looked at her torturer helplessly. Then she cried out:

"There are no bodegas on upper Fifth Avenue!"

"Try Madison, then. No, scratch Madison, everything on Madison will be closed by now. Lexington, Fern. I guess that means that you'll have to try Lexington. Well, what of it? You're a lithe young thing, aren't you? What are you staring at me for? Run, Fern, run!"

She had a pleasant vision of Fern's Bambi-like legs prancing buoyantly into the night.

"But Cassandra. Aren't you going to give me any money?"

"What are you, a retard? I never have any money on me, remember!"

Fern ran. While she was waiting, Cassandra noticed in a stack of magazines arranged next to the toilet a copy of the most recent Bennington alumni magazine, addressed to Jude St. James's father. She flipped toward the back pages to the alumni notes, searching for updates from the Bennington class of 2003. Bitsy Citron, she read, had founded a sarong importing business. A couple of years from now, when her father died, she would inherit millions; diamonds are forever. Meanwhile, that other heiress, Penelope Entenmann, and her son, Prajeetha, had relocated from living on a private beach in Hawaii to one in Ibiza.

Cassandra read on, and on. Angelica Rocky-Divine had gotten married. Lanie Tobacco, of all people, had also gotten married, to the very same man of whom she had once uttered the immortal words, "Rough night. I fucked a hippie," which only went to show you the mysterious nature of love itself. Vicky Lalage, meanwhile, wrote in that she was living on the Vineyard year-round and "still working on her art." Cassandra took away from that rather austere encapsulation that Vicky, at least, was still single. (The maniacal Tess Fox had indeed dumped her and had moved on to men.) Gala Gubelman was not married yet but would be engaged by this time next year, to a mediocre young man, met on OKCupid, who co-owned a distillery next to the Lorimer stop. And oh how Gala Gubelman, once, had hated earth tones—

How all of them, all of them had been unable to conceive of their own lives as ever being anything other than fantastical, beautiful, richly and expensively textured!

"Ready?" said Jude St. James's father, having just appeared in front of Cassandra carrying an Italian weekender bag.

"Ready," said Cassandra, and she surrendered.

The hell with the breath mints, she kissed him.

Cassandra was not just plain kissing, but French-kissing, Jude St. James's father when Fern Morgenthal, her Bambi-like legs prancing buoyantly, buoyantly into the night, was crossing Park Avenue and was hit by a taxicab and killed. Luckily, unlike Sylvie and Cassandra and the rest of the Bennington class of 2003, Pansy Chapin, Gala Gubelman, Angelica Rocky-Divine, the notorious Lanie Tobacco, Bitsy Citron, Penelope Entenmann, Vicky Lalage, and nameless others, Fern had graduated seven years afterward and had not lived long enough to be unhappy or to concede, in her final, blinkered moments on earth, that New York City had lost its luster. Because it hadn't, yet. The lights were still brilliant when she was called.

ACKNOWLEDGMENTS

I would like to thank, as ever, my loyal and lovely agent, Emily Forland. I would also like to thank Coralie Hunter, for her initial faith in *Bennington Girls*, and Melissa Danaczko, for smoothly seeing it to publication, as well as Bill Thomas and the rest of the splendid team at Doubleday.

ABOUT THE AUTHOR

Charlotte Silver is the author of the memoir *Charlotte au Chocolat: Memories of a Restaurant Girlhood* and the young adult novel *The Summer Invitation*. She is a graduate of Bennington College and lives in New York City.

DISCARD